The Butcher's Bill

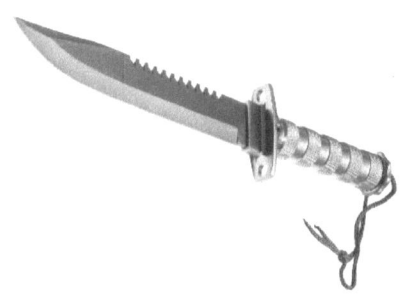

MARTIN ROY HILL

32-32 North

San Diego, CA

Published by

32-32 North

An imprint of
M. R. Hill Publishing
San Diego, California

ISBN-0692802932

ISBN-978-0692802939

For information contact
www.martinroyhill.com

Cover design by RebeccaCovers

Images by Belchonock, Nightman1965, and Zeferli
Depositphotos.com

Books by Martin Roy Hill

Duty: Stories of Mystery and Suspense from the Cold War and Beyond (2012)

The Killing Depths (2012)

Empty Places (2013)

Eden: A Sci-Fi Novella (2014)

The Last Refuge (2016)

Butcher's Bill: Old naval slang term for the dead
and wounded on board after battle.
— *The Oxford Companion to Ships and the Sea (1976)*

CHAPTER 1

HE STAYED IN THE THICK growth of the hillside, hidden by the shadows of its trees, and looked down on the training camp. A good twenty yards lay between him and the cyclone fence of the compound. The cleared area would give the guards an unobstructed view of anyone approaching during the day. At night, however, the poor positioning of the security lighting left deep shadows that extended from the fence to the trees. The bright lighting inside the compound also compromised the guards' night vision, making those shadows even darker.

Bill Butcher raised the small set of binoculars to his eyes and scanned the camp again, just as he had for the past four hours. There were four guards on duty—one at the gate, two walking the fence line, and one inside the main building manning a radio. Every hour on the hour, the guard in the building would relieve one of the guards outside and they would rotate positions. It was a good routine for watch standers on a ship at sea, but it was a terrible routine for compound security.

"Amateurs," Butcher muttered. He shook the rucksack next to him as if trying to wake someone. "And you guys call yourselves professionals."

The guard nearest him paused and lit a cigarette. The flame lit up a dark Hispanic face framed by a thick, black beard, and topped with a khaki baseball cap. Butcher couldn't see it, but he knew the front of the cap bore the logo of Gideon Security International, the so-called contract security company that ran this training site. Far beyond the security lighting, Butcher knew the compound extended another twenty acres. Built on that acreage were training areas used by Gideon to train its own security operators—mercenaries, really—as well as legitimate law enforcement and military personnel, a bunch of wannabes, and the occasional drug cartel member, though Gideon would never confess to the latter.

The guard took a drag, blew smoke, and carelessly tossed the match into a clump of bushes at his feet. He continued walking toward Butcher's left, never looking outside the fence. Butcher knew the guard would walk on for five more minutes, turn, and walk for ten minutes to Butcher's right. Fifteen minutes to complete the length of his part of the fence; thirty minutes for a complete lap.

Butcher timed it that way. Five minutes from that clump of bushes to one side, ten minutes on the other side. The innocuous bushes were a major factor in Butcher's plan. They grew close to the fence, their branches poking through the links from the inside. Their presence so close to the fence violated the most basic security precautions. It cast a shadow along the fence and the ground beyond, and offered a prowler concealment. There, as the guard made his ten-minute trek to the right, Butcher would cut his way into the compound.

The guard came back. He passed the bushes and flicked his finished cigarette over the fence. It arced through the night like a small meteoroid, a flash then gone. Butcher shrugged into the rucksack and began his crawl across the clearing. He moved slowly, carefully, the way he was trained, his dark clothes and rucksack blending into the shadows. The guard retraced his steps and, as he neared the bushes, Butcher stopped entirely, lying still. The guard marched on to the right, onto the long leg of his route.

It was winter and cold in the rural backcountry of San Diego County. Without the nighttime warmth of the Pacific Ocean felt by coastal Southern California, the backcountry would often see snow this time of year. Despite the cold, Butcher felt sweat drip down his face and soak into his black balaclava. He felt it dampen his black, long-sleeved sweater. He ignored it and crawled on.

When he reached the fence, his breathing was heavy from exertion. He drew a pair of wire cutters from the cargo pocket of his dark trousers and snipped the links, covering each one he cut with a gloved hand to muffle the noise. He snipped six up, ten over, and six down, removed the freed section of fence and hid it beneath the bushes. It left a hole twelve inches high and twenty inches wide, enough to let him crawl through without snagging his clothes or gear.

Butcher crawled through, pulling the ruck after him. Concealed by the bushes he listened for the guard's footsteps. They were still at a distance and diminishing, moving away from him. Butcher rose and glanced over the top of the bushes. Other than the guards, the compound was empty, the students having left for the day. In front of him was the main building that held the administration offices. That's where Cavendish would be.

The main entrance was at the front of the building. It was well lit and in direct view of the both the gate guard and the man on the radio. There was a back entrance, too; a large, solid utility door Butcher knew was unlocked so the guards could enter the building to use the toilet. Butcher considered that another sign of their lack of professionalism.

The guard's footsteps grew louder. The guard was on his way back. Butcher lowered himself and waited for the man to pass. When the guard was a safe distance away, Butcher stood and, gripping the ruck in his hand, trotted to the building, his soft-soled boots barely making a crunch on the gravel. He reached the side of the building and slid against the wall toward the rear. A quick glance around the corner showed him the guard on the other side of the building was out of sight. He slipped around the corner and tested the door. As he expected, it was unlocked. He opened it, and slipped in.

The compound had once been a military camp, a relic from some long-forgotten war. The buildings were of simple, practical design; a hallway ran the length of the building, with rooms or offices on either side. The hallway was dark, the only light coming from the front of the building where the guard sat with the radio, and from under the door of a room in the middle of the hallway to Butcher's right.

That had to be Cavendish's office.

Butcher knew Cavendish was in. He had watched him walking the grounds a few hours earlier, saw him enter the building, and never saw him leave. He stepped closer to the door and listened. A television was playing, and he heard a grunt of laughter. One live voice. No others.

Butcher shouldered the rucksack, drew a KaBar knife from a sheath on his belt, and entered the room.

Charlie Cavendish sat at his desk, his feet up on the desk. A half-empty bottle of whiskey sat on the desk, and he held a glass of whiskey and ice in his hand. He didn't turn from the television.

"Yeah," he grunted, "What is it?"

"Special delivery, Cavendish," Butcher said, closing the door behind him.

Cavendish turned and froze.

Butcher's beefy six-foot frame crowded the doorway. He pulled the balaclava from his head, revealing a deeply tanned face with a wide mouth, a prominent nose, and cold gray eyes. A cleanly shaved head glinted in the lamp light. Cavendish let the drink fall from his hand and shatter on the floor.

"You? But—"

Cavendish tried to stand, but Butcher was across the room in two steps and had him by the throat. Cavendish's face went red. His eyes bulged. He tried to yell but only a small screech came out.

"Why?" Butcher demanded. Cavendish shook his head. Butcher squeezed tighter. "Don't lie."

When Cavendish still feigned ignorance, Butcher shrugged off the rucksack and held it out. The top flap straps hung loose. Butcher smiled.

"I know," he said. "I know you sent them after me. I have a snitch." Butcher flipped open the ruck. "Meet my little friend."

Butcher let the ruck fall. It hit the wooden floor with a thump, and Butcher kicked it over. A man's severed head rolled out, wobbled, then steadied. Opened eyes stared blankly at the ceiling, and the mouth stood agape. Butcher let go of Cavendish's throat, but the man didn't move. He stared at the head and gasped for air.

"We have a little talking to do, Cavendish."

When he had finished a few minutes later, Butcher studied his work. Cavendish sat dead in his chair, his throat slit and gaping like a second mouth. Butcher quickly searched Cavendish's office, finding nothing. That was okay. Cavendish had told him what he needed.

Butcher picked up his ruck, leaving the severed head on the floor, and started for the door. Then he stopped. His mouth puckered in thought. He turned back to the dead man, dipped a gloved finger into the pool of blood, and began writing on the wall. When he finished, he stepped back, admiring his work. A grin stretched across his face. The message read:

BRING ME LINUS SCHAG

Replacing the balaclava, Butcher retraced his steps and left the building. When the guard walking inside the fence line turned away, Butcher trotted back to the bushes and slipped through the hole he had made in the fence. Then he disappeared into the dark.

CHAPTER 2

MONDAY
Naval Air Station China Lake
California
0700 Hours

THE DRIVER-SIDE WINDOW ROLLED down and a blast of chilled morning air slapped Linus Schag's face, ruffled his gray-flecked, light-brown hair, and fogged his silver-rimmed aviator eyeglasses. It was winter and the temperature at China Lake had dropped to thirty degrees during the night. With the sunrise, the temperature rose somewhat, but it still had some ways to go, and the wind-chill factor made it seem colder than it was.

Schag pulled the sedan up to the gate guard and held out his identification. The guard, dressed in the Navy's dark-blue camouflage uniform and a black foul-weather coat, stooped and studied the ID a moment, straightened, and waved him through.

"Welcome to Naval Air Weapons Station China Lake," the guard said. "Have a nice day."

Schag nodded his thanks and drove onto the base, passing several decommissioned Navy jets on static display.

China Lake was a two-hour drive to the east of Los Angeles, just outside the city of Ridgecrest in California's high desert. It was a desolate swath of scrubland suited for nothing more than what the Navy used it for—a sophisticated, high-tech bombing range. There the Navy tested its latest means of destroying enemy aircraft and ships. In fact, every airborne weapons system developed since World War II experienced its explosive birth in the hundreds of acres of desert wasteland surrounding the main area of the base and its airfield.

Schag parked the sedan outside of a squat, whitewashed structure built two or three wars before. Inside, in what the Navy called the quarterdeck, Schag used his proximity card to unlock the security door and walked up the stairwell to the second deck. In the Navy, all floors were decks, even those located two hundred miles from the nearest hint of salt water. On the first door to the left, a sign read in large block letters: NAVAL CRIMINAL INVESTIGATIVE SERVICE. Smaller letters below read: Special Agent Linus Schag, Resident Agent.

Schag unlocked his office door and entered, closing the door behind him. He removed his sports coat and hung it on a hook. Then, just as he had done for the past five months, he unlocked a file cabinet, removed his Glock 40 and holster from his belt, placed them inside, and locked the cabinet again. If this day was like any other day in the past five months, in another eight hours he would unlock the file cabinet, take out the gun and clip it to his belt, retrace his steps to his car, and drive back to his motel with little to show for the day.

Schag's assignment to China Lake began five months earlier. As the resident NCIS agent, he was a civilian investigator responsible for investigating major crimes like murder, fraud, and espionage involving Navy and Marine Corps personnel or assets. The biggest crime wave to hit the base since Schag reported aboard, however, was a series of minor infractions by sailors that were in the purview of the base's uniformed master-at-arms police force, not his. For Schag—who preferred duty as an agent afloat investigating crimes at sea with the fleet—this temporary assignment was nothing less than exile.

Schag's duty aboard the aircraft carrier USS Halsey ended when he was called to testify before a board of inquiry about the crew member deaths and near loss of the attack submarine USS Encinitas a year before. Schag went aboard the sub to investigate an apparent suicide of a crewmember, only to discover it was a murder and only the first of several more to come. He blamed himself for that. If he'd been a little more alert, he might have discovered the suspect's identity before the killer's rampage almost destroyed the sub.

It is naval tradition that a ship's captain answer to a board of inquiry for any untoward incident aboard his vessel. The inquiry board correctly determined that the submarine's skipper was not culpable for the deaths aboard his ship, but it mattered little. The officer's career was over. He was "on the beach," as he had put it, and he retired from the service. Schag's impatience with the members of the board—it was rare when he was not impatient with authority—had a similar effect on his career. Banished to China Lake, he would cool his heels until the Navy brass determined he'd suffered enough.

The desk phone issued a strange, tinny warble, and Schag answered it.

"NCIS. Special Agent Schag speaking," he said.

"Lin, it's Tom Riley."

Tom Riley was the special agent in charge of the NCIS Southwest Regional office in San Diego. Despite a popular TV show's claim otherwise, there was no NCIS office in Los Angeles County for the simple reason there hadn't been any Navy presence in that area since the Long Beach Naval Ship Yard closed in the mid-1990s. San Diego, however, was homeport for the Third Fleet and boasted one of the largest concentrations of Navy and Marine Corps personnel and assets in the world.

"Tom," Schag said cautiously. Riley was Schag's boss, and getting a call from him was unusual enough to raise suspicion. "To what do I owe this honor?"

"We need you down here," Riley said. "Can you break free?"

"Let me check my calendar," Schag said. If Riley noted the sarcasm, he didn't mention it. Schag didn't even bother to check his calendar. "I think I can squeeze you in. What's up?"

"I don't want to go into details over the phone," Riley said, his voice almost hushed. "Don't know if those pricks at NSA are listening in." Schag smiled at Riley's comment. Then Tom said more softly, "We may have a rogue agent."

Schag straightened. "What? Who?"

"What part of 'I don't want to go into details over the phone' did you not understand?" Riley answered.

"Come on, Tom," Schag said. "No games."

"Okay, but sit down, Lin. It's Bill Butcher."

Schag's brain sputtered to a halt. He stared at a blank

spot on the wall and said nothing. Did he hear right? Bill Butcher?

He heard Tom Riley's voice again. "Lin, you still there?"

"Ah, yeah," Schag said. "Yeah. Did you say Bill Butcher?"

"I'm afraid so," Riley said. "The Butcher himself."

"Can't be," Schag insisted. "Not Bill Butcher."

"It's Butcher," Riley said. "Look, when can you get down here?"

"Three, four hours," Schag said, "depending on traffic." He paused a moment before asking, "Tom, you sure you want me on this? I mean, Bill Butcher and I are close friends. You don't want to taint the investigation by having a conflicted agent on your team."

"We don't have a choice, Lin," Riley said. "Butcher asked for you."

Schag drove through the main gate a half hour later, right after notifying the command of his absence. He was heading south on the freeway only a few minutes later. He didn't need to stop at his hotel. Everything he needed was already packed in his trunk—a go-bag with a couple of changes of clothing and a spit kit, an evidence kit, and a locked box with two spare magazines and extra ammo for his service Glock and his backup weapon. His weathered flight jacket, which he won from an inebriated pilot in a poker game, lay neatly in the back seat next to his carelessly tossed sports jacket.

The news station on the radio reported the San Diego Sheriff's Department was investigating a murder of a man at a rural training center operated by Gideon Security

International, a company that provided tactical training and security services to law enforcement agencies and militaries around the world. Hearing the company's name, Schag reached over and turned up the sound, but there wasn't much more information, only that deputies still had no suspects and the name of the victim was being withheld pending notification of relatives.

Schag felt an uneasiness form in the pit of his stomach. He didn't know much about the company itself, but he remembered the last time he'd heard the name. It was three years before, in a hotel bar in Bahrain. The last time he had seen Bill Butcher.

"I tell you, Lin," Butcher said. "You won't believe the corruption going on in Iraq. It's like the Wild West. Totally lawless."

They were sitting at a table in the Dublin Club, a bar and nightclub popular with American sailors. Hardwood tables sat on a well-varnished hardwood floor. Lamps with ornate shades lit the bar where a few sailors in civilian clothes were throwing back shooters. Other customers dug into steaks and chicken wings at the tables, the overhead lighting just enough to let them know what they were putting into their mouths. An empty stage reputed to host the best bands in Europe dominated the far end of the club. Large-screen plasma televisions hung from two walls, flashing a never-ending stream of sports news.

Schag had flown into Bahrain on a COD flight, escorting a prisoner from the Halsey's battle group to the regional NCIS office for transfer back to the States for a court martial. COD officially stood for Carrier Onboard

Delivery, but most passengers felt Crash on Deck was a more fitting title. Butcher came over from Iraq to assist the regional staff with an investigation. They had run into each other at the regional headquarters, and decided to have dinner and drinks at the Dublin Club.

"Those damn contractors—my god, don't get me started." In truth, Butcher didn't need prodding to go on. "They're all crooks in my book."

He leaned his elbows on the table and pointed a finger at Schag, the overhead light glinting off his cleanly shaved head.

"The Navy contracted with one company to build some barracks. They did such a shitty job they managed to electrify a shower stall. It electrocuted the first sailor who took a shower. We started an investigation, but orders came down to drop it. The company skated."

"Who ordered you?"

Butcher's eyes lifted toward the ceiling, a gesture meaning the order came from higher up.

Schag asked, "How high up?"

Butcher rolled his eyes even higher, looked at Schag and shrugged. "Pretty damn high, Lin. It seems the fucking contractors have immunity from prosecution."

Butcher barely paused before rushing on.

"You remember the battle of Fallujah?" he asked. Schag nodded. Fallajah was an Iraqi city that insurgents had taken over. Two battles were fought for control of the city, the second the bloodiest of the war. "We were taking so many casualties, our docs and corpsmen ran out of medical supplies. The corpsmen were going into homes and tearing sheets off beds to use as bandages. We started to investigate why our medical warehouses were so low on supplies. You know what we found?"

"Black marketeering?" Schag said.

Butcher nodded his head, again with exaggeration.

"Some of these security firms were drawing medical supplies, more than their motley numbers would need," he said. "Know where we found them? On the dead and wounded insurgents. The contractors were selling them on the black market."

Schag sipped his beer and shook his head. "That's not unheard of," he said.

Butcher leaned over the table and tapped it with an index finger.

"Yeah, but it isn't just your run of the mill black marketing," he said. "We've got evidence of them smuggling drugs into Iraq to sell to our troops, and weapons to sell to the insurgents."

"And you couldn't bust them?"

Butcher sat back in his chair, a look of disgust twisting his face.

"A couple got their hands slapped and sent home, but not one of those shit heads went to jail."

Schag sipped his beer and let Butcher vent. His friend seemed to have a need to let go of pent-up frustration and anger. The best thing he could do for Butcher was to act like a psychiatrist, and shut up, and listen.

"The worst group," Butcher said, "is Gideon Security International. Ever hear of them?"

Schag nodded.

"Yeah. Big outfit. Lots of political mojo, right?'

Butcher blew air through pursed lips and rolled his eyes up.

"Big mojo," he said, "and they use it to pull off every scam they can think of. They claim to have nothing but the top security operators in the world, and the guy who runs it, Aidan Black, claims to be a former Green Beret. Yeah, well we ran backgrounds on some of his guys. We found ex-cons and a bunch of former Latin American death-squad members."

Snorting, Butcher shook his head again, slower this time.

"And it turned out this Aidan Black was a psychological warfare officer assigned to Special Forces to write propaganda. The son-of-bitch never even deployed. He trained up for two missions. The first was Somalia, but he ended up breaking his leg at the last minute and couldn't deploy. I don't know what the second mission was, but I heard he came down with some heart palpitations or something, and they held him back. After that, he was given some kind of medical discharge, and the teams were happy to see him go."

Butcher sipped his beer. His eyebrows rose, and he set the glass down.

"I doubt he realizes it, but Black chose the perfect name for his company," he said.

Knitting his brow, Schag mulled it over before saying, "Gideon? It's from the Old Testament. He was an Israelite general, wasn't he? Won some big battle." Butcher, a devout Catholic, nodded. "So, Black wanted to project a sense of strength and protection. Makes good business sense."

"Not for a man who claims to be a church-going Christian," Butcher said.

Schag watched Butcher's toothy smile spread across his face. Schag's eyebrows rose in question.

"Gideon won that big battle by fooling the Midianites with a phony army, just like Black is fooling the U.S. government with a phony security service."

They shared a laugh over that. Bill Butcher sat back and rubbed his lips thoughtfully. When he spoke again, his voice was lower, sadder.

"It would be fine if all they were only harmless fools, but they hurt people, and not only Iraqis. There was this one young girl, a college student hired to work in one of the gedunks—you know, the PX or something. Why the hell such a young girl would want to go work in a war zone, I don't understand. Maybe she was saving up for college, who knows? Anyway, this Gideon op named Cavendish and two his goons slipped her some ruffies, and gang raped her. They left her unconscious in a cargo container to sleep off the ruffies, and forgot about her. You have any idea how hot those containers get during the summer in the desert? By the time someone found her, her body temperature was so high she had suffered irreparable brain damage."

Butcher fell silent again. His head shook with disgust at the memory. Schag watched his friend a moment, then asked the obvious. "No prosecution, right?"

The ends of Butcher's lip tugged down and he shook his head. "I heard later that the girl's family tried a civil suit, but Gideon claimed immunity again."

He grabbed his beer and took a savage draw from it. He swished the beer around in mouth as if ridding himself of some awful taste. When he finished, he looked across the table at Schag.

"But the big thing," he said, "the biggest scam that happened out there was—" His voiced lowered to a confidential murmur. "—the money."

"What money?"

Butcher leaned across the wooden table toward Schag.

"Did you know the administration confiscated some forty billion—*billion*—dollars from Saddam's overseas bank accounts?" Schag nodded, having read news reports of the administration's plans. "Yeah, well, did you know it was in cash? They just packed up that cash and shipped it to Baghdad. Planeload after planeload. Most of it went to contractors for building stuff, but no one bothered with niceties like receipts. But we know $8.9 billion of it simply disappeared. Disappeared. Came off the plane and was never seen again. Nearly nine billion in cash. The largest bank heist in history and no one investigated it."

Schag had read news reports of the disappearance of the money, but he considered them rumors rather than fact.

"Are you saying that actually happened?"

Butcher nodded once, and hit the table with his beer bottle. "As real as I'm sitting here."

"And you're saying no one investigated it?"

"We weren't allowed to," Butcher said. "And I mean no one, Lin. Not NCIS, Army CID, Air Force Special Investigations, not the FBI, DEA, or CIA. Nobody. We had a task force set up for joint investigations and when we started to look into it, we got our chain pulled hard."

"Nine billion in cash can't just disappear, Bill. Someone had to know where it went."

Butcher shook his head. "Lin, the Viceroy's staff was handing out duffle bags stuffed with cash. They couldn't fully account for the cash they know they handed out." Viceroy was the nickname given to the Administrator of the Coalition Provisional Authority of Iraq, the American-led military occupational government. It harkened back to the days of European imperialism when a viceroy appointed by a king lorded over an overseas colony. Many in the military and the State Department felt there were strong similarities in the American occupation of Iraq. "But this nine billion just vanished."

Butcher stifled a beer-generated belch. "Well, there's nothing I can do for that kid," he said. "But that money? That I can still do something about."

Schag didn't like the look on Butcher's face. He wondered if his friend was getting drunk. "What's that mean, Bill? You said you were told to stand down on that investigation."

Butcher smirked and pointed the mouth of his bottle toward Schag.

"The joint task force was ordered to stand down, Lin," he said. "But I've got time on my hands. I've made a few inquiries. I'll make some more."

"Bucking orders is dangerous, Bill. Good way to end up on the carpet."

"Since when does the Linus Schag I've come to know and love care if he gets called on the carpet? I've seen you cuss out a Marine Corps full colonel as if he was a boot recruit. You getting soft in your old age?"

Schag smiled at the memory and sipped his beer.

Butcher glanced at the large dive watch on his left wrist, and stood. "I've got to run, Lin. Gotta Skype the old lady and kids." He held out his hand, and Schag shook it. "Listen, next time you're back in the States, come see us. I know Yolanda would love to see you. The kids, too."

"I'd like that, Bill," Schag said. "And keep your damn nose clean, for your family's sake."

Butcher didn't respond. He was already winding his way through the tables toward the door. Schag watched him sidestep a couple of drunken swabbies, swing open the door, and disappear into the night outside.

That had been three years before, and as Schag drove south toward San Diego, his hands gripped the steering wheel until his knuckles turned white.

"My God, Bill," he murmured. "What have you done?"

CHAPTER 3

MONDAY
Point Loma Yacht Club
San Diego, California
0830 Hours

THE SECURITY GUARD WATCHED THE gray pickup truck approach the gate and stood up. He waited for the driver to pull opposite the guard shack. It was raining, and he didn't want to get any wetter than he needed to. His arthritis was already acting up.

"Can I help you?" he asked the driver.

The driver hooked a thumb toward the truck's cargo bed behind him. "I'm here to clean a hull," he said.

The guard glanced into the back of the truck and saw scuba gear, brushes, and hull scrappers. Underwater hull cleaning services were regular visitors to the yacht club. It was cheaper to hire a diver to scrape off barnacles while a boat was still in the water than to have a boat yard haul it into dry dock to do the job.

"Where you going?" the guard asked.

The driver wore a dark-blue watch cap, a wet suit, and, despite the overcast, dark wrap-around sunglasses. He picked up a piece of paper from the passenger seat and read off a dock number.

"Okay," said the guard. He pointed to a group of parking slots reserved for club guests. "Park over there and carry your gear through that gate. It should be to your right."

The driver flashed a wide, toothy grin, thanked the guard, and drove on.

The yacht club sat on the edge of San Diego Bay's Shelter Island, and stretched its finger-like docks out into the cove created by the man-made island's southern spur. A squat two-story wooden clubhouse overlooked the docks like a Scottish castle brooding over the moors. The great, wide windows, fogged by the early morning chill, looked down on vessels representing the gamut of pleasure boating, from small single-masted daysailers to large ocean-going motor yachts and multi-masted sailing vessels. There were few members in the clubhouse at this hour to look out. Even fewer stirred on the rain-dampened decks of the boats. Bill Butcher was counting on that.

He sat on the edge of the dock, a single air tank strapped to his back, flippers on his feet, and looked out over the water. The gray overcast reflected off the surface and gave the water the color of pewter. Rainbows of color danced here and there on the surface, created from the sheen of spilled fuel. Butcher spat into his mask and smeared it around with his fingers, coating the glass to prevent it from fogging underwater. After placing the mask over his face, he gripped the air regulator in his mouth, took two test breaths, grabbed a hull scrapper, and slipped into the water.

He had no use for the scrapper, or any of the cleaning equipment he carted down to the dock. It was all decoration, part of his disguise to get into the yacht club. Nor did he have any interest in the yawl he appeared to be cleaning. His target was a large motor sailer tied up three docks over. He swam over to it, keeping under the moored yachts as much as he could to hide his air bubbles. What he wouldn't give for a rebreather. But he had to settle for whatever he could steal from the dive shop he broke into during the night after driving back from the Gideon compound.

Butcher surfaced, his mask barely above the water, and eyed his target. The motor sailer was one of those half sailboat, half motor yacht vessels that rich people chose when they couldn't decide what kind of yachtsman they wanted to be—canvas slapper or a stink pot. With a built-in engine and a single tall mast, the motor sailer could cut through the sea under power or slice through it under sail. But it did neither very well.

This one had a fifty-foot, dark-blue hull topped by a white gunwale, deck, and cabin. He recognized it from the photos he'd studied, but to be sure he swam toward the stern and read its name: *FREE ENTERPRISE*. No surprise there, Butcher thought. What else would he name it?

Slipping beneath the water again, Butcher moved toward the bow of the boat. There he pulled a black, brick-like object from a bag hanging from his weight belt. At one end was a small propeller. Two flanges angled out from the top, with two screw holes in each flange. Pulling a small, pump-action hand drill from the same bag, he placed the object against the hull and drilled holes through each of the screw holes. He replaced the drill in the bag, removed four screws, and fingered them into place. He replaced the bit drill with a screwdriver head, and used the drill to tighten the screws. When he finished, he removed a small cotter pin from the propeller shaft and tested its free movement. Butcher paused to admire his work, his mouth forming a grin around the regulator.

This would be his ace in the hole. The brick-like object held a quarter pound of improvised plastic explosive. *Ah, the things you can whip up in the kitchen if you only had the right cookbook.* This little specialty was courtesy of the CIA training he'd received in the SEALs. If his primary plan went to hell, this would complete the mission.

Half an hour later, he was on Interstate 8 heading for the mountains, smiling contentedly. Only three days before he'd had no idea how to proceed. He'd been stumped, stonewalled at each attempt to bring to light what he had discovered. Those idiots at NCIS wouldn't listen. They ruined his reputation, forced him out of the agency, and they weren't about to admit they were wrong and take his evidence to court.

Then they had come after him. There were two of them, a short Hispanic with a Boston Blackie moustache and a taller white guy with a shaved head and muscular build much like Butcher himself. He recognized them as Gideon mercenaries; the Hispanic was in Iraq the same time as Butcher. Caught with a cache of illegal weapons, he was sent back to the States with a slap on the wrist. Butcher tried to recall the guy's name. Was it Ruiz? Yes, that was it. Ruiz, a Rambo wannabe.

They were both amateurs, like most of Gideon's mercs, and Butcher easily spotted them tailing him. He didn't try to lose them, but let them follow him south from Salinas, where he'd been visiting his children, down to San Diego County and up into the mountains. Butcher's family had a summer cabin up there, and he'd been living in it since he and Yolanda separated. He used the time driving to think about what the two men wanted. Were they tailing him to see whom he was meeting, if anyone? Were they afraid he might go to the press? Maybe they planned to run him off the road, rough him up a bit, and threaten him to back off. Yeah, right. I'd like to see them try that, he told himself. Then another possibility came to mind. If that was it, Butcher knew he couldn't wait and see. He had to act first.

He led the Gideon men up the I-8 to Alpine, a small mountain town outside the Cleveland National Forest, and stopped for dinner at a mom-and-pop diner he frequented. It was tucked beneath a copse of trees well off the beaten path. It had been snowing, and the undisturbed blanket of snow covering the diner's parking lot told Butcher there would be few people inside.

He took his time eating, watching the Gideon mercs' dark-blue Nissan parked a several yards down the road, close enough to watch the entrance to the restaurant and his own car, but far enough away, they assumed, not to attract his attention. He didn't see anyone leave the vehicle, so he knew they both were still inside it.

Butcher rose, paid his bill, and walked toward the single, unisex restroom. He knew there was a backdoor next to the restroom. He tested the backdoor's handle. It was unlocked. He slipped out the door and trotted quietly past the trash dumpsters into the woods, angling obliquely to the left, going deeper into the woods, and moving toward the Nissan. In five minutes, he was parallel to them but still hidden in the shadows of the trees. He pulled up his right trouser leg, revealing an ankle holster holding a Glock 26, the so-called Baby Glock for its compactness. He drew it and crept forward.

Focused on the diner and Butcher's car, the two men never saw Butcher approach. The vehicle's closed windows were fogged over from their own breathing. Butcher watched them repeatedly wiping down the inside of the windshield. *Amateurs.* They had no idea Butcher was near them until they heard his voice and turned to find the Glock staring at them.

"Either of you twitch, I blow your fucking heads off," Butcher said. "Driver, put your hands on the wheel. Passenger, put your hands on the dashboard."

They both did as told.

"Good," Butcher said. "Now, driver, I'm going to open this door, and you're going to ease out and lie face down on the ground. Passenger, you stay as you are. Understand?"

The driver, the white guy with the cleanly shaved head, nodded.

"Do you understand, amigo?" Butcher said to the Hispanic.

"Y-yes, sir," the darker man said.

"Okay, then." Butcher opened the driver's door, never letting his pistol divert from the driver's baldhead. The dome light glinted off the man's head. Another careless mistake, Butcher thought. Always keep the dome light turned off when you're following someone or on a stakeout. "Now slide out."

The white man slid from the car seat and knelt in the snow.

"All the way down," Butcher barked. "Face in the snow."

The man did as he was told.

"Now, hands on the back of your head, fingers interlaced, and cross your ankles." The position would make it harder for the man to attack Butcher. When the man complied, Butcher shifted the Glock to his left hand to cover the Hispanic, crouched, and felt along the other man's waistband with his other hand. He found a .45 caliber 1911 Colt automatic in a holster in the small of the man's back and removed it. Butcher hefted it in his hand, admiring its weight and balance, before turning his attention back to the Hispanic man.

"Now, what am I going to do with you?" he said. He thought a moment, then turned toward the man on the ground. Without warning, Butcher kicked the man in the temple with his boot. The man's head snapped to the left. He grunted and lay unconscious.

Butcher grinned. "Always wear steel-tipped boots," he said to the Hispanic. "Safety always comes first."

Butcher crouched so he was level with the second Gideon mercenary. "Remember me?"

"Yeah," the man said. "You're that NCIS guy who tried to bust me back in Iraq. Butcher's your name."

Butcher nodded. "And your name is Ruiz, right?" The man nodded. "What was your first name again?"

"Hector."

"Okay, Hector," Butcher said. "I'm going to move around the back of the car. You're not going to move one bit. If you do, I'll blow the back of your head off with either one of these guns. Then I'm going to open your door and you'll slide out—slowly—and lay on the ground. Do you understand, Hector? "

"Yes, sir"

Keeping both weapons trained on Ruiz, Butcher moved around to the passenger's side, stuck the .45 in his waistband, and opened the door. He watched closely as Ruiz laid himself face down in the snow, arms and legs stretched at angles as if he were making a snow angel.

"You know the routine, Hector," Butcher said. "Hands on your head, fingers interlaced, ankles crossed." When Ruiz did as told, Butcher asked, "Where do you keep your gun?"

"On my side in a belt holster," Ruiz croaked.

Butcher felt the man's right hip but found nothing.

"Other side," Ruiz said. "I'm left handed."

Butcher found the gun and stuck it in his back pocket. He patted down Ruiz's legs, finding nothing. Stepping away from the car, Butcher said, "Okay, Hector, I want you to get up slowly. Do it now."

Ruiz's uncrossed his legs and unlaced his fingers. Moving with great deliberation, he pushed himself to his knees and stood, his hands held high. Butcher grinned.

"Well done, Hector. Now move around the back of the car."

Without turning his back to Butcher, Ruiz sidestepped around the vehicle until he stumbled over his partner. He looked down, then back at Butcher, his eyes large with fear.

"Is—is he dead?"

"To be honest with you, I don't know," Butcher said. "But just in case he isn't, you're going to tie him up."

"Tie him up? With what?"

"Use your belt and his," Butcher said. "I need my belt to hold all these guns I've been taking from you guys." He gestured with the Glock. "Go ahead, do it. And make it tight."

While Ruiz trussed up his partner, Butcher moved to

the driver's door and reached in for the keys. When Ruiz finished, Butcher unlocked the trunk and lifted the door.

"Put him inside," he said.

"Wait a minute," Ruiz protested. "You can't do this. You ain't no agent now."

"But I have all the guns," Butcher said. Ruiz didn't argue.

With the bald man locked in the trunk, Butcher ordered Ruiz into the driver's seat while he covered him from the passenger seat. He told the Hispanic to start the car and head back to the main road.

"Where are you taking us?" Ruiz asked.

"I've got a place a couple more miles up the road," Butcher said.

"Then what?"

"I only want to talk."

" 'Bout what?"

" 'Bout why you two have been following me."

"What makes you think that?"

"Oh, stop it," Butcher said. "I spotted you four hundred miles back. You still working for Gideon?"

Ruiz didn't answer. Butcher aimed the Glock directly at Ruiz's head. The man flinched.

"Okay," he complained. "Yeah. I still work for Gideon."

"And your orders were . . .?"

"Just to follow you," Ruiz said, with a side glance at Butcher.

"Why?"

"'Cause you keep sticking your nose where it don't belong."

"You mean like where the money went?"

"I don't know nothing about money."

That, Butcher figured, was probably true.

"And what else were you to supposed to do?"

"Like I said, just follow you."

Butcher pressed the barrel of the Glock hard against Ruiz's head. The man tried to move his head away but Butcher pushed it harder against his temple.

"Okay, damn it. Okay!" Ruiz said. "We're supposed to kill you. Make it look like suicide. You know? You got fired from the Navy, separated from the old lady. Who'd think otherwise?"

Butcher mulled over what Hector told him. His lips pursed, and he nodded.

"You used to work for . . . what was his name? Cavendish?" Ruiz nodded. "Still work for him?" Ruiz bit his lower lip and nodded again. "Take the next right, Hector."

Ruiz turned the Nissan down what looked like a rarely used dirt road smothered in snow. The road quickly petered out, and he stopped.

"What's this about," he asked.

"Where can I find Cavendish these days?"

"Down in Campo," Ruiz said. "At the new training camp. He runs it now." He swallowed hard. "You going to let me go?"

"Sure, I am, Hector," Butcher said. "I can walk home from here. Get out. Let's untie your friend."

Butcher opened his door and, still covering Ruiz, climbed out. Ruiz slipped out and moved toward the trunk, fumbling with the key to open it. When he looked up, he froze. Butcher was pointing the bald man's .45 at his chest.

"Thanks for all your help, Hector."

The pistol jumped twice in Butcher's hand. Thrown backward by the double blows, Ruiz landed heavily in the snow, twitched twice, and lay still.

Butcher put the .45 on safe and stuck it back into his waistband. He raised his left pants leg and drew a KaBar knife from an ankle sheath. He looked at it once, then at Hector Ruiz, and stepped closer to the dead man, a wide, tooth baring grin on his lips.

That was three days before. Butcher hadn't slept much since then, but he didn't feel particularly tired. After he left Ruiz in the woods, he'd driven the Nissan to his family cabin and left it, then jogged back to the diner to retrieve his own car. He'd spent a day forming his plan, making the improvised bomb, then another day doing a recon of the Campo training camp, watching the guard routines, and spotting and identifying Cavendish.

After getting the information he needed from Cavendish, he'd driven the Nissan back to San Diego, breaking into a dive shop along the way, then drove to the Navy's Anti-Submarine Warfare base and rented a room at the Navy Gateway Inn. He stayed there only long enough to get a few hours of shuteye. Outside the inn, he stole the gray Toyota pickup truck he was driving and left the Nissan in the parking lot.

Lack of sleep and the adrenalin rush from the last few days' activity was making him giddy. He couldn't stop grinning, and he found himself humming along with the music on the radio. It wasn't a song he'd ever heard, but he seemed to know every note. He reached down to turn up the radio's volume, but couldn't feel the knob. He glanced down to find it, but all he saw was an empty slot where the radio should have been and a rat's nest of wires. The music in his head stopped, and Bill Butcher was suddenly very worried for himself.

CHAPTER 4

THE FIRST U.S. NAVY WARSHIP to enter San Diego Bay was the frigate *USS Cyane*, which landed Marines as part of the American takeover of California from Mexico in 1846. A hook-like peninsula pointing like a finger to the south toward Mexico formed the bay. Called Point Loma, the peninsula provided a natural barrier from the onshore westerly winds and storms. The U.S. Army recognized the importance of the natural harbor and six years later began building coastal fortifications to protect it. However, other than a small coaling station, there was little naval presence in San Diego Bay until after the First World War, when the Navy purchased a small tract of land on the east shore of the bay to build a repair depot.

Today, the bay is homeport to the Navy's Pacific Fleet. The peninsula that once bristled with Army coastal artillery is now home to hunter-killer submarines moored near where the old coaling station once stood. Across from Point Loma is Coronado Island, largely man-made and home to Naval Air Station Coronado. In the days before air power made them obsolete, battleships tied up here. Today the island provides moorings to some of the world's most powerful aircraft carriers.

Farther south, along a narrow strand of beach, is the West Coast home of the Gator Navy, the amphibious ships used to set Marines ashore anywhere in the world, and the Navy's commando elite, the SEALs. Across the bay from the amphibs, where the Navy built its small repair depot in 1919, now sits the San Diego Naval Station. Better known to locals as the 32nd Street Naval Station due to the name of the street in the suburb of National City where its main gate is located, the base is home to the fleet's "small boys," as cruisers, destroyers, and frigates are called. It is also home to the NCIS Southwest Regional headquarters.

The Navy guard at the main gate gave Schag's credentials a cursory look, and waved him through. The agent steered the rented car through a labyrinth of narrow streets cutting between office structures and warehouses until he came to the moorings and dry docks that stretched into the dark, sheen-covered waters of the bay. Rolling down the driver's window, Schag's car filled with the scrape and clang of shipboard maintenance and the briny smell of the bay. He felt he was home.

He wound through the bayside parking lots for a good ten minutes before finding an empty slot within reasonable walking distance to the building housing the Southwest Regional offices. Squinting against the glare of the sun, he could barely make out the two-story building's red-tiled roof as he put his sports jacket on. After walking for five minutes, he could see the building's white outer walls and the entrance to the parade area it surrounded. Built as a public works project during the Great Depression, it originally served as barracks and chow hall for the sailors stationed there. Construction of better facilities decades later allowed conversion of the old barracks and chow hall into offices, and the parade area became a parking lot.

Another large, white structure drew Schag's attention. The *USNS Mercy* hospital ship, its sun-glistened white hull punctuated by medical red crosses, towered above all other ships moored nearby. In the 1980s, at the height of the Cold War, the Navy converted two commercial oil tankers into 1,000-bed sea-going hospitals—the *Mercy* and her East Coast sister ship, the *Comfort*. Designed to care for large numbers of casualties in a Soviet Union vs. NATO conflict, both ships had become relics, too slow to keep up with a fast-moving fleet and too large to be staffed by a smaller, post-Cold War navy. Instead, both ships sailed humanitarian missions, showing the flag while giving medical care to Third World nations. These days, with continuing government belt tightening, even those missions were fewer and farther in between.

"Schag?"

Schag turned at the sound of his name and saw his boss, Tom Riley, walking out of the one-time barracks building. He was shorter than Schag and stockier. His hair was jet black, well cut, and so stiffly lacquered into place the ocean breeze couldn't ruffle it. With his dark business suit and power tie, and the briefcase he carried in his left hand, Schag thought Riley looked more like an attorney than a law enforcement agent. Schag grinned slightly at the irony of that thought. Schag himself had once been a Wall Street lawyer.

"I thought that was you," Riley said, shaking Schag's hand. "Glad you could make it. What were you watching?"

"Just admiring the big, white target," Schag said.

"Big white rust bucket's more like it." Riley took Schag by the shoulder and guided him toward a car. "You're just in time. There's been a report that Butcher was seen at the Anti-Submarine Warfare base. We're heading there now."

"We?" Schag asked.

"Special Agent Parker," Riley said, pointing to a white, unmarked sedan ahead. "He's waiting in the car."

When they reached the vehicle, Riley motioned Schag into the back seat. Behind the wheel was a younger man in a gray suit. Thinning blond hair framed a long, narrow face punctuated with a prominent sharp nose.

"Special Agent Linus Schag meet Special Agent Timothy Parker," Riley said.

As the two shook hands, Schag recalled Riley had a habit of referring to all his agents with the former title of special agent, even in the office.

"Call me Lin," Schag said.

"Tim," Parker said.

Riley impatiently waved his hand at the two men. "Okay, enough with the introductions," he said. "Let's get going."

Schag waited until Parker pulled out of the parking slot and wended his way onto the street before speaking.

"Are you lead on this investigation, Tim?"

Parker started to answer, but Riley jumped in.

"None of us are," he said. "The county sheriff has the lead. Bill Butcher is no longer connected with the Navy. The man—or men—he killed were civilians and killed in county territory."

Schag's stomach lurched.

"The news story I head on the way down mentioned only one victim," he said. "There were more?"

Riley nodded.

"At least two," he said, and explained about the severed head. "Anyway, it's a county case. We're only liaising and providing manpower and support as needed."

Parker drove out the gate and guided the car toward the Interstate 5 freeway.

"But you just said Bill was seen at the ASW base—"

"And if he's there, that changes everything," Riley said. As they merged into the northbound lanes, three black-and-white police patrol cars flashed past, followed by two motorcycle units. All five vehicles had their red and blue lights flashing. Riley added under his breath, "Or maybe not."

Schag watched another two police vehicles flash past. "There's an awful lot of cop activity in this county. I've been seeing black-and-whites everywhere since I crossed the county line. Is it connected to Bill?"

"What do you think," Riley asked brusquely, "they're going to the Policeman's Ball?" After a moment, Riley apologized. "You've been on the road. You haven't been briefed on the latest developments. Here."

The agent reached into his briefcase, removed a swath of stapled pages, and handed them to Schag.

"This list of accusations and demands was discovered on a Facebook page used by Butcher," Riley explained as Schag leafed through the pages. "The media got hold of it, and they've already given it a name—The Butcher's Bill. Sweet, huh?"

"I don't understand that name," Parker said. "I mean I get the reference to Butcher. Obviously, it's his name. But why call it a bill? It makes it sound like the Bill of Rights or something."

Riley shrugged. "Maybe it refers to the old days when people use to run a bill with the local meat shop?"

"No," Shag said, still flipping through the pages, "it was probably a reporter with knowledge of naval history."

Parker shot Schag a questioning look in the rear-view mirror. Riley turned to him and said, "What?"

"The butcher's bill is an old naval term referring to the number of men killed and wounded in a battle," Schag said. He looked up at the two other men. "What I don't understand is how the media learned about Bill's nickname, The Butcher. It's not mentioned anywhere here." He gestured toward the pages in his hands.

"He's ex-Navy," Riley said, facing forward again. "Maybe one of his old buddies ratted on him."

"Bill didn't get that nickname until we were at the academy in Glencoe," Schag said. "None of his Navy buddies would call him that. Only NCIS agents."

Riley shrugged. "Who knows?" With an irritable wave of his hand he added, "Let's speed it up, Parker. Hit the lights."

A light bar secured to the inside of the windshield flashed red and amber as Parker sped through traffic. Schag read the so-called The Butcher's Bill quickly, then again with greater care. His jaw clenched harder as he read.

"Most of you who personally know me will be in disbelief to hear from media reports that I have decided to end my life," it began. "You are saying to yourself that this is completely out of character for the man you knew who always wore a smile wherever he was seen. But since I got home from Iraq, that smile had become more of a mask than a sincere expression.

"I know I will be vilified by the NCIS, which will say that since I returned from my tour in Iraq my investigative work has suffered, that I have been obsessed by make believe crimes I convinced myself were committed by U.S. officials and contractors. They will call these 'conspiracy theories' and 'X-files plots' and such. They even called me Fox Mulder, said I should wear a tin foil hat. They will tell you I returned from the war afflicted with severe depression and was no longer stable. They will tell you I was terminated from NCIS because of this.

"I have decided they were right.

"I have lost everything which made me me—my Navy career, my NCIS career, now my wife and two children. I no longer can function as the man I once was. I cannot provide for my wife, Yolanda, or my children, Bill Jr. and Beatrice. I've decided they can do better without me. I hope someday they can come to forgive me."

Schag nervously bit his lower lip, and looked out at the other cars on the freeway. Nothing in the words sounded like Bill Butcher, a man whose zest for life Schag envied. In a profession that often turns even the most charitable people hard and callous, Bill Butcher always remained a staunch believer in the goodness of mankind. More importantly, he always believed in himself. Schag turned back to the printout.

Two or three line spaces separated the next section of writing. Schag thought that curious. It looked added on as an afterthought or, maybe, like it was supposed to be separate from the words written above.

"But when I am gone, I hope others will take up my challenge. I call on all journalists and honest law enforcement investigators to demand the answers to this list of questions.

"1. Who received the nearly nine billion in cash shipped to Iraq by the Bush Administration and which disappeared without a trace?

"2. What role did Charles Bennett the Third and Gordias play in the disappearance of the money?

"3. What role did Gideon Security International play in the disappearance of the money?

"4. Why has the government refused to prosecute contractors who committed egregious crimes including rape and murder, and even protected them by paying off the families of victims?

"5. Why has the government done so little to ferret out the hundreds of bribes contractors have paid to otherwise honest military officers?

"These should be more than just questions. These should be demands, demands for the truth. Every American citizen should demand the answers to these questions. We owe to the men and women service members who risked their lives in Iraq and, especially, to those sacrificed their lives."

Schag knitted his eyebrows as he reread these last lines again. It seemed to him like an entirely different person wrote the last section—not the sad and depressed loser in the first paragraphs, but a confident, determined leader. It sounded like Bill Butcher.

The Navy's Fleet Anti-Submarine Warfare Training Center—also known as the ASW base—sits on a small point of land that juts into the bay like a movie star's square chin. Despite its name, there are no sub-chasing destroyers or helicopters here, no depth charges or anti-submarine torpedoes waiting for the kill. The moorings here are either unused or filled with pleasure craft. The only clues it was a military base were the welcoming sign at the main gate and the uniformed guard checking vehicles. Unlike the noisy workshops and warehouses at 32nd Street, the ASW base looks more like a college campus than a naval base, with modern classroom buildings, barracks that look like dorms, a parking structure, even a hotel for visiting personnel. Most times the base shows the same level of activity expected on a college campus during summer break.

This, however, was not most times.

North Harbor Drive, the wide, four-lane street that snaked past the base, was normally full of traffic. But as the agents approached, they saw nothing except dozens of black-and-white police cars, ambulances, and news vans with telescoping antennae lining its curbs. There were patrol cars from at least half a dozen different agencies, including the San Diego city police, the sheriff's department, the harbor police, even the Border Patrol. The parked cars led to a tighter knot of vehicles forming a semi-circle around the main gate. Parker slowed to show his credentials to a traffic cop who waved them through without a word. Up ahead, Schag saw a SWAT team line up to climb into an armored assault vehicle. The men wore camouflaged fatigues, ballistic vests and helmets, and carried a variety of automatic weapons. His heart sank into his stomach.

Parker pulled up to another traffic cop and flashed his badge again. The cop pointed to a large black-and-white bus bristling with antennae and said, "Incident command's right over there." Parker drove as close as he could to the bus and parked. The three agents got out and made sure their badges could be clearly seen before walking up to the incident command center.

Uniformed and plain-clothes officers crowded the bus, including a SWAT lieutenant Schag assumed was the weapons team's leader. He was talking to a tall, uniformed city police captain with thinning gray-blond hair and matching moustache. The officer looked up, saw Tom Riley enter the bus, and waved him over. The two shook hands before making introductions.

"Captain McManus," Riley said, "these are Special Agents Schag and Parker."

The police officer shook both agents' hands, then introduced the SWAT officer. He was a baby-faced man with sun-reddened skin and angry blue eyes. His name was Whitney. He gave each of the agents a dark glare.

"Schag?" The captain pointed a finger of recognition at Schag. "You're the agent Butcher asked for."

Schag shrugged. "I'm afraid I am."

"You have any light on why the suspect did what he did," McManus asked softly.

Cringing at the thought of Bill Butcher as a suspect, Schag said, "Sorry, but no. I'm as much in the dark as everyone else. I haven't seen Bill in nearly two or three years. We exchanged some emails, but just routine stuff. Family and work."

"So this guy writes your name in blood on a wall and you say you don't know anything about it?" Whitney snarled.

Schag bristled at the SWAT officer's tone. Checking himself, he turned to the captain. "As I said, I hadn't even received an email from him in months. I didn't even know he'd left NCIS until this morning."

"That's right," said Riley. "I called Agent Schag this morning to tell him about—what happened. He was as surprised that Mr. Butcher was no longer with NCIS as he was about what he did to those men."

"*Allegedly* did to those men," corrected Schag.

"Yeah," Whitney sneered. "*Allegedly.*"

Schag drew a deep breath, then let it out. His teeth clenched. He turned to look the baby-faced cop in the eyes, his own gray eyes hard and cold.

"You don't know how to play nice with others, do you?"

"Hey, he's your wacko friend," Whitney shot back. "We don't let that type in our department."

Schag stepped forward and grabbed the officer's ballistic vest so fast, the cop didn't have time to react.

"Bill Butcher is a former Navy SEAL with a couple dozen

combat deployments under his belt and an equal number of citations for valor," Schag said. "He could take you and your whole damn team apart single-handedly."

Whitney swatted Schag's hand away as his own went for the pistol grip of the assault rifle hanging from a three-point rig.

"Lieutenant Whitney!" The police captain's voice echoed through the command bus, causing heads to turn. "Tend to your team. Now!"

Whitney glared at the captain, then at Schag. As he turned to leave, he muttered, "Looks like NCIS has more than one whacko agent."

Riley started to speak, but Schag interrupted him.

"I apologize, captain," he said. "Bill Butcher was—is a very good friend and colleague. I'm having trouble believing he's done the things . . . that people say he has."

McManus shook his head. "Understandable, Agent Schag," he said. "Every agency has had good people go bad. As for Lieutenant Whitney, he has his own personal stake in this. He took a leave of absence from the department a couple years ago and went to Iraq with Gideon, and he still works as a part-time instructor for them. He knew one of the victs, a guy named Cavendish."

Great, thought Schag. Another mercenary.

"And, as you said," McManus continued, "Whitney doesn't play nice with others."

CHAPTER 5

AFTER LIEUTENANT WHITNEY'S EXIT, THE hubbub of conversations in the bus returned.

"Captain McManus, why don't you brief us on the situation here?" Riley asked.

"Sure," McManus said. He turned and scanned the others in the bus, caught the eye of a sailor at the far end and waved him over. The sailor wore the Navy's blue camouflaged fatigues and a black nylon duty belt with a M-9 Beretta in the holster, and a handheld radio with a microphone clipped to the front of his uniform. On his right chest above his nametape he wore a base security shield. "This is Senior Chief Fredericks. He's our liaison from base security." McManus introduced the NCIS agents. "Could you fill them in on the activities here last night?"

Frederick nodded, pulled a small, dark-green notebook from his thigh pocket, and flipped through the pages. Clearing his throat, he began his brief.

"At approximately 0530 this morning, our office received a BOLO from the San Diego County Sheriff's Department that they were seeking a retired Navy service member and former . . ." The senior chief looked at the agents nervously, cleared his throat, and continued. ". . . a former NCIS special agent named William Butcher on suspicion of murdering two indivi—"

"Senior chief," Riley interrupted, "that part we know. Please cut to the chase."

Fredericks cleared his throat again, and nodded. "Yes, sir. Ah, anyway, we immediately alerted our patrols to look for anyone matching the suspect's description. We also alerted the front desk of the BOQ—that is, the Navy Gateway Inn on base to notify us if anyone matching the suspect's appearance or name checked in. The Gateway Inn notified us that a Mr. William Butcher had checked in earlier in the morning at approximately 0230, using a retired Navy ID card. We locked down this base and every other Navy installation in the Point Loma area. No one was allowed in or out.

"Our patrol units responded to the Gateway Inn and sealed off all exits. The front desk confirmed the suspect's identity and description, and provided our officers with Mr. Butcher's room number and a pass-key card. After rousing and evacuating everyone else on Mr. Butcher's floor, our officers approached the suspect's room. When there was no answer to our officers' knock and demands to open the door, they used the hotel key card to unlock the door and tactically enter the room."

The senior chief stopped reading and looked up at the agents expectantly. After a few moments of looking at each other, Riley said, "And?"

"The room was empty, sir. No suspect. No luggage. Nothing."

"Any chance Bill—that is, the suspect, could have left the

floor with the other guests?" Schag asked.

"Not likely, sir," Fredericks said. "Everyone's identification was checked before they left their room and again when they were secured in the Inn's restaurant."

Schag nodded approvingly. "Well done, senior chief."

"Thank you, sir."

"What about a vehicle," Riley asked. "Any information on what he was driving?"

Fredericks shook his head. "Guests at the Inn are required to fill in a form describing their vehicle with its license plate. It appears Mr. Butcher failed to fill it in and the desk clerk didn't notice."

"So, we don't know what kind of car he's driving," Riley said flatly.

"Perhaps, sir," the senior chief said. "But we did have another incident that might be related. Shortly after 0600, our dispatch received a call from a sailor staying in the student barracks saying his pickup truck had been stolen. We rarely get stolen vehicle reports on base, sir."

Schag looked at Riley then at Parker. "It's possible Bill stole the truck to cover his tracks."

"Senior chief, we'll need information on the stolen vehicle," said McManus. "Year, type, color, etc."

"Yes, sir."

"That would mean the car he came in is still parked on base," Schag said.

"I could have some of my men run the plates on all the vehicles parked around the Inn," McManus said. "See if we can identify which car was his."

"If I may suggest, sir," Fredericks said, "once we have finished checking all the buildings on base and lift the lockdown, we could have the Inn's guests show us which vehicles are theirs. That would reduce the number of plates to run, sir."

McManus and the NCIS agents looked at each other, nodded, and smiled. "You ever thought about a career in NCIS when you retire, senior chief?" Riley asked.

"Oh, no you don't, Riley," McManus said. "I saw him first."

The senior chief stifled a grin, but the proud flush of his cheeks betrayed his satisfaction.

Schag saw Riley glance at a Rolex watch on his wrist. The agent couldn't tell if it was a real Rolex or a knockoff. Either way, it was an unusual item to see a NCIS agent wearing, even if he was agent in charge for the Southwest Region.

"Captain, you're aware there's a joint meeting at the county emergency operations center at 1400?" Riley asked.

McManus nodded and glanced at his own watch, which Schag noticed was a moderately priced sports brand.

"I think our bird has flown the coop here," he said. "I'll hand off to my second-in-command and meet you there." He nodded at Schag and Parker. "Pleasure meeting you, gentlemen." He turned and wound his way to another part of the bus.

The county emergency operations center, or EOC, stood on a side street away from the main flow of traffic, next to the county administration center. While the administration center was open to the public, the fenced-off EOC was only accessible by two locked gates. Parker pulled up to one and pressed a button on an intercom mounted on a pole.

"May I help you?" a disembodied female voice asked.

"Agents Riley, Schag, and Parker from NCIS," Parker announced, holding his badge up toward a video camera pointing at their car. "We're here for the 1400 joint task force meeting."

"Thank you," the voice answered. "Standby."

"Aren't EOCs used for disasters and such?" Schag asked as he watched the gate slide open. "Why here rather than the sheriff's department?"

"More room," Riley said, turning to look at Schag. As he did, he laid his arm across the backrest, revealing the Rolex again. It certainly looked real to Schag, who once considered buying one. That, however, was in another career, when he made much more money than he did as a federal agent. "The EOC is set up better than the sheriff's OC for a joint task force. Besides, the top floor of the EOC is the sheriff's dispatch center, so the department has office space here anyway."

The EOC was a massive three-story, wedge-shaped structure. The front of the building was at the base of the wedge where three wings formed a ragged tooth-like facade. Schag imagined that, from the air, the building resembled a B-2 stealth bomber. The entire structure was sitting on giant metal springs set deep into the earth and designed to let the building ride out severe earthquakes, which happened with great frequency in this part of the country. Parked next to the EOC was a group of mobile command vehicles in various sizes, from a large truck to a bus-size vehicle like the one Schag had seen at the ASW base.

Parker found a slot to park in, and the three agents got out, again adjusting their badges to be readily identifiable. Two glass doors made up the entrance to the EOC, and standing at these doors were three men and a female Navy officer in khakis. Schag noticed a certain degree of uneasiness among the four. As they got closer, one of them spoke.

"Would you gentlemen know how to open these doors?" a man with a ring of ruffled hair circling a baldpate asked.

"And you all would be?" asked Riley.

"My name is Dr. Winslow," the bald man said. "And this is Dr. Porter and Dr. Davis."

Like Winslow, the two other men wore conservative dark suits and carried leather brief cases, the type that opened from the top. They shook hands with the agents and Riley asked, "Physicians?"

"No," Winslow said, "PhDs. We're psychologists, experts in deviant behavior, PTSD, and so on. We were asked to attend a meeting of the joint task force, to be their brain trust, so to speak."

"I'm the only real doctor here," the Navy officer said, with a condescending smile aimed at Winslow, who had ignored her in his introductions.

She was short, with a wide, childlike face sprinkled with freckles, and medium-brown hair cut short and pulled back beneath a black beret. Her light-brown eyes were large and spaced far apart, and her nose small, above a wide, full-lipped mouth. Schag thought it a very nice face, and the figure beneath her shirt and skirt looked just as nice.

"Lieutenant Commander Clarke," she said, holding out her hand. "Unlike these gentlemen, I wasn't invited. I asked to attend and my commanding officer at Balboa Hospital—Admiral Mattson—made it so."

"Now that we have established everyone's bona fides, did any of you try knocking on the door?" asked Riley.

The three PhDs and Clarke looked at each other a moment, then toward the ground.

"Ah, no," Winslow muttered.

With a smirking glance at Schag and Parker, Riley rapped his wedding ring against the glass. A sheriff's deputy leaned over a counter barely visible from the door, saw the group, and held a finger up indicating, "Just a moment." Seconds later, the deputy rounded the corner and opened the door.

"Joint task force?" he asked, eying the badges worn by the agents.

"NCIS," said Riley, pointing to Schag and Parker. Then, nodding toward the three men and Clarke, he said, "Brain trust," not trying to hide his sarcasm.

The deputy held the door open and pointed to an elevator at the end of a long hallway.

"Second floor," he said. "Can't miss it."

With a sidelong glance at the PhDs and physician, Riley muttered, "I wouldn't bet on that."

The operations center was a large room separated into

sections by long, horseshoe-shaped tables bristling with computer monitors and phones. Vests of blue, yellow, or red draped the back of each chair. Each vest held the name of a position in the incident command system, the organizational structure used during emergencies such as wildfires, earthquakes, even manhunts. The largest flat-panel television screen Schag had ever seen dominated the front of the EOC. During an emergency, the screen could display a single video picture or as many as a dozen separate video shots, whatever the emergency managers needed to maintain their situational awareness. That day, however, the screen was dark. This was an informational meeting, not the actual command system overseeing the manhunt for Bill Butcher.

As agent in charge, Riley took a seat at the table while Schag and Parker took seats at the back of the room against the wall. The "brain trust" took chairs reserved for them at the big table. Seated at the end of the table was a man with gray thinning hair and wearing a crisp sheriff's uniform. Four stars twinkled at his collar, identifying him as *the* sheriff of San Diego County. Schag considered the stars superfluous. Watching the trio of deputies dashing back and forth at each twitch of the bald man's gray moustache was enough to identify his authority even if all he wore was a Speedo.

The sheriff stood and glanced about the room with cold, gray eyes, waiting for the hubbub of conversation to die down. When it did, he cleared his throat and looked over the room, nodding his head.

"I trust we've all had an interesting morning," he said, raising a few hushed chuckles. "I know mine has been. Murder isn't exactly a stranger in this county. We've even had a few headless corpses in my time. But a head without a body? That's something new."

More chuckles filled the room. The joke may have been off color, but everyone in the room knew that black humor at a time like this was often the only way to stay sane. Still, Schag didn't join in the laughter.

"I won't stand here and make a speech," he said. " I'm not

up for re-election yet." Again, more laughter. "But I did want to thank you all for responding so quickly to our request for assistance. We all know we have had some desperadoes in the county before, but when one is as highly trained as this suspect is . . . well, it's good to have friends."

Around the table heads nodded. Only Riley and the other two agents' heads remained still. The sheriff appeared to notice.

"I also want to assure our colleagues from NCIS," he said, nodding toward Riley, "that we appreciate the position this tragedy puts them in. None of us here has not seen one of our own go bad. And I want you to know, Tom, we've got your back."

The room filled with the sound of polite applause, and Riley nodded in thanks.

"I appreciate that, Sheriff Betz," Riley said.

Parker leaned over so his mouth was close to Schag's ear. "That guy is a supreme politician, isn't he?"

"Which one," Schag whispered back, smiling, "the sheriff or Riley?"

Parker thought a moment, and grinned. "I guess you're right."

A door opened and Captain McManus entered the EOC with an exaggerated attempt at being quiet. The sheriff noticed him anyway.

"Oh, Mike," he said. "Glad you could join us."

"Sorry about that," McManus said. "We had a busy morning."

"Not to worry. The briefing just started." The sheriff turned and whispered something to one of his aides. The aide nodded, and the sheriff again addressed his audience. "As I promised, no more speeches from me. I want to introduce Commander John Hanes, the head of our emergency services division." A younger man with well-groomed dark hair and only one star on his collar stood and nodded at the others. "Emergency services contains both the special enforcement detail—that's what we call our SWAT team—our hostage negotiation team, and ASTREA, our aviation unit. It also holds most of our reserve deputies, many of whom were activated for this . . . crisis. John, would you bring us up to speed on the search and the investigation?"

Commander Hanes thanked the sheriff and took his place at the head of the table. In a slow, dry voice, he briefed the gathering on the number of regular and reserve deputies that were on duty, the number of fixed- and rotary-wing aircraft the department had available, and the number of tactical officers staged throughout the county. Schag watched several attendees take notes. Occasionally, someone raised a hand and asked a question. His eyes fell on the brain trust. The three men—the PhDs—appeared enthralled with the minute details Hanes was dishing out. The woman, Dr. Clarke, appeared less so. She stared at a spot on the opposite wall, her hands playing absently with a ballpoint pen. She seemed to sense Schag watching her and turned her face toward him. Schag smiled and nodded, but Clarke only turned her stare back to the spot on the wall.

"The office of Customs and Border Patrol offered us the use of one of their new surveillance drones," Hanes said. "You'll be more familiar with this aircraft as the Predator used extensively by the military in Afghanistan. It will provide us with much more sustained flight time than normal aircraft. Of course, the CPB Predator isn't armed."

"We're working on that," said one of attendees, bringing about more laughter.

"Now I understand NCIS is available to give more background on the suspect, Mr. William Butcher, that might shed some light on his actions," Hanes said. "Tom?"

"Thank you, John," Riley said, rising. He half turned and held his hand out toward Schag. "I brought with me today Special Agent Linus Schag—"

"The guy whose name was painted on the wall with blood?" the sheriff blurted.

Every set of eyes in the room turned and stared at Schag as if he were some mysterious, grotesque creature. Schag felt his stomach churn.

"That's right, sheriff," Riley continued. "Agent Schag knows William Butcher better than anyone. They went through basic agent training together. I thought he could provide some background on the suspect."

Schag swallowed hard, his mouth dry. He had no idea he was to be used this way. Riley should have warned him. He stood, shooting a hard glare at his boss. Riley's face remained impassive.

"Perhaps Agent . . . Schag . . ." Winslow, the deviant behaviorist, pronounced Schag's name as "skag."

"Schag," the agent said.

"I beg your pardon?" Winslow looked at Schag over his reading glasses.

"My name," Schag said. "The C is silent. It's pronounced 'shag.'"

Winslow looked at the agent as if he were an impertinent schoolchild. "The agenda," he said, "has your name spelled S-C-H-A-G. Is that correct?"

Schag hadn't known there was an agenda that might have warned him of this ordeal. He nodded.

"Well, then, it should be pronounced Skag, just as school is pronounced."

Schag closed his eyes for moment, relishing the thought of using a police baton on the psychologist's head. "With all due respect, Dr. Winslow, it's my family name, and we'll pronounce it the way we want."

The others at the long table snickered, much to Winslow's consternation. Schag glanced at Riley who mouthed the words "brain trust."

"Very well, Mr. . . . Schag." This time Winslow pronounced it correctly. "Perhaps, you could give us some insight into Mr. Butcher's background. Something that might help us understand his actions."

"Agent . . . former Agent Butcher was one the best agents I've ever worked with, sir," he said. "I cannot imagine why he would commit these murders or make those demands—if he did do so. As for his background, he was a former Navy SEAL—that is, a sea, air, and land special operations commando. I think you all know that already. Bill—Mr. Butcher—suffered a serious injury in a parachute accident, and took a medical discharge from the Navy. He recovered and applied to NCIS about the same time I did. We became roommates at the academy in Glynco."

"We understand how friendship can sometimes blind a person to his or her friends' less than desirable traits," said one of Winslow's companions. "But did this Mr. Butcher ever display a temper or a tendency towards violence?"

The stupidity of the question made Schag burn. "Mr. Butcher was a former SEAL, one of the most elite warriors in the world. He was trained to kill, if necessary. But I never once saw him be violent without cause—"

"Without cause," the psychologist interrupted. "What does that mean?"

Schag took another deep breath.

"We are law enforcement agents," he said through clenched teeth. "We sometimes get involved in violent situations with people who are violent. Sometimes we need to meet that violence with violence per the established tenets of the continuum of force."

Schag felt the muscles in his neck tighten, and with that tightness came a stab of pain in his shoulder that reminded him of the last time he faced one of those violent people, a crazed serial killer who almost shattered Schag' shoulder with a heavy wrench.

The same shrink started to ask another question, but Schag continued.

"I knew Bill Butcher professionally and as a friend, and I never knew him to be hot tempered or unduly violent," he said. "I know his family—his wife Yolanda and their two kids. He was madly in love with all three of them. He was like a teddy bear around his family."

"Then why did Mr. Butcher and his wife separate?"

"I didn't know they'd separated until I read his list of

demands," Schag said.

"Ah, yes, The Butcher's Bill, as the media so whimsically calls it," said Winslow.

"Agent, when *was* the last time you saw your close friend, Mr. Butcher?" Winslow's companion asked.

"About three years ago," Schag answered. "Maybe more. Bill was working a case in Bahrain and I was transporting a prisoner. We ran into each other at the NCIS offices there. Tom—Agent Riley, you remember, don't you? You were working out of Bahrain then."

Riley nodded. "Yes, I remember that case. About two years ago, I'd say."

"And what did you talk about?" the psychologist asked.

"Just caught up on life, work, and his family."

"And nothing since then? Winslow asked.

Schag shook his head. "We exchanged emails occasionally. Might be six months since the last time I heard from him. I sent him emails but never heard back."

"You weren't aware Mr. Butcher was dismissed by the NCIS six months ago?" Again Winslow.

"No."

"So," Winslow concluded, "you weren't such close friends, after all."

Schag didn't answer.

"Perhaps the agent could explain to us why such a nonviolent person as this Mr. Butcher would call himself The Butcher?" the third psychologist asked.

Schag bit the inside of his mouth, trying to keep his anger in check. He crossed his arms behind his back and balled his fists until the knuckles turned white.

"Bill Butcher never called himself The Butcher," he said. "That was a nickname we gave him in the academy."

"Was there a particular reason you named him that?" Winslow asked.

"There was a lead instructor in D-Tac who was . . ."

"I'm sorry," Winslow interrupted. "An instructor in what"

"D-Tac," Schag repeated. "Defensive tactics. Hand-to-hand

combat. The lead instructor liked to get . . . overzealous when demonstrating tactics on trainees, sometimes injuring them. When he tried to get . . . overzealous . . . with Bill—well, being an ex-SEAL, Bill knew more about hand-to-hand combat than the instructor. The instructor ended up face down on the mat in an arm lock he couldn't get out of. That's when we—all the trainees—started calling Bill 'The Butcher.'"

Winslow removed his reading glasses and looked at Schag. "So, Mr. Butcher lost his temper with this instructor and assaulted him."

Schag glared at the psychologist. "That is not what I said. Bill demonstrated his superior knowledge of defensive tactics. Afterward, the instructor asked Bill to help teach the D-Tac classes. And the instructor never got overzealous with the trainees again."

Winslow stared back at Schag a moment, his lips puckered. "Very well, thank you, Agent . . . Schag," he said, making sure he pronounced it correctly. He looked at his colleagues. They both shook their heads. "You've been most helpful."

Winslow turned away, as did everyone else at the table. Schag continued standing for another minute, struggling with his own anger. With a deep sigh, he sat back down.

CHAPTER 6

MONDAY
San Diego County Emergency
Operations Center
San Diego, California
1230 Hours

SCHAG BARELY HEARD THE REST of the meeting. Someone asked whether Butcher could have developed post-traumatic stress disorder—PTSD—since his tour in Iraq was in a noncombatant role. The Navy commander said something about participation in combat was not necessary to get PTSD, that exposure to the stress and horrors of war was enough. Schag wondered why none of them realized that as a SEAL, Bill was involved in both overt and covert combat operations dating back to the first Gulf War, but he said nothing.

One of the shrinks wondered if Butcher was a victim of something he called "mobbing."

"If his co-workers thought his work actions were jeopardizing their own self-interests," said Winslow, waggling his ballpoint pen in the air, "if they thought he was jeopardizing their promotions or, say, raises—whatever—they might gang up on him, to *mob* him as we say, and create a hostile work environment that would force him to leave his position. If so, he could still harbor great grievances against his co-workers. We see this all the time in work place dynamics."

Tom Riley protested the speculation.

"The NCIS, like all U.S. government agencies, has programs in place that ensure any employee with a grievance can have that grievance heard," Riley said.

"Have you ever heard the phrase 'going postal,' Agent Riley?" Winslow asked. "Last time I checked, the U.S. Postal Service was a U.S. government agency."

Riley rolled his eyes and sat back with a sigh.

"We should acknowledge, however, that Mr. Butcher has yet to harm any of his fellow NCIS agents," said one of Winslow's colleagues.

"He did write Agent Schag's name in blood at a murder scene," said Hanes. "That could be taken as threatening."

"Or a request to have an old friend called in who could talk to him," said Riley.

Lieutenant Commander Clarke tried to break in several times, but the three men of the brain trust ignored her. Commander Hanes interrupted the psychologists and asked Clarke to make her point.

"We hear a lot of talk of PTSD and suicide among veterans," she said. "But research indicates there may be another cause of emotional turmoil among veterans. It's called agueloquine psychosis."

"That's utter nonsense. The reports of psychosis caused by agueloquine are anecdotal, at best," Winslow said. "It's been prescribed to thousands, perhaps millions, of people around the world with no harmful side effects."

"And just what is this . . . what did you call it?" asked Hanes.

"Agueloquine," she said. "It's an anti-malarial drug developed by the Army that's been given to thousands of our service members. In most people, it's harmless. However, in a small minority of people, it appears to cause a form of psychosis."

"Oh, really," said Winslow, his head shaking along with his two colleagues. "And what research would that be?"

"Research we're conducting at the naval medical center," she answered. "We've been looking into this—"

"I'm sorry, young lady, but we are wasting our time with this avenue of discussion." Winslow turned his back to Clarke, as did his two fellow psychologists.

Schag didn't hear any more. Telling Parker he needed to use the restroom, he left the EOC and paced the corridor outside. He stopped at a window and looked out at the county administration building next door. There people walked calmly to their offices. Some sat outside in the shade, working on laptop computers. Others sat outside the cafeteria, eating late lunches. No one seemed to care there was a madman running loose, a madman who was one of Schag's closest friends. He removed his glasses, squeezed his eyes until he thought they might pop, and ran his hand across his entire face. He didn't hear the voice behind him say his name.

"Mr. Schag?" It was a woman's voice. When Schag didn't respond, she tried again. "I'm sorry. I should say Agent Schag."

Schag turned and found Lieutenant Commander Clarke looking up at him with her large brown eyes. He slipped his glasses back on.

"That's correct, isn't it?" she asked. "NCIS agents should be called Agent So-and-So, right?"

"As long as you pronounce my name correctly," Schag said.

"I've never met an NCIS agent before," she said, "so I wasn't sure."

"Is there something I can help you with, commander?"

"I hope so," she said, nervously. "I mean, I hope I can help you . . . and your friend, Agent Butcher."

"Your colleagues in the 'brain trust' don't seem eager to

help *former* Agent Butcher," he said.

"They aren't my colleagues, agent," Clarke said. "They're psychologists. I'm medical corps."

Schag glanced at the gold insignia on Clarke's khaki collar. Unlike the Army, which used the medical caduceus to identify medical personnel, the Navy used a golden oak leaf to identify medical officers. Clarke's leaf had an acorn centered on it, the emblem of a physician.

"I see," Schag said. "You're a *real* doctor."

"Quite," she said. She looked up and down the hallway. "Look, is there a place we can talk? Someplace not so heavy with testosterone?"

Schag glanced out the window again.

"There's a cafeteria over there," he said with a jerk of his head. "I could use some coffee."

"Great," Clarke said. "Me, too."

They walked across the compound in silence. Clarke sensed Schag was too preoccupied for small talk, and she was still steaming about her own treatment at the hands of the *brain trust*. Clarke insisted on buying the coffee and Schag let her, sensing her own need to establish herself as more than a mere woman after her mistreatment by the psychologists. She ordered a nonfat cafe latte, Schag a black coffee, and they took a table outdoors.

Schag took a hesitant sip from his steaming paper cup and asked, "You said you could help Bill Butcher?"

Clarke sipped her own drink and nodded. "I think so, at least," she said.

Schag eyed her the way he'd eye a suspect. "How?"

"You heard what I was trying to explain earlier?"

Clarke nodded. "When you were shut down by the so-called brain trust. Some of it. I was a little preoccupied with my own thoughts."

"I can imagine," Clarke said. "You don't think Mr. Butcher could do the things he's accused of, do you?"

Schag took another sip of coffee, looked around, then back at Clarke.

"I don't know what I think right now, commander," he said. "I guess he did do it. I mean he left a message at the murder scene—well, one of them. That was pretty much a confession. But . . ." Schag shook his head. "Bill was a good friend. A great guy. Everybody liked him. He was a conscientious agent. A good husband and a loving father. I can't believe he'd just turn like this."

"And that's what I believe, too," Clarke said. "I'm a neurologist, Agent Schag, and I'm involved in a study looking at the neurological effects of agueloquine on service members who have been given it as a malaria prophylactic. Our data show several service members have had psychotic breaks after taking agueloquine, resulting in acts of violence against themselves or others."

"Themselves? You mean suicide?"

Clarke nodded and took a sip of coffee. "Sometimes worse. Sometimes horrific. Have you ever heard of an army sergeant named Bales?"

Schag thought a moment, remembering. "You mean the soldier who went off post in Afghanistan and murdered several Afghani civilians?"

Clarke nodded again.

"Mostly women and children," she said. "He walked off post once and used his service weapon to murder families in their sleep—men, women, and children—then calmly walked back on post. After a while, he went back and did it all again. Now I don't want to defend what he did, but there has been some discussion whether Sergeant Bales was a victim agueloquine psychosis."

Clarke reached into her black brief case, pulled out a manila folder fat with sheets of paper, and thumbed through the sheets. Finding what she wanted, she handed Schag several photocopied newspaper articles.

"Bales was only one incident," Clarke continued. "In the summer of 2002, four separate soldiers, all previously deployed to Iraq, murdered members of their families. All four soldiers took agueloquine while deployed. In 2004, another soldier was court-martialed for cowardice. Prior to that, he had an exemplary service record. The Army eventually determined his acts of cowardice were due to agueloquine psychosis and acquitted him."

She let Schag scan the papers. They were all United Press International news stories about the Army linking agueloquine to a 2004 series of murders committed by soldiers stationed at Fort Bragg. Schag finished reading them and handed them back.

"I could go on, agent," Clarke said, sliding the photocopies back into their folder, and the folder into her brief case. "Suicides, murders, you name it. Both in the military and civilian communities, and all linked back to agueloquine."

"Just what is this . . . agueloquine, commander?" Schag asked.

"It's an anti-malaria drug developed by the U.S. Army to replace doxycycline as a prophylactic to prevent malarial infections," she said. "Doxy is an antibiotic, but it also prevents most malaria infections. The problem is, you need to take it every day, and getting service members to do that is difficult. With agueloquine, you only take it once a week. That was the nice thing about it. Service members were more likely to adhere to their dosage regimen."

Clarke took a sip of coffee, and dabbed her lips with a paper napkin.

"Unfortunately, the Army rushed agueloquine through testing," she continued. "There were . . ." She wagged her hand. "There were also some irregularities in the testing. Before it was discovered there was form of neurotoxicity to it, agueloquine was in widespread use around the world, not only by the military but civilians, too."

Schag thought a moment, thinking back to his deployments to the Middle East.

"When I've deployed, I've been given a pill to take once a week for malaria," he said. "That had to be this agueloquine, right?" Clarke nodded. "Does that mean I'll lose my mind?"

"No, no, no," Clarke said, shaking her head. "Not

necessarily. It seems only to have a neurological effect on a very small number people. It may have to do with genetics or a predisposition to mental illness. Some research shows a relationship with mild traumatic brain injury or post-traumatic stress disorder. Other research indicates the psychosis may present after the drug bioaccumulates in the brain or the body. We simply don't know. That's why it's so important we find your friend Mr. Butcher and—how do you say it? And bring him in . . . *alive*."

"How do you know for certain Bill was taking agueloquine?"

"It would be unlikely he didn't," Clarke answered. "The military didn't stop prescribing the drug until 2013, well after Mr. Butcher's tour in Iraq."

Schag leaned toward Clarke, pounding the table with his finger as he spoke. "They continued to give this drug to service members even though they knew it was unsafe?"

"It was a matter of necessity, agent," she said. "Understand this, malaria kills more than half a million people each year. Compare that risk to the very minute risk of agueloquine toxicity affecting only a handful of people each year."

Schag tugged at his lower lip, thinking. He asked, "If this agueloquine is so . . . neuro toxic, why were the shrinks in the meeting so dismissive of your theory?"

Clarke leaned her elbows on the table, interlaced her fingers, and rested her chin on them, looking at Schag with mock wide-eyed wonder.

"Because, Agent Schag," she said in a sarcastic, sing-song way, "they're not here to help the police understand Mr. Butcher. They're here to cover the government's ass."

"What?"

"They're not the local police or sheriff's experts," Clarke said. "They weren't asked to come here. The U. S. Department of Justice sent them to deflect blame for everything that's happening away from Uncle Sam." Clarke made a gesture with both hands as if shoving them into pockets. "You know, everyone's uncle with the deep pockets?"

"Why the government?"

"The government created it. The government issued it to service members. Who else will people blame?"

Schag took a deep breath, thinking. "So, they throw Bill to the wind and deny he might have been impacted by this agueloquine so anybody hurt by him can't sue the government?"

Clarke resumed her mocked look of wonder. "Now you're beginning to understand, agent," she said. "Sure, it'd be a long shot, but there is always some scumbag Wall Street lawyer willing to take a chance at a big settlement."

"I used to be one of those scumbag Wall Street lawyers," Schag said.

Clarke raised her eyebrows. "Sorry," she said.

Schag waved a hand, dismissing the subject. In truth, when he worked on Wall Street, he did feel like a scumbag.

"But you can't know for certain Bill was prescribed the drug, can you?" he asked.

"We're sure," Clarke said, nodding. "As part of our study, we have access to the medical records of uniformed and civilian Navy and Marine Corps personnel deployed to Iraq and Afghanistan. The military's ability to capture medical data on deployed personnel greatly improved during these two wars. We didn't want to happen what occurred at the end of Vietnam and Desert Storm, where we had to guess at what service members were exposed to."

"No more Agent Orange or Gulf War Syndrome debacles," Schag said.

"Exactly," Clarke said.

Agent Orange was a toxic herbicide used to kill jungle growth during the Vietnam War. Thousands of American service members and millions of Vietnamese later suffered severe, even lethal, health problems from exposure to Agent Orange. During the First Gulf War, service men and women suffered health problems from exposure to airborne toxins from burning oil wells, bombed fighting vehicles, and the latest in armor-piercing depleted uranium munitions. In both cases, years often passed before symptoms appeared. It was a nightmare for the veterans and the government to prove if an illness resulted from a wartime exposure or was naturally occurring.

"As soon as I heard the news reports about Mr. Butcher, I checked our database for his medical records. They showed he was prescribed agueloquine not only while deployed as an NCIS agent, but earlier, too, when he was with the SEAL teams."

"And if we do catch him and . . . *bring him in alive* . . ." Schag winced at the phrase. ". . . what can you do for him? Is there a treatment, or some kind of antidote?"

Clarke leaned back, took a deep breath, and shook her head.

"I'm not going to lie to you, Agent Schag," she said. "I don't know if we can do anything for Mr. Butcher. But we can *try*. The more people we can find like Mr. Butcher, the more testing we can do, the better chance we have of understanding how this happens."

"In other words, make him a guinea pig," Schag said, not trying to hide the distaste in his voice.

"Better a guinea pig than a corpse," Clarke said. "Wouldn't you agree, Agent Schag?"

CHAPTER 7

SCHAG'S BLACKBERRY VIBRATED IN HIS coat pocket. Pulling it out, he checked the caller ID and saw Tom Riley's name.

"My master's voice," he told Clarke. Pressing the answer button, he said, "Yeah, Tom, what's up?"

"Where the hell are you, Lin?" Tom demanded.

"Having coffee with Lieutenant Commander Clarke," Schag answered.

"Who?"

"The doc that spoke at the meeting."

"Where?" Tom sounded confused.

"Just across the compound from the EOC," Schag explained. "There's a cafeteria of sorts here."

Riley grunted. "Well, this is no time to pick up strange women," he said. "Get your butt back here pronto. We've got to get back to the base. The former assistant secretary of the Navy is meeting us there."

"Charles Bennett?" Schag asked, though he knew the answer.

"Charles Bennett *the Third*," Riley corrected. "Old Bomber Bennett himself."

"On my way," Schag said. He pressed the End Call button and put the Blackberry back in his jacket. "I've got to go, Commander."

Clarke's eyes were wide. "Something to do with Charles Bennett?" she asked.

Schag nodded. "*The Third*," he said, standing.

Clarke stood, too. "Old Bomber Bennett?"

"The one and only," the agent said, nodding.

"Oh, my," Clarke said, slinging her brief case over her shoulder. "What have you done to deserve such punishment?"

Tom Riley and Tim Parker were waiting in the agency car with the engine running when Schag and Clarke reached the EOC. They exchanged business cards before Schag climbed into the vehicle's front passenger seat.

"What the hell was that about?" Riley growled. He threw the car in reverse and pulled out of the parking slot before Schag could fasten his seat belt.

"Commander Clarke is a physician," Schag said, buckling the belt. "She's a neurologist and medical researcher. She had some information on what may have caused Bill Butcher to go over the edge."

Schag recounted their discussion about agueloquine

and its psychotic effects on certain people. When he finished, Riley shrugged.

"So, what's that mean to us?" he asked. "Can she fix him?"

"She's not sure, but she does feel strongly she needs to study him to find a cure," Schag said. "She wants us to capture him *alive*."

Riley grunted as he turned the car onto the freeway, and sped south. "That'll be a neat trick, considering the temper he's in. Besides, it's not our case. It's in the hands of the cops."

Schag remembered the SWAT lieutenant at the ASW base and felt a bitterness rise in his throat.

"And what are the cops doing now?" he asked.

"Yeah, while you were flirting with the good doctor, we got a call from security at the ASW base," Riley said. "They were able to identify Butcher's car, though it wasn't registered to him."

Schag's brow furrowed. "If it's not registered to Bill, how do they know it was his car?"

"You remember that severed head Butcher left at the Gideon compound?" asked Parker. Schag nodded. "Well, base security pried open the trunk of the suspicious car. Inside they found everything south of the head."

The sour taste in Schag's throat increased. He closed his eyes, pushed up his classes, and squeezed his eyes with his finger and thumb.

"We figure Butcher took the victim's car to the Gideon compound, then drove it to the ASW base," Parker continued. "In the morning, he left the sedan and stole the pickup truck to throw us off his trail."

"The sheriff put out a BOLO out on the stolen truck," Riley said, "and he's got air units looking for it on all of the freeways. That includes that Predator drone the

Customs boys have." Riley shook his head. "What the fuck do they need a Predator for?" He switched lanes to avoid a slow driver, muttering, "Homeland Security gets all the good stuff."

What passed as the conference room for NCIS Southwest Regional HQ was less impressive than those envisioned by Hollywood. People who thought the military had the latest in high-tech equipment always amazed Schag. It was a false impression generated by movie scriptwriters with no military background. Anyone with military experience understood the equipment bought with the taxpayers' money rarely performed as advertised, if it performed at all. When it came to computers and broadband, the Navy had less than even a moderately well-off corporation. Open and secured Internet connectivity was intermittent at best. Computers were old and filled with so much security software they barely operated. The intent of the security software was to combat Chinese hackers who broke into DoD systems with too much regularity. The fact that most computers used by the U.S. military were built in China was never mentioned as the problem.

The secured conference room was crammed into a windowless room lined with flat-panel video displays for teleconferencing. A camera mounted at the front, along with tabletop microphone-speaker assemblages, provided for video teleconferencing or VTC—when it worked, which it wasn't. A technician cursed as he tried to fix the problem, all the time blaming Congressional budget cuts for all the woes in the country, including his crappy equipment.

"Those bastards in the House work four days out of every ten and still draw a full-time salary," he grumbled, as he ran a diagnostic program. "Then they say us civil servants make too much money and furlough us one day a week. How do they think things get done in the Navy?"

"Wah, wah," Riley said. "Poor little you. Just be happy you still have a job, which you won't if you don't get this stuff running in the next fifteen minutes."

Schag checked his email on his Blackberry. "I thought you said Bennett was meeting us here," he said.

"That's what I was told," Riley said, looking through some papers in front of him. "He decided differently. He's currently in hiding. Apparently, he believes Bill Butcher is coming after him. He decided it was safer for him to do a VTC." Riley glanced at his watch. "Where the hell is Parker with our coffee?"

"I'm right here," Parker said, entering the room carrying a carton loaded with three tall cups of coffee and two piles of sugar and sweetener. He handed one to Riley with an apologetic look. "Sorry. The line at the coffee stand took forever."

He handed another coffee to Schag, who thanked him and grabbed a packet of sweetener. Riley dumped three packets of sugar into his coffee, stirred it, and tasted it. The sweet concoction didn't change his sour mood.

"You got that thing working yet?" he grumbled at the technician.

"Just finishing it up," the technician said.

He booted up the computer and, in a few minutes, the screen at the front of the conference room came alive, showing a field of blue except in one corner where a small box showed the three NCIS agents and the technician in the conference room.

"There you go. Happy?" The technician stood up and

adjusted the video camera that didn't seem to have any effect on the small video picture. "When your party logs in, he'll automatically show up on the screen."

"About time," Riley said.

"Could've had this fixed last week if'n all us techs wasn't furloughed for a day," the technician said, heading for the door. "Next time you have technical problems, call your congressman."

Schag looked at his watch and asked, "When's old Bomber Bennett supposed to call in?"

Riley looked at his own watch. "Should be any minute. But he'll make us wait to show us how important he is."

"Why do they call him Bomber Bennett?" Parker asked.

"He was part of the old administration's big push to invade Iraq," Schag said, catching a warning glance from Riley. "You've heard of Shock and Awe?" Shock and Awe was the cute media name the previous administration had given its intense bombing of Iraq prior to the land invasion. Parker nodded. "Well, Charles Bennett *the Third. . .*" Schag tossed a quick grin at Riley. ". . . was the real political power behind Shock and Awe, only he wanted it to be more shocking and awesome. He was quoted as saying he wanted to bomb Iraq back to the Stone Age."

"And so the media called him Bomber Bennett," Parker said, catching on.

Schag nodded. "But it had less to do with his fighting nature than with the fact he had a half dozen draft deferments during the Vietnam War when he could've done all the bombing he wanted himself. Now he's been nominated to become defense secretary."

"That's—strange, isn't it?" Parker asked. "I mean he's not exactly an ally of the president. They're from different parties."

Schag shrugged. "Hands across the aisle?"

"Maybe the new administration wants to appear strong on defense," Riley said. "Bennett has the experience."

"He also has enough money to buy the Pentagon, and all the politicians in it," Schag added softly.

"That's enough of that," Riley said, with even a stronger look of warning. Schag merely shrugged. "He should be logging on anytime now."

At that instant, the video screen blinked twice and the stern, angular face of Charles Bennett III stared down at them like an angry schoolteacher.

"Sir, good afternoon, sir," Riley said. "My name is Special Agent Tom Riley, the agent in charge for the NCIS Southwest Region."

Bennett nodded and said, "Agent."

Riley waved a hand toward his subordinates. "These are Special Agents Schag and Parker."

Bennett turned his mouth down. "Schag? That would be this Linus Schag that the madman called for?"

"That would be me, yes," Schag responded. He knew what the next question would be.

"And what do you think . . . triggered this man Butcher's action, special agent?"

"I'm afraid I'm as bewildered by Bill Butcher's actions as everyone else," Schag replied.

"Sir, we just returned from a meeting with local law enforcement authorities. They've retained the services of a . . ." Riley paused and pursed his lips. ". . . of a brain trust of psychologists to try to determine Mr. Butcher's motivations. They are looking at a number of possibilities, including PTSD, traumatic brain injury, and—" Riley turned to Schag. "What was it that doctor told you about?"

"Agueloquine," Schag said, surprised Riley had actually paid attention to his description of Clarke's theory.

"Yes, agueloquine."

Bennett's eyes narrowed. "Agueloquine?" His thin lips pressed tighter together. "What about agueloquine?"

Riley turned to Schag again and waved at him to answer.

"Agueloquine is an anti-malarial drug," Schag began. "A preventative. In some people, it can have an adverse neurological impact, a kind of toxicity that can cause psychosis. Lieutenant Commander Kendra Clarke is a Navy neurologist who's been studying this problem. She told me she's confirmed Mr. Butcher was prescribed this drug while he was deployed to Iraq. She thinks his behavior might be caused by agueloquine."

Bennett nodded, his lips still pressed together. After a moment, he said, "Very well. And what are your plans on how to deal with this man?"

"Sir, since Mr. Butcher is no longer a Navy employee, the murders he apparently committed fall under the jurisdiction of local law enforcement, more precisely the local sheriff's department. Our role is merely to liaison with the sheriff's investigators and provide assistance as needed."

"I had hoped your office would be a little more proactive in this matter, Agent Riley," Bennett said. Schag noticed Riley blanch.

Riley cleared his throat.

"Sir, we are limited by our jurisdiction—or lack thereof in this case," he said. "However, our jurisdiction does include providing protection to former Navy officials who may be threatened by Mr. Butcher. As former assistant secretary of the Navy, sir, we are ready to provide you with protection. Now, I understand you're here in town. Our agents can take you to a safe house and—"

"Thank you, but no," Bennett said. "I have arranged for my own protection, agent. Your help will not be needed."

"But, sir—"

Bennett shook his head and held up a hand.

"Not needed, Agent Riley. But I thank you." He glanced at the watch on his wrist. Schag noticed it was a Rolex, but Bennett's looked far more expensive than Riley's. "I have to go. I would appreciate regular updates on this matter, agent. I'll have my office provide you with information on how you can contact me."

Then the screen went blank.

The three agents looked at each other, dumbfounded.

"Provided his own protection?" Schag said. "Who?"

"I read somewhere he did that when he was assistant Navy secretary," Riley said. "He would go off for days with no official guard detail. He'd hire his own bodyguards."

"Who?" Schag asked.

"Gideon Security," Riley said.

The three agents looked at each other again.

"Considering happened last night," Schag said, "who's going to guard the bodyguards?"

CHAPTER 8

MONDAY
Gideon Security International
Training Compound
San Diego County, California
1600 Hours

AIDAN BLACK WAS NOT IN a good mood. The events of the past night—the deaths of two of his operators at the hands of a psychotic maniac—did not make good publicity for Gideon Security International. As Gideon's chief executive officer, he had built what had once been a security guard company providing rent-a-cops to shopping malls and sporting events into one of the largest security and tactical training companies in the world. Gideon currently had contracts not only with the U.S. government and its military and law enforcement agencies, but also with governments around the globe. He built the company a reputation for high-tech, low-drag operations. However, he had used the knowledge of propaganda tactics he learned in the Army to build that reputation. It didn't matter what the customer saw, it was what they believed, and Aidan Black could make most people believe anything. Black saw nothing wrong in that; every company did it. They called it public relations, advertising, or whatever. He simply did it better than most.

Sitting at the desk in Cavendish's office, Black flipped a Gideon challenge coin between the fingers of his right hand and thought about the consequences. Black was tall and thin, with thinning, dark hair and a closely cropped mustache. The mustache was part of the facade. He had copied it from a sergeant major in the British Special Air Service. It had the effect of imparting the air of a professional soldier. He encouraged his operators to adopt similar mustaches, which they did to the point the moustaches became known as the Gideon Brush.

The challenge coin slipped from his fingers and clattered on the desk. He picked it up and stared at it, first one side, then the other. It was the color of pewter, gray with a touch of color for highlights. Both sides sported a rendition of the American eagle, wings spread wide on one surface, furled on the other. He copied that, too, from a Department of Homeland Security challenge coin. The side with the spread-eagle wings read GIDEON SECURITY INTERNATIONAL. The other side read UNITED STATES OF AMERICA. The eagles, the bold words, and the weight of the coin itself imparted the feeling of strength and patriotism to the customers he gave them to.

The problem, as Black knew damned well, was that Gideon Security was a house of cards that could tumble down with one wrong move, a move like having two of his operators— possibly three since one was still missing—killed by one man. It was particularly appalling that Butcher had infiltrated Gideon's Southern California training center, killed its director, and escaped into the night undetected. My God, no one at the center knew anything had happened until someone went looking for Cavendish in the morning. Black had flown out from the east coast as soon as he had heard the news. By the time he arrived in San Diego, Twitter was alive with sarcastic tweets about Gideon. With the sheriff's forensics team finished in Cavendish's office, he sat at the desk wondering how he was going to salvage Gideon's reputation.

In a fit of pique, Black threw the coin across the room. It hit the wall, bounced off, and landed on the carpeting where Cavendish's blood had pooled. *That* would need dealing with straight away, he thought to himself.

The sound of Black's cell phone interrupted his thoughts. He glanced at the number. *Oh, God, what does he want?*

He pressed the answer button and said, "Aidan Black."

After listening for a minute, he pulled a pen and small, green, military memo pad from his pocket.

"I don't understand," he said. "What? Who?"

He jotted a name on the pad.

"And who is she?"

He made another notation on the pad.

"Just discredit her? That's all you want?" he asked. "No wet work?"

Black held the phone away from his ear as it blasted the caller's reply.

"Fine. Fine," he said. "I'll get on it right away."

He ended the call, laid the pen down, and looked at his notes. The right side of his mouth twisted down as he rubbed the bristles of his moustache thoughtfully. The name of a private investigator he'd used a couple of times came to him. Trustworthy enough for a price, and not too encumbered with scruples. He found the name still in his phone's contacts list and called it.

"It's Aidan Black," he said. "I've got a job for you. We need information on someone, preferably something nasty. The subject's name is . . ." Aidan looked at his note pad again. ". . . Clarke, with an 'e.' Lieutenant Commander Kendra Clarke."

"Tom?" Riley's attractive executive assistant leaned through door. "Yolanda Butcher's here. A couple of the guys just brought her in."

Riley looked up from his desk, reading glasses perched on his nose, looking every bit the corporate executive. "Fine. Bring her in." He stood and quickly put on his black suit coat, and waited in the center of his office. When the woman came in, he offered his hand.

"Mrs. Butcher," he said. "Thank you for coming."

"I didn't have much choice," Yolanda said. "Your agents were very insistent."

She was Hispanic. Riley guessed her to be about thirty-five only because he knew she and Bill had been married more than ten years and had two kids. She looked younger. She was medium height, about five foot seven, he guessed. The jeans and blouse she wore revealed a slender, athletic build. Riley figured she was as much into physical fitness as her ex-SEAL husband was. Her deep brown eyes probed his.

"Yes, well, in light of everything happening with Bill," he said. "I mean, with you two being estranged, we worried your safety might be endangered and wished to offer you our protection. We like to think of you as still part of the Navy family. Please have a seat."

Yolanda sat in a padded chair in front of Riley's desk. He sat on the edge of the desk and asked, "Did you bring your children?"

"No," Yolanda said. "I've already sent them to my parents, and they are flying out with them today to my sister's place in Texas. My brother-in-law is a police officer there, and he's taking time off to guard them until . . ." She sighed. "Until this is over."

Her voice waivered on the last word, and she swallowed hard.

"Ha-Have you been in touch with Lin Schag?" she asked.

Riley nodded. "In fact, he's just down the passageway in the bull pen. I'm surprised you didn't see him."

Yolanda's eyes widened. "He's here? Can I see him?"

"Certainly." Riley picked his phone and dialed a number. "Tim? Riley. Could you tell Schag to come to my office?" He replaced the phone. "He should be here soon."

Two minutes later Riley's executive assistant opened the door again and announced, "Special Agent Schag to see you, Tom."

"Lin!" Yolanda propelled herself out of the chair and almost bowled Schag over as he walked through the door. "Lin! Oh, my god, what's happening?"

Schag embraced her, a warm, friendly embrace, and stroked her glistening black hair.

"I wished to god I knew, Yolanda," he said. "I-I didn't know that you and Bill . . . that you two had broken up."

She stepped back and looked at him.

"Bill didn't tell you?"

"I haven't heard from Bill in the better part of a year," he said, shaking his head. "I sent him emails, but he never replied."

Yolanda turned away from Schag and rubbed her nose with the back of her hand.

"Oh, Lin, this is how it's been," she said. "Ignoring old friends . . . and family."

Schag guided her to the chair in front of Riley's desk, and she sat down. She took a tissue from her purse, dabbed her eyes, and wiped her nose.

"I don't know what you mean by that, Yolanda," Schag said.

"It's . . . it's . . ." Yolanda took a breath, looked at Schag, then Riley. Schag got the hint. Talking about her marriage problems with an old friend was one thing. Talking about them in front of a stranger was something else.

"Maybe we can find someplace quiet to talk," Schag said.

He offered his hand to Yolanda to help her stand, but Riley waved him off. "No, no," he said. "The only place you'll find privacy here is the interrogation room—not very comforting. Stay here. I've got people to talk to anyway."

Riley picked a stack of file folders off his desk and turned to Yolanda.

"But, Mrs. Butcher, I'm serious about giving you protection. We don't know for certain what kind of state of mind Bill is in. We can set you up in a nearby safe house. You'll be comfortable there, and you'll have two agents guarding you around the clock."

Yolanda looked at Schag, her eyes questioning. He nodded.

"Can Lin come?" she asked.

Riley shook his head. "I'm afraid not. We need Agent Schag here. It's not our investigation, but we still need to liaise with the local authorities, and Agent Schag knows Bill better than anyone does. Except for you, of course."

Yolanda stared at the floor a moment, sniffed, and nodded. Her answer was barely audible. "Okay."

"Fine," Riley said. "I'll have two agents waiting for you when you two are finished. But take your time." Riley turned the doorknob and paused. "And, Lin, I'll have my assistant book you a room here on base at the Gateway Inn. You'll be here for a while."

"Actually, Tom, I've already booked a room at the Gateway at the sub base on Point Loma," Schag said. Riley cocked his head questioningly. "Better view," Schag said, nodding toward Riley's office window.

Riley glanced out the window at the gray steel hulls towering above sun-drenched docks, the skeletal stairways leading up to the ships' brows, and the parked cars crowded in front of them.

"A better view than this?" he said. "You must be kidding." Then he left the room, closing the door behind him.

"Lin, I don't know what happened to Bill," Yolanda said, turning to Schag. "He'd been on deployments before with the SEALs. There were some bad ones, but he would never let it affect the family. He would go get counseling and deal with it. But this time . . ."

"I saw him in Bahrain," Schag said. "We had dinner and a couple beers. He seemed fine."

"And he was . . . at first," Yolanda said. "Then things

started happening. He'd come home from the office angry or sullen, complaining people wouldn't listen to him."

"About what?" Schag asked.

Yolanda shook her head, and brushed a long strand of fine black hair back behind her ear. "Something about a bunch of money someone lost in Iraq—"

"You mean the nine billion dollars that disappeared?"

"Yeah, that's it," Yolanda said, nodding. "You know about it?"

"Bill mentioned it when we had dinner that night."

"Bill was obsessed by it. He said they wouldn't let him work on it at the office, so he worked on it at home. He'd stay up late working on the computer, looking stuff up. I'd beg him to come to bed, but some nights I don't think he got any sleep at all before going back to the office."

Schag bit his lower lip, thinking. "Do you know what he was looking at on the computer?"

Yolanda shook her head again. "No, but they looked like some kind of business sites, maybe investment sites or bank sites. Something about money transfers and stuff."

Schag nodded. "Go on, Yolanda."

"He began acting . . . The only way I can describe it is paranoid. He thought people were talking behind his back at the office, that people would look at him funny when they didn't think he could see him."

Schag remembered something from the sheriff's briefing.

"Some psychologists at a briefing this morning were talking about something called workplace mobbing," he said. "Did Bill ever complain that people at work were angry at him, blaming him for things?"

"No. No, I don't think so," she said. "Not at first, at least. He was upset they wouldn't let him work on the missing money thing. Oh, I don't know." Yolanda's hair moved in glistening waves as she shook her head. "But he started becoming suspicious of everyone. He thought he was on to some big conspiracy. He'd start ranting about it at home. The children would run to their rooms and hide. They were afraid of him, Lin."

"Was he drinking a lot?"

"No, Bill hardly ever drank," Yolanda said. "Maybe a beer now and then."

"He didn't hurt them, did he?" Schag asked. "Or you?"

"Certainly not," Yolanda said. "Bill adored the children. He'd never hurt them or me. I only sent them away . . . as a precaution."

"Same reason we want to set you up in a safe house," Schag said.

Yolanda looked at him, her eyes moist with tears. An ironic smile played on her lips. "Yeah, I guess so."

"When did you two separate?" Schag asked. "And why?"

"Six months ago, almost," Yolanda said. "Bill was becoming too irrational. His rants. His late nights on the computer." She paused and carefully wiped a tear from her eye. "And the distance. He had no time for the family. And then . . ."

Schag waited for her to go on. When she hesitated, he touched her hand.

"When I realized . . ."

She stopped, collecting her thoughts, trying to figure out how to describe it. She leaned forward toward Schag, looking straight into his gray eyes.

"One day we were out jogging. There's a stretch of ocean bluff where we used to run together. We're going along, enjoying the scenery, and talking a little. All of a sudden, Bill stops and turns around and starts screaming at someone. I jogged back to him and asked him what was wrong. He said some asshole had said something to him he didn't like."

"Said what?" asked Schag.

"I don't know," Yolanda said. "Bill never said. He just kept screaming at whoever it was."

"And who was it—this guy Bill called an asshole? Did you get a name?"

Yolanda's eyes blinked at Schag, and he saw them grow even sadder.

"That's just it, Lin," she said, her head shaking. "There was no one there. That's when I realized it was all in his head. He was hearing voices, Lin. Like a madman."

CHAPTER 9

MONDAY
NCIS Southwest Regional
Headquarters
Naval Station San Diego
2200 Hours

"HOW'S SHE DOING, LIN?"

Schag looked up from the small, gray, military notebook in his hand. He had spent another thirty minutes talking with Yolanda, then stood outside Tom Riley's office, jotting down notes from the conversation. He was concentrating so much, he hadn't noticed Riley walk up to him.

"Oh, ah, she went to the ladies' room to . . . you know." Schag circled his pen around his face. "Makeup stuff."

"Crying?"

Schag nodded. "She's scared," he said. "She's worried to death about Bill."

Riley gestured to Schag's notebook. "She said anything that can help?"

"Not really." Schag shook his head. "Well, you might say it may help us understand what Bill's going through. She's afraid Bill had some kind of mental breakdown. Problems at work and at home. And he was hearing things."

"Hearing things? Riley repeated. "Like voices?"

Schag nodded.

"Was he taking drugs or medications?"

"Not that she knows of." Schag slipped the notebook into his jacket. "But Lieutenant Commander Clarke said one of the symptoms of agueloquine psychosis is hallucinations. I assumed she meant seeing things, but I guess hallucinations could include hearing things. I'll check with her later. Anything new on Bill's whereabouts?"

Riley pulled his own notebook from his coat pocket and flipped through the pages. "I got a call from the sheriff's. Some gate guard reported he saw someone who looked like Butcher drive into a yacht club in a pickup truck similar to the one stolen from the ASW base. The guard said the man in the truck claimed to be a diver there to clean a boat hull." Riley shrugged. "I guess boat hulls need to be cleaned? Who would have thought? I mean they're in water all the time."

"Barnacles attach to the hulls of boats," Schag said. "They need cleaning off periodically or they build up and slow the boat down."

"Since when do you know so much about boats?" Riley asked.

Schag looked at Riley with raised eyebrows. Riley knew Schag not only spent most of his time aboard Navy ships, but he had also attended the Naval Academy at

Annapolis.

"Oh, yeah. Never mind. Anyway, the local PD is checking it out, but the guard said this diver was there for thirty or forty minutes, then drove out the same gate."

Schag rubbed his hand against his jaw and felt the bristle of a five o'clock shadow. He looked at his watch and for the first time realized how late it had gotten.

"I can't imagine why Bill would go to a yacht club," he said.

"Maybe he wanted to steal a boat and make a get away," Riley offered, shrugging. "Likely nothing to it anyway. Just a rent-a-cop trying to be helpful." Riley licked his thumb and paged through his notebook. "Anyway, a highway patrol chopper pilot spotted a pickup truck matching the one stolen from the ASW base heading eastbound on Interstate 8 toward Alpine. It was getting dark and the chopper was low on fuel, so he had to break contact. Homeland Security is sending up their drone. It has forward-looking infrared and what they called a 'longer loitering capability.'" Riley made air quotes when he said the last words.

"Alpine?"

Both men turned to find Yolanda standing behind them, her makeup refreshed, her brow knitted in thought.

"The highway patrol reported a vehicle matching the description of one Bill may have stolen heading into the mountains," Schag said, reaching out and touching her shoulder. "Does that mean something to you, Yolanda?"

"Yes," she said. "Bill's parents used to have a cabin up near Alpine. We stayed there two, maybe three times."

"Do you remember how to get there?" Schag asked.

"No, it was quite a while back," she said, shaking her head. "Bill always did the driving up to it. When his parents died, they left it to Bill and his brother, Peter. Bill was still with the teams, and we were having some money problems, so he sold his half to Pete. We haven't been back since."

"Could you call Pete and get directions to the cabin?" Riley asked.

Yolanda pulled her cell phone out, looked through its directory, and selected a number. She listened for a few minutes, then shook her head.

"No answer," she said. "It's going into voicemail." After a moment, she said into the phone, "Pete, it's Yolanda. I guess you've heard about Bill. I'm with the NCIS in San Diego, and they need to know how to get to the cabin in Alpine. Can you call me when you get this?" She cleared her throat, stifling another sob. "Thanks, Pete."

Yolanda put away her phone and looked at Schag and Riley. "Sorry."

Schag shook his head. "No, problem. County records should have a copy of the deed. All I need to do is go by and search for a piece of property owned by Peter Butcher." He turned to Riley. "Yolanda's ready to go to the safe house. I can run by the county administration center and check their records."

Riley looked at his watch and shook his head. "Too late. They're closed by now. It can wait."

"Okay, then I'll get on the phone and wake someone up," Schag said. "For that matter, the information might be online. I can check it out in the bull pen."

Riley held up his hand, stopping Schag before he could move.

"Look, Agent Schag," Riley said, suddenly officious. "It's getting late and we need to get Mrs. Butcher to the safe house before it gets dark. I don't want her or our agents walking into a dark house. Remember, it's not our case. Our responsibility is to Mrs. Butcher's safety."

Riley pursed his lips and knitted his brow. "So, I want you to follow Mrs. Butcher and her guard detail to the safe house. The only people who'll know where she is will be the agents assigned to her detail, you, and me—and the only reason I'm letting you in on it is because of your relationship with her. Make sure she's comfortable and safe, then *you* go get yourself some rest. In the meantime, I'll call the sheriff's department and let them know about this cabin, and *they* can go do the footwork to find it. Understood, agent?"

Riley looked at Schag with expressionless eyes. Schag stared back, bewildered. He looked at Yolanda. She, too, looked confused. Then Schag nodded. "Fine," he said. "Understood."

"Good," Riley said, smiling. "I'll go make that call and see you bright and early in the morning." He turned and shook Yolanda's hand. "I'm sorry we had to meet like this, Mrs. Butcher. But I assure you we will do everything to keep you safe—and try to keep Bill safe, too."

Riley strode into his office, leaving Schag and Yolanda exchanging questioning looks.

Linus Schag stood on the balcony of his hotel room, sipping a drink, and staring at the ocean. He had followed Yolanda and the agents to the safe house, a small bungalow-style home in Kensington, a small neighborhood in San Diego. Entering first, Schag searched each room, weapon drawn, then the back and side yards. He went back inside and checked each cabinet, drawer, and closet. When he was confident the house was safe, he waved the guards and Yolanda in. He helped her settle in, turning down the bed, unpacking her small overnight bag, and ensuring the kitchen was adequately stocked with food. When he felt content enough to leave, he stood by the door and looked at her. Her deep dark eyes were wide with worry and glistened with tears. He wanted to tell her he would stay with her, but he couldn't. Instead, he put an arm around her, and she fell into his embrace like a scared animal seeking the safety of shelter.

"Look," he said, "you'll be okay here. I'll call tomorrow morning to see how you're doing. And if I can, I'll come by."

He felt Yolanda's head nod, felt her body sob. Uneasy, he stepped back, holding her at arm's length, and looked at her.

"You're strong, Yolanda," he said. "Bill wouldn't marry a weak woman, would he?"

Yolanda smiled feebly and used a finger to wipe a tear from her eye. "You're right," she said. "Bill would be pissed if he saw me right now."

"Bill would be holding you and comforting you if he saw you right now," Schag corrected.

Yolanda smiled again, more brightly this time.

"Thank you, Lin," she said. "Thank you for everything." She reached up and took Schag's face in both hands, pulled him forward and kissed him lightly on the lips.

Back in his hotel room, Schag tried to forget about that kiss. There was nothing emotional about it, nothing erotic. Just a quick, almost motherly peck, but it stirred in Schag feelings he didn't want, something he thought best left buried as deep as possible. Yet, no matter how hard he tried to push it back down, it kept resurfacing, forcing him to look at it.

He had always liked Yolanda, admired her, and

thought Bill lucky to have found a woman like her. She was everything Schag's ex-Wall Street wife hadn't been—caring, thoughtful, passionate, and strong. Staring out at the star-speckled night hovering over the dark, open sea, Schag had to accept the truth he had always avoided, always denied.

He was in love with Yolanda Butcher.

He poured another Scotch, happy for the first time he wasn't aboard a dry U.S. warship, and gulped half of it down without tasting it. A row of lights out beyond Point Zuniga, the breakwater that marked the eastern border of the harbor's main shipping channel, drew his attention. It was a ship anchored in the stream, the open ocean outside the channel. Taking a small set of binoculars from his bag, he focused on the lights and could see the unmistakable outline of a large oil tanker.

That was strange. San Diego Harbor had no oil refineries; those were farther north in Los Angeles/Long Beach Harbor. Huge crude carriers like the one at anchor rarely if ever made side trips or port stops other than the oil terminals where they loaded cargo, or the portside refineries where they offloaded it. After watching the tanker for several minutes, Schag shrugged, finished his drink, undressed, and went to bed.

Six hours later, the buzz of his Blackberry woke him. He slipped on his glasses and stared at the caller ID. Tom Riley again.

"Schag here," he answered.

"Lin," Riley said, "they've found Bill Butcher."

"Who?"

"The sheriff's," Riley said. "He's dead, Lin. Bill Butcher is dead."

CHAPTER 10

MONDAY
Cuyamaca Mountains
San Diego County, California
2330 Hours

BUTCHER SAW THEM COMING.

He expected them. Or, rather, he expected someone. Earlier in the day, he had noticed the highway patrol helicopter patrolling the interstate as he drove into the mountains. Later, he noticed navigation lights of an aircraft high overhead running a search pattern over the forest. The spacing of the lights looked too narrow to be a regular aircraft, the altitude too high for a manned aircraft to search from, and Butcher assumed it was a drone with night vision or infrared capabilities, or both. He knew they were looking for him, and it was only a matter of time before someone stumbled onto his old family cabin.

He had ditched the pickup truck in the woods, and retrieved his own car from the copse of trees where he had killed Hector and incapacitated the bald Gideon operator. The car was parked on the side of the cabin, in plain sight of the men he watched moving in the dark. Too late to use it to escape. By his count, there were at least five of them, possibly more, dressed in dark fatigues and heavily armed. He couldn't be a hundred percent certain, but he didn't think they were cops. Law enforcement wouldn't come sneaking in the dark with so few men. They would come big time, with lots of people and lots of noise. Butcher figured they were from Gideon.

Butcher moved to the rear of the cabin and, looking out, saw no one. No doubt, they were planning to make a frontal assault, thinking him asleep. More amateurish tactics, he thought to himself. Still, running out the back door wasn't an option. There was too much open space between the cabin and the woods. His father had created the firebreak to protect the cabin from the frequent wild fires that plagued these mountains.

Butcher walked back into the small, darkened front room. His foot bumped into the bundle on the on floor. He eyed it as if he hadn't seen it before. A thought came to him. Fire. Fire destroys. It blinds. It hides. He glanced back into the kitchen, at the propane stove sitting there, and the decision came to him in a flash. No matter what happened to him, he was determined to take as many Gideon men with him as possible.

Moving quickly, he entered the kitchen and fired up two burners on the stove. Stepping onto the back porch, he found two more full propane tanks in the storage locker, and carried them inside, one in each hand. Without any effort, he lifted each one onto one of the lit burners. Back in the front room, he pulled his Glock 26 from its ankle holster. He studied the pistol closely, his mouth tugged down into a frown, then touched its barrel to the side of his head. No, he thought, not there. He tried it again on his forehead but, no, that wasn't good either. He placed the barrel into his mouth—cops called it "eating your gun"—but that didn't feel right either. He tucked the barrel under his chin and realized, yes, that was the proper place. He sank to the floor and, sitting cross-legged, waited.

A single shot. The Gideon operators froze, waiting for the sound of a bullet impacting something or someone. Nothing happened. They looked at each other, shook their heads, and waited. Still nothing. The leader used hand gestures to order men to the right and left of the cabin while he took the front. They moved silently, their boot steps muffled by the snow. Once in place, they peered cautiously into the darkened windows.

"Anyone see anything?" the leader whispered into his wrap-around mike

"Roger," someone replied. "I see a body on the ground. It looks like Butcher."

"Are you sure?"

"Roger that. He's big, bald and . . . Jesus, it looks like he put a gun in his mouth."

"Roger," replied the leader. "We still need to make sure he'd dead. Everyone stack up on me and we'll go in."

Within a minute, the five men had formed a tight stack to the right of the front door. The leader aimed a tactical shotgun at the doorknob and fired a solid slug into it, shattering the lock and a good chunk of the door. The team leader kicked the remainder of the door open and rushed through, followed closely by the others. They each peeled off left or right, crouching, weapons to their shoulders, peering over the sights. The leader hovered over the body on the floor, his shotgun aimed at the figure. The others cleared the bedroom, and started to clear the kitchen. As they entered the kitchen, the leader heard one of his men say, "Oh, shit."

It started with a shriek, then another shriek—the pressure relief valves on the tanks trying to vent the building pressure. Two simultaneous blasts formed massive fireballs that flowed through the cabin with the speed of quicksilver. The flames held deadly shards of metal from the tanks and whatever debris the blast wave picked up. Fire engulfed each of the Gideon men in turn, the shards ripping through them, the flames searing them. The blast first blew out the windows. Next, the walls of the cabin came apart. Then there was only the crackling of flames consuming what was left of the cabin and the smell of burnt human flesh.

"We think we found your man," said Travis, the lead technician on the sheriff's crime scene team. He wore a blue Tyvek hazmat suit. An N-95 respirator mask hung beneath his chin, and his safety glasses rested atop his head. The hazmat suit did not breath, and despite the frosty winter mountain air, he was sweating heavily. "At least he looks like he fits the description despite being badly burned. And he's the only one not carrying a long gun."

Alerted by the Border Patrol, sheriff and fire units raced to the scene only to find little left of the Butcher family cabin. Only one wall remained standing, the fireplace providing support for its charred timbers. To the side sat the remains of a scorched sedan, its windows shattered by the blast, and its body battered by the debris of the explosion. Inside the ruins lay six corpses, covered by blue tarps. Travis's CSI team and technicians from the coroner's office, all dressed the same as Travis, milled around the remains, still searching for anything that could be evidence.

Schag, Riley, and Parker had sped up the mountain road after rendezvousing at the naval base. Despite using their lights and sirens, by the time they arrived on scene there was little to do but watch the firefighters pack up their gear and the crime scene investigators unpack theirs. They had spent hours sitting and watching TV helicopters orbiting like vultures waiting for the chance to snatch a quick carrion meal. It was an apt analogy, Schag thought.

"Can you determine the cause of death?" Schag asked.

"For your man? It looks like he took himself out," Travis said. "We found a Glock still gripped in his hand, and a good portion of his face and head are missing."

"And the others?"

"Killed by the explosion. It looks like your guy wanted to go out with a blast." Travis noticed the sour looks the NCIS agents gave him. "Sorry, I didn't mean that as a pun. He intended to blow the place up. From what we can tell so far, it looks like he placed two, maybe three, full propane tanks on the stove, and lit a fire under them. Then he shot himself. When the other people came in, the tanks blew."

"Like giant pipe bombs," said Parker.

"Bigger than that," Travis said. "Technically, it's called a BLEVE—boiling liquid expanding vapor explosion. The heat increases the contents of the tanks to the point the container can't withstand the pressure and ruptures. All that heated propane spills out and forms a cloud of explosive vapor. And when that's exposed to flame . . . boom. It's more like a thermobaric explosion than a pipe bomb, agent."

"A thermo what?" asked Parker.

"Thermobaric explosion," Schag answered. "Air gas mixture they use to clear jungles to make landing zones for helicopters."

"Creates a blast wave that knocks everything over—" Travis nodded toward the devastated cabin. "I think this is your man coming out now."

The three NCIS agents turned and saw two Tyvek-cladded coroner technicians carrying a litter loaded with a black, sealed body bag. Travis waved the litter bearers over. "Someone's got to do an eyes-on identification sooner or later," he said. "Want to look at him now?"

Riley made a face and shook his head. Parker blanched at the thought. They both looked at Schag.

"Yeah," he said. There was no way he would make Yolanda do it. "Let's take a look."

Travis placed the N-95 back over his nose and mouth, and pulled opened the bag's long zipper. Within an instant, the miasma of burnt flesh assaulted the agents. Despite the respirators, the coroner's techs turned away from the stench.

Schag pulled a set of nitrile gloves from his pocket and put them on before spreading the sides of the body bag. He pulled a small LED flashlight from another pocket and flicked it on to examine the bag's contents. With the clothing burned away, only charred skin remained. The wrecked face was unrecognizable. He reached in and pulled on the corpse's left arm, ignoring the churning in his stomach when some of the burnt tissue sloughed off into his hand. Taking a better grip, he pulled the arm up and studied its hand.

It was there. On the third finger, instead of a wedding band, was a large signet ring. Schag rubbed soot off the ring until he saw letters encircling the gemstone. First were the letters "U.S.," then the word "Navy." Schag tried to swallow, but his mouth was dry. He rubbed more, and the final word became clear: SEALs.

Schag respectfully replaced the arm and nodded. "That's his Navy SEALs ring," he said, choking. "That's Bill Butcher."

Then he turned away and retched into the snow.

CHAPTER 11

AIDAN BLACK SAT IN THE dark of the late
Cavendish's office, absently swirling a tumbler of Stoli on
ice. The blood-stained carpet was gone and the splatter
on the wall cleaned, but the stain on Gideon's
reputation—and his—remained. He took a deep gulp of
the vodka, making a face as he let it drain down his
throat. He didn't usually drink, but the events of the
preceding two days were threatening to make him take up
the vice.

True, Butcher was dead and Gideon had its revenge.
But at what cost? Five more of his operators were dead.
It was supposed to be a covert op—find him, trap him,
kill him, then extricate without leaving clues that it was a
Gideon job. With his operators killed, however, it was

only a matter of time before the police put the pieces together and called on Black for an explanation. With his psy-ops background, he had one ready for them. It was an unauthorized operation, he told the detectives, undertaken by a few of Cavendish's pissed off co-workers to seek revenge for his murder. Always careful to protect himself, Black had made sure the only person who knew he had ordered the hit was the team leader himself. And he was dead.

Taking another swig, Black thought about the further damage the operation had done to Gideon's reputation. Having one of his top men murdered *inside* a guarded Gideon compound was bad enough; having an entire tactical team killed by the last crazed act of just *one* man was something else. With a sigh, Black drained his glass and refilled it.

Black's cell phone rang in the holster on his belt. He pulled it out, looked at the caller ID, and took another long drink of vodka before thumbing the answer icon.

"Aidan Black."

"Well?" boomed the voice on the other end. "Is it true?"

"Is what true?" Black asked, knowing full well what the caller meant.

"Don't fuck with me, Aidan," the man said. "What they're saying on TV. That Butcher's dead."

"Yes, he's dead." Black took another drink. "Along with five more of my men."

"I heard there was a fire and the body was burned beyond recognition. How do they know it's him?"

"My source said one of the NCIS agents did a visual ID on the body," Black said, noting the caller didn't mention the deaths of his own men. "He found a Navy SEAL ring that Butcher wore."

"Good," breathed the caller, as if letting go of a breath he'd been holding.

"You do realize there were other problems, don't you?" Black asked.

"Problems?" the other man said. "Like what?"

Black rolled his eyes and fought to hold his temper.

"Five of my men were killed in that cabin along with Butcher," he said. "That's eight Gideon operators altogether taken out by one lone madman. How's that going to play in the press?"

"Not important," the caller said sharply.

"It might be important if it impacts some of our government contracts," Black insisted. "Plus, the little matter of the police coming by, asking questions about those men killed in the cabin with Butcher."

"You don't worry about those contracts," the man said. "My people will make sure they're secure. They always have, even after your people left that girl for dead in the cargo container."

Black closed his eyes and gritted his teeth, remembering that fiasco. That was Cavendish's fault. *Couldn't keep his prick in his pants. A lot of good it'll do him now.*

"Yes, your people helped a great deal with that," Black conceded.

"Along with the gun-running and drug-smuggling accusations," the caller added. "What did you tell the police about your five dead men?"

"Rogue operation," Black said. "Some of Cavendish's friends out for revenge."

"You think they bought that?" the caller asked. "What if they start hauling your people in for questioning?"

"They can give them lie detector tests as far as I'm concerned. The only person who knew I gave the order is dead."

Black heard a satisfied grunt on the other end. "Good." A pause and then, "What about the other matter?"

"Better luck there," Black said. "My PI came through faster than I thought he could. He managed to hack into the good doctor's personal email account and found some interesting exchanges."

"Like what?"

Black told him.

"Good. That's very good," the caller said with a tone that was the closest to a laugh that Black had ever heard from him. "But can he prove it?"

"He went out this morning and got a signed affidavit from the other person," Black said, "and delivered it to Dr. Clarke's commanding officer this afternoon."

"Excellent," the caller said. "What about this other man, this—what his name? This NCIS agent?"

"What about him?"

"I didn't like the way he looked at me," the man said. "He gave me a distinct impression he didn't know his place."

Black lowered the phone and took another long drink of vodka, letting it drip down the back of his throat while his shook his head in dismay.

"Well?" the voice boomed.

"Linus Schag," Black said. "Spelled S-C-H-A-G. He's a special agent with NCIS."

"I know that, you idiot," the caller said testily. "What's he got to do with this whole mess? Why did Butcher write his name on your wall in . . . you know?

"He and Butcher were old friends," Black said, watching the ice turn sluggishly in his glass as he rocked it back and forth. "They went through training together. As to why Butcher wanted him here, I don't know."

"I didn't like his looks."

I'm certain he didn't care for yours either. God knows, I don't.

"He's known for being insubordinate," Black said. "He was involved in some a covert operation several months back that resulted in the court martial of a Navy officer. The convening board considered Schag a hostile witness and exiled him to the weapons base at China Lake."

"They should have kept him there," the caller said. "Do you think he knows anything? Did Butcher tell him anything?

"No," Black said. "There's no evidence Schag met with Butcher during his rampage, and NCIS examined Butcher's email records and found no email exchanged between Schag and Butcher for the last several months."

The caller grunted. "Not good enough. He's a loose end and he needs to be contained. There's too much riding on this."

Aidan Black sat up straight and slammed his glass onto the desk.

"You can't expect me to take out an NCIS agent now," he said. "Not with the cops knocking on my door about the cabin fiasco. No way."

"Calm down, Aidan," the man said. "I only said contain him. Keep an eye on him, a close one. Make sure he doesn't know anything. If he doesn't, fine. If he does—well, we'll do what we have to."

Do what *we* have to? Black thought. Since when do *we* take chances?

"Did you hear me, Aidan?"

"Yes, sir," Black said. "I'll put some men on him and I'll make sure my source keeps tabs on him, too."

"Fine, fine. You do that," the caller said. "And don't

let me down again, Aidan. The top dog never gets bitten, remember that."

Then the line went dead.

The man who called Aidan Black clicked off his mobile phone and sat back in his chair, his head cocked to the left as usual, and his lips pulled down in a frown. Despite the stern appearance, he felt satisfied for the first time in months. In fact, he almost felt giddy with pleasure. Butcher had been the proverbial thorn in his side for too long. First, there was the attempted joint investigation in Iraq. The man got that squashed easily enough. However, unlike the agents from the other agencies, Butcher kept at it even when he returned to the U.S. When the agent's appeals to restart the investigation began gaining traction among the NCIS leadership, the man had to pull in some heavy artillery to get it stopped—the kind of artillery that only resides in the seat of government power. No one in government wants to be noticed by the White House or by Congress, and when it does happen, everyone goes to ground. Butcher's evidence for a new investigation became radioactive, untouchable. Butcher himself became as welcomed as the Ancient Mariner with the albatross around his neck.

With Butcher's dismissal from NCIS, the man had thought the matter settled. But the damned son of a bitch kept at it, prying into every aspect of the man's business dealings, and prying too damned successfully. Things were too sensitive for that, too volatile. Something had to be done to quiet Butcher once and for all.

The man looked around at his surroundings. He was aboard a ship, his safe house afloat until the Butcher mess finished. Despite being an avid yachtsman, he hated this confinement aboard what he considered a tub. He had taken over the captain's cabin, the best quarters aboard ship, and yet to him it was worse than a roadside motel. Many years ago, after using up his college draft deferments during the Vietnam War, the man's father had suggested he avoid the conflict by becoming an officer in the Navy. His father had enough political connections to ensure his son would never set foot on the Asian mainland. Yet the man couldn't bear the idea of living aboard a ship with cramped quarters, sleeping in a threadbare bunk, and going months without comfort. He married instead. At the time, married men were exempt from the draft. When only married men with children were exempt, he demanded his wife have a child. After the draft ended, he left both the wife and the child.

With a grim smile, he tapped his fist on the desk twice and stood with earnest. He stepped across the cabin's small living room to a cabinet. Inside, he found glasses and an array of liquors. Thank god, this wasn't a U.S. flagged merchantman, he thought. They were dry ships, like the U. S. Navy's. He took a glass and a bottle of bourbon, found ice in a small refrigerator, and poured a drink.

Butcher was dead, he thought with grim satisfaction. The next day, he would arrange to go ashore.

CHAPTER 12

WEDNESDAY
Naval Base Point Loma
San Diego, California
1900 Hours

LINUS SCHAG THREW OPEN THE curtains in his hotel room and stared hard and long at the ocean beyond. He took a long swig of his single-malt Scotch, taking great satisfaction in the burning sensation as it flowed down his throat. He took another long drink to feel the burn again, as if the fiery sensation could consume and purify the horrors and emotions of the previous three days. The sight of his friend's charred corpse was bad enough. Having to tell Yolanda Butcher the man she adored had killed himself and five other men in a fiery blast gut-punched him harder than seeing Bill's body.

She refused to believe it at first. That was natural enough. Shock and denial comprise the first stage of grief. Schag tried to convince her without mentioning the fact he had identified Butcher's burnt body, but she kept insisting Bill would never commit suicide.

"Lin, you know Bill and I are Catholic, right?" Schag nodded. "We're devoted Catholics. Bill would never kill himself—the Church says suicide is a sin. He knows he couldn't be buried in consecrated ground. Bill would go down fighting. He'd sacrifice himself for others, but he would never commit suicide."

Schag explained that the crime scene team had found Bill's body with his face destroyed by a gunshot wound, and a pistol in his hand.

"Then it was somebody else's body, Lin," she insisted. "Maybe the body was one of the men trying to kill him. I mean, you said there was a fire. How could you be sure it was him?"

Schag saw no other way but to tell her.

"I made a visual ID, Yolanda," he said. "I found his SEAL team ring on his wedding finger, where he always wore it."

Yolanda stared at him, not moving, not saying a word. She collapsed onto the sofa, buried her head in a pillow, and sobbed.

Staring into the gloom beyond his hotel window, Schag watched the elongated reflection of the oil tanker's anchor lights on the flat sea, looking so much like shimmering stalactites. Like Yolanda, he could not accept that Bill Butcher's life would end like this, without reason, without cause. He, too, always thought Bill would go down like a Roman gladiator, fighting to the finish. That, however, was the old Bill Butcher, the man he was before he was poisoned by the medication the Navy had given him. Schag was becoming increasingly convinced that Butcher's actions were due to this drug agueloquine. It was the only thing that made sense.

He finished his Scotch, considered pouring another, thought better of it, and slammed the empty glass down on the dresser.

Perhaps there was one way to make something good come of this. Maybe if Lieutenant Commander Clarke could get tissue samples, she could prove it was the drug and not Bill Butcher himself that caused all this havoc. For the sake of Yolanda and the kids, he told himself. And for Bill's, too.

Schag went to the closet and pulled out his sports jacket. He fumbled through the pockets for Clarke's business card but couldn't find it. Damn it, he thought. No telling where he dropped it. No matter. He'd drive over to Balboa Hospital in the morning and talk to her. First, however, he would need to pick up the appropriate paperwork at the base and go talk to Yolanda.

He woke early and reached the NCIS offices before Riley or Parker arrived. After logging into a computer, Schag located the forms he needed and filled in the necessary information. He finished printing them out as Riley walked in. He folded the forms and slipped them into the inside pocket of his leather flight jacket.

"Aren't you the early bird today?" Riley commented, not noticing Schag's quick movement with the papers.

"I wanted to go see Yolanda," Schag said. "See how she's doing."

Riley nodded. "With Bill dead, she'll be able to go home today."

"Bill's not officially dead until the county M.E. confirms his identity," Schag said, referring the county's medical examiner.

"That shouldn't be long," Riley said. "They're doing the autopsy today."

"That doesn't mean they'll ID him today," Schag protested. "You heard the crime-scene tech. The gunshot destroyed most of his jaw and mandible. There may not be enough to do a dental comparison. And trying to resurrect fingerprints on a burnt corpse can take days, if it's possible at all."

Riley eyed him curiously. "What are you saying, Lin? That the crispy-critter wasn't Bill Butcher?"

Schag winced at Riley's description of his friend's corpse, but bit his tongue. He shook his head and said, "Not at all. I just think we need to proceed cautiously on this."

Riley snorted and grinned mockingly. "You know what I think?" he said. "I think you don't want to go back into exile at China Lake." Riley waved his hands, giving in. "All right, fine. We'll wait until Bill's identity is confirmed. But then . . ." Riley pointed his finger at Schag. "Then she goes and you go. *Capisce?*"

Schag nodded, back peddling out of the office.

"How long do you think you'll be, anyway?" Riley called after him.

"Don't know," Schag said, turning and opening the door. "I'm stopping by Balboa, too."

"You sick?" Riley asked.

"No, I want to talk to that doctor—Commander Clarke."

"What about? About that crazy theory of hers about the medication Butcher was given?" Riley's voice was getting louder as he spoke. "It's not our case, Schag. It's still not our case."

"I know. I know," Schag said, waving a hand. He closed the door and was gone.

CHAPTER 13

BALBOA PARK HAS BEEN HOME to Naval Medical Center San Diego since 1915, when a tent hospital was erected where the Natural History Museum sits today. Four years later, construction began on a permanent hospital atop Inspiration Point overlooking what was then the wide-open Florida Canyon. Like most of the early Navy buildings in the area—including NCIS regional headquarters—the hospital sported a Spanish Colonial Revival design, with pale-colored buildings topped with peaked, red-tile roofs. During World War II, Balboa Hospital—its common name—grew to accommodate the wounded returning from the Pacific Theater. During the Vietnam War, Balboa grew still more, becoming the largest military hospital in the world.

The old hospital was replaced in the 1980s with a sprawling modern facility built in the canyon it overlooked. All that remains of that original hospital is the administration building.

As Schag walked between its buildings, he saw the only thing that distinguished the modern Balboa Hospital from any civilian medical center was the large numbers of young men and women missing limbs. Some walked on prosthetic legs or rolled along in wheelchairs. Others carried their personal items with artificial arms or hands. Casualties of war, they all looked incredibly young to Schag, and old at the same time.

Following signs, Schag wended his way through the corridors of the hospital until finding a plaque next to two swinging doors that read: Neurology. He found a nurse's station beyond the doors and asked for Lieutenant Commander Clarke.

"I'm sorry," a nurse said, "But Dr. Clarke isn't available."

"Do you mean she's not here today, or she's not taking visitors?" Schag asked as he showed the nurse his credentials.

The nurse's mouth opened into an astonished "O," a reaction Schag hadn't expected. She stood quickly, murmuring, "Please wait here," turned and hurried down a hallway. A minute later, the nurse scurried back, saying, "Dr. Clarke can see you now. Third door on the left."

Schag thanked her and eyed her curiously as she stared back at him, mouth still agape. He found the door, rapped twice, and turned the nob. Clarke was sitting at a desk, staring at a document in front of her.

"Dr. Clarke?"

She didn't look up.

"I don't know what I did to you, agent," she said, "that you would do this."

"Ma'am?"

"Why?" Clarke asked, looking up. From the redness of her eyes, it was clear she'd been crying. "I only offered to help your friend."

"Doctor, I'm . . ." Schag, stunned, grasped for words. "I don't know what you're talking about. What do you think I did to you?"

"This, goddamn it!" she yelled, tossing the document at him.

The paper fluttered to the floor. Schag picked it up and read the first few lines. "It's an affidavit from someone who says she's your lover? Is this true?"

Clarke, eyes lowered, nodded and sniffed loudly.

"Don't ask, don't tell is gone, commander," Schag said, still not understanding. "It's not a court martial offense anymore."

"It is if my lover is an enlisted woman under my command," Clarke said. "And you know that damn well."

Schag finally understood. While being gay in the military was no longer illegal, fraternization with the lower ranks still was, no matter what your sexual preference. In the old days, the Navy turned a blind eye to the offense or allowed the offender to discretely retire or resign his commission. Under the new procedures, however, the Navy dealt with fraternization quickly and publicly.

"What made you think I had anything to do with this?"

"Oh, I don't know," Clarke said, waving her hand. "You're the only NCIS agent I've talked to in the last forty-eight hours and then this shows up on my C.O.'s desk."

"That's not the way we operate, commander," Schag said, shaking his head. "I—we—have no reason to investigate you. As for this, it's not even a real witness affidavit. It doesn't say NCIS had anything to do with questioning this sailor. It's only signed by her and a notary public."

Clarke looked up, brow knitted, mouth tight. "Are you saying it's not real?"

"It's real as far as your sailor wrote it, signed it, and had it witnessed by a notary, but it's not an official Navy document, not something NCIS did." Schag thought a moment, and cleared his throat. "Did you and, uh, the young lady have a falling out?" Clarke shook her head. "Have you talked to her about this?"

"My C.O. ordered me to stay away from her and have no communication with her of any kind," Clarke said.

"That's SOP," Schag said, nodding. "Better keep it that way, too, commander. In the meantime, where is she now? Still here in your department?"

Clarke shook her head with minute movements. "The admiral transferred her to the emergency department immediately after receiving that."

Schag held up the affidavit. "You mean this?" Clarke nodded. Schag studied the document again, his brow knitted. "Can I have this?"

Clarke's blue eyes narrowed. "Why?" she asked.

"I want to check out this notary," Schag said. "Maybe I can figure out how or why all this came about. It wouldn't change your situation, commander. The die is cast on that. But intel is always helpful."

The doctor nodded, sniffing. "Take it then," she said. After a moment, she looked up. "Then why are you here, agent?"

"You heard Bill Butcher killed himself?"

Clarke nodded. "It's all over the news," she said.

"The M.E. is doing the autopsy today," Schag explained. "I thought you might want to get some samples—you know, blood and tissue, whatever you need—maybe find out if this agueloquine was the reason Bill went rogue."

Clarke didn't say anything.

"Look, commander, I'm trying to find some good to come from all this mess," Schag said. "If Bill went off the reservation because of this medicine, it might help take some of the tarnish off him."

"He becomes a victim instead of a victimizer," Clarke said. Schag nodded. She considered what the agent said, then shook her head. "Can't be done. We need the approval of Mr. Butcher's next of kin."

Schag pulled the forms from his flight jacket pocket and handed them to Clarke.

"We have it," he said. "I visited his wife this morning and she agreed. All the forms are signed. I also called the M.E.'s office. You're invited to observe the autopsy."

Clarke studied the documents, sat back in her chair, and blew air from her pursed lips.

"You do work fast," she said. "I give you that." She handed the documents back. "What the hell? My Navy career is finished. What more can they do to me? Send me back to Iraq?"

"*Deja vu*," Clarke said. "Haven't we been here before?"

"Yes, we have," Schag said, resignation in his voice.

He aimed his leased car into a parking spot in front of the building housing the medical examiner's office. The building, a modernistic patchwork of asymmetric angles, stood across the street from the county emergency operations center where Clarke and Schag met. They had walked past the building on their way to and back from having coffee. Schag remembered the dread he felt on seeing the short concrete wall with the gray metallic sign and raised letters reading MEDICAL EXAMINER & FORENSICS CENTER. Somehow, he knew he would be visiting this place before too long. And here he was.

Inside, a technician handed them visitor badges and dark-blue scrubs to wear and, after dressing, escorted them into the autopsy room. It was a cavernous space lined on two walls by stainless steel autopsy tables, sinks, scales, and computer screens. The stainless-steel tables glistened in the overhead fluorescent light. The surface of each table canted toward a central drain where blood and other bodily fluids could flow. The room was vacant save for one man in scrubs and a face shield. The miasma of burnt flesh hung in the air. Schag took a small tube of Mentholatum from his pocket, opened it, and offered it to Clarke. She looked at him questioningly.

"Put it around your nostrils," he said, showing her on his own nose. "It helps with the stench."

"Dr. Carter?" Their escort called out. "Your visitors are here."

The man turned, raising the face shield. He was in his fifties, thin, with a long, bearded face. The beard and his short, thinning, curly hair were both gray.

"Oh, you must be Agent Schag and Dr. Clarke," he said. "Come. Come."

Schag and Clarke crossed the room, and Dr. Carter greeted them with a friendly smile that seemed out of place for the location.

"I'm Dr. Jason Carter, deputy M.E.," he said. "I'd shake your hands, but as you can see I had to start without you." He held up gloved hands smeared with thickened blood in explanation.

Behind Carter lay the naked, burnt body of a man. A

Y-incision had already opened the trunk of the corpse from the shoulders to the pubis, revealing his internal organs. Schag glanced at the body's left hand. The Navy SEAL ring was missing. He looked over at a nearby table and saw the ring sealed in a plastic evidence bag.

"That's Bill Butcher, I take it," Schag said.

"I'm afraid so," Carter said, sensing the agent's pain. "He was your friend?"

Schag nodded. "And we worked together before all this happened."

"A terrible thing," Carter said, turning to Clarke. "And you are researching the impact of agueloquine on the emotional stability of those prescribed it?"

"Basically," Clarke said, nodding. "Mr. Butcher was prescribed agueloquine on his last deployment overseas. I believe it may be responsible for the psychosis that led to this." She nodded to the body. "I thought a few tissue samples might give us better insight to Mr. Butcher's state of mind."

"By the way, doc," Schag said, pulling the papers from jacket pocket. "I have Bill's wife's authorization papers right here."

"Excellent," Carter said. "Put them on the center table there, please." He waved a hand toward a table that almost ran the length of the room. He turned back to Clarke, moving her closer to the autopsy table. "You know, I've read quite a few of the journal articles on this agueloquine problem. What tissue samples would you need to help you prove your hypothesis?"

Schag laid the papers on the table and looked around, not eager to see Bill's body sliced and diced. Like most law enforcement officers, he attended autopsies for training and for evidence collection. He remained detached for those carvings, but this was different. He spotted a large flat-screen computer monitor on the center table, and studied it. A dozen smaller screens divided the larger screen. In each square was an X-ray. Schag looked closer, saw Bill Butcher's name on each of the squares. Schag knew X-rays were part of the autopsy, but one of the small squares seem to stand out to him. He looked closer, squinting at the tiny image of a leg. A small L in the corner of the image indicated it was the X-ray of someone's left leg.

"Doc?" he said.

Carter and Clarke both turned and answered in unison. "Yes?"

"Sorry. I meant Dr. Carter."

"What can I do for you, agent?" Carter asked, clearly not pleased with the interruption.

"These X-rays," Schag said, pointing to the monitor. "These are all of Bill Butcher?"

"Yes. We had them shot this morning in preparation for the autopsy," Carter said, eager to get back to his discussion with Clarke.

"Can I see this one here?" Schag pointed a finger at the X-ray of the left leg. "I mean full size."

"Touch the image and it will enlarge," Carter said gruffly before turning back to Clarke.

Schag touched the image as told and it blossomed to fill the screen. He studied it closely, following the shape of the tibia and fibula—the two bones of the lower leg—up to the knee, then to the femur, the large, thick bone of the upper leg and hip. He pursed his lips in thought, and looked at the L again to make sure he was looking at the correct leg.

"Dr. Carter?"

Carter's back stiffened and he sighed before answering.

"What is it, Agent Schag?"

"You're certain these X-rays are from that corpse?" Schag asked, turning and pointing to the body on the table.

"Of course," Carter answered tartly.

"And this is an image of the left leg, correct?"

"If it has a little L in the lower corner, then it's the left leg," Carter said, turning back to the corpse and Dr. Clarke.

"Forgive me, doctor, but would you look at this X-ray?"

"Why?" Carter's voice was no longer able to hide his impatience.

"Please, take a look," Schag asked. "You, too, commander. Does this leg look like it was ever broken?"

Both physicians stepped over to the monitor and studied the X-ray. They looked at each and shook their heads in agreement. They turned and faced Schag.

"No, agent," Carter said. "This image shows perfectly intact bones. This extremity has never been broken. Why?"

Schag scratched his head, aware his gloom was beginning to fade.

"Bill Butcher's Navy career as a SEAL ended when he had a parachute malfunction," Schag said. "He landed hard, very hard, and shattered both the tibia and femur of his left leg. He had to have pins inserted in each bone—pins which are still there." Schag tapped the monitor. "This leg has no pins."

Carter looked more closely at the X-ray. He called up another image, this one of the right leg to make sure there were no pins in that one. There weren't. He looked up at Schag.

"Then . . ." Carter let the sentence hang.

"Then what?" Clarke asked.

"Then that body is not Bill Butcher," Schag said.

CHAPTER 14

WHEN SCHAG REPORTED HIS DISCOVERY to Riley, the agent-in-charge's profanity-riddled response made it painfully clear Butcher's survival didn't delight him. Schag understood the anger. He knew it would fall upon Riley to notify the sheriff's department that the burnt body sitting in the medical examiner's office was not the man they thought it was. Schag and Riley both knew what the response would be. Certainly not good. Riley even considered delaying the call to the sheriff, giving the county M.E. time to notify the lawman first. But since it was his own man who made the first identification of the body, then discovered the error in that identification, Riley knew the sheriff would consider it NCIS's responsibility to notify him first.

Riley and the sheriff weren't the only ones upset. In

the three days since Schag misidentified the corpse, the small army of law enforcement officers and agents demobilized. That army must mobilize again—and at great cost. Not only that, but valuable time was lost, time in which Butcher could have fled the area because the dragnet spread to catch him had been pulled in empty. Recriminations flew at the press conference called by the sheriff to announce the renewal of the manhunt, with Tom Riley, red faced but stoic, enduring an onslaught of accusatory questions and innuendo from the press.

The only person to receive the news with enthusiasm was Yolanda. By the time Schag arrived at the safe house, she already knew about his discovery. Riley notified the agents on her guard detail, and they, in turn, told Yolanda. The instant the agents let Schag in the door, Yolanda wrapped him in her arms, kissing his cheek, and burrowing her head into his neck. He felt her warm breath on his skin, the press of her body against his, and felt guilty for the desire it raised within him.

"I knew Bill wouldn't kill himself," she said as they separated. Tears streamed down her face, smearing her eyeliner. This time, however, Schag understood these were tears of relief. "I told you, didn't I?"

"Yes, you did, Yolanda," Schag said. "I'm sorry."

"Sorry? For what?"

"For what I put you through when I thought Bill had shot himself," he explained. "I know how much your beliefs mean to you and Bill."

Yolanda smiled sadly, leaned forward, and kissed his cheek again. "You're a good friend, Lin," she said.

Schag threaded his car through downtown traffic,

looking for the address of the notary public who notarized the affidavit of Lieutenant Commander Clarke's lover. After returning the doctor to Balboa, Schag had stopped by the hospital's emergency department to talk to the commander's lover. She was a first class corpsman, a senior petty officer who should have known better than to get involved with a senior officer. Her name was Braxley, and she was about the same age as Clarke. Unlike the shorter and more curvaceous physician, Braxley was tall and lanky, with black hair pulled tight around her head. Schag took her into a private office, where she stood nervously at attention.

"Stand at ease, sailor," Schag said, taking out his notebook and pen.

Braxley remained at attention, as if too nervous to relax her muscles.

"Sir, I already told the other agent everything I have to say," she said. "On the advice of my lawyer—"

"Relax, petty officer," Schag said. "I'm not here to discuss your relationship with Dr. Clarke. I'm here to talk about this other 'agent,' as you call him."

As soon as Schag explained, it was clear to her she had been tricked into confessing her relationship with Clarke. The realization made her muscles weaken, and Schag had to help her into a chair. Braxley stared at the floor, aware her blunder had ended the career of her lover and maybe her own as well.

"I should have looked closer at his credentials," Braxley sobbed. "I just saw a badge and assumed . . ."

"Did it look like my credentials?" Schag asked, handing her his flash wallet with the NCIS badge and identification card.

Braxley studied the badge. "No," she said, shaking her head. "This guy's badge looked more like a police officer's badge—you know? Silver and kind of egg-shaped. Yours is gold and kind of … squatty."

Schag's eyes rolled at the description. "Did he give you a name?"

"Riley," Braxley said. "Special Agent Thomas Riley."

Schag looked up from his notebook. "He called himself Tom Riley?"

"Thomas Riley," Braxley corrected. "Why do you know him? Is he a real NCIS agent?"

Schag ignored her question. "What did this man look like, petty officer?"

Braxley closed her eyes and concentrated a moment.

"Somewhat heavy set—not obese, but heavy," she said. "Short hair, really short like a Marine's and light brown with some graying. About so tall." Braxley held her hand up to her shoulder height.

Schag sighed with relief. "Yes, there is a Special Agent Tom Riley," he said. "My boss. But he doesn't match that description. Where did he approach you? At Balboa?"

"No. At home. In the evening after duty."

"What did he say?"

Braxley screwed her face up, thinking. "He said he was from criminal investigations and that he knew all about Kendra and me. I mean Dr. Clarke."

"Criminal investigations?" Schag asked. "Not NCIS or Naval Criminal Investigative Service?" Schag knew that was the proper way for an agent to identify himself.

"No, I'm certain he just said 'criminal investigations.'"

"Okay. Did he have any evidence?"

"Email," Braxley said, nodding. "Intimate. Love letters, you know?"

"Do you know how he got them?" Schag asked.

Braxley shrugged. "You guys have ways to do that, don't you?"

"Yes," answered Schag. "But it requires getting a court order. Then what?"

"He made me write my affidavit on my computer and print it out," Braxley said. "Then he drove me to this notary public and had me sign it."

"And afterward, he took you home and left you?" Braxley nodded. "That was it?"

"Yes, sir."

The notary public's second-story, walk-up office was on the outskirts of downtown San Diego in a neighborhood that bypassed by the city's redevelopment district. The business occupying the first floor was a bail bondsman that promised fast service for any offense. Two tough-looking youths with long hair and shiny badges clipped to their belts walked out the door as he passed by. Agents of the bail bondsman, Schag assumed. Bounty hunters.

Schag took the stairs to the second floor two at a time, prodded by the stench of stale beer and piss. At the landing, he paused, looking up and down the corridor at the office doors until he found the right one. He rapped twice on the door and opened it.

The office was small and crammed with a desk, a desktop computer with an aging cathode ray tube monitor, and a scanning device Schag recognized as the type used for making live-scan fingerprints. A plump, middle-aged woman sat behind the desk, typing on the computer's keyboard. Her hair was mousey brown, curled, and sprayed in place. She peered at Schag over half-moon reading glasses.

"May I help you?" she asked, smiling.

Schag's credentials were already in his hand and

flipped open so she could read them.

"Sandra Goodkin?"

"Yes," she said. She held out her hand. "May I see those a little closer, please?" Schag handed the ID wallet to her. "There are so many people running around with badges these days, you can't be too certain who's who. Navy? Well, that's different. Never met an NCIS agent before. Not in real life. Just that show, you know?"

Schag rolled his eyes as Goodkin handed the wallet back to Schag, and he replaced it in his flight jacket pocket.

"How can I help you, agent?" Goodkin asked.

The agent handed her the affidavit. "That was delivered to the commanding officer of a Navy unit this morning. It contains an allegation about one of the officers under his command, and it appears you notarized it. Do you recognize the document?"

Goodkin flipped to the last page and studied the signature and notary mark. "Yes, that's my mark and signature," she said.

"So you recognize the document?"

"I didn't say that, agent," the woman said, handing the papers back to Schag. "I said it was my signature and my mark—my state number."

"But you don't recognize the document itself?"

Goodkin reached into a drawer and took out a pack of cigarettes, chose one, and lit it. "Agent," she said, blowing smoke, "I don't read every document that comes across my desk. If I read every business contract or bond agreement I notarized I'd have a bigger headache than I have now. All I do is witness the document being signed, check the signer's ID, and stamp it."

"If you don't recognize the document, would you recognize the people?"

She took a drag on her cigarette and thought about it. "Maybe," she said. "Why? You got a picture?"

"No, but it was a man and woman," Schag said. "Older man, short and stocky, Marine Corps haircut, and graying. The woman was younger, tall, thin, with long black hair, maybe pulled back?"

"Oh, them," Goodkin said. "Yes, I remember them. Came in here late last night, just before I closed. The guy called and asked me to keep my door open."

"Do you know him?" Goodkin shook her head. "But you kept your business open for him?" She nodded. Schag was growing weary of this game playing. "Look, Ms. Goodkin—"

"Mrs. Goodkin," she corrected, dangling her left hand out so Schag could see her wedding ring.

"Mrs. Goodkin," Schag said. "I'm investigating a case involving a man who is impersonating a federal agent. If you don't cooperate, I'm going to start thinking you might be an accomplice. That's a federal felony."

Goodkin sat back, no longer amused. "Who said I wasn't cooperating? I never saw the man before, agent. But the girl called him Mr. Riley."

"We know that's not his real name. You have no idea what the man's real name is?"

The woman pulled more smoke into her lungs and considered the question. She exhaled and said, "Okay, like I said, I never saw this guy before. But he paid me cash and as he was taking money out of his wallet, I noticed he had a badge. Next to the badge was a private investigator's license. PIs are good business for me around here, being so close to the courthouse. I didn't want to rat him out if he was going to do return business with me."

"Did you get his name?" Schag asked impatiently.

Goodkin nodded. "Just a glance of his last name," she said. "It was Gavin. Nice and short."

"What do you mean he was impersonating me?" demanded Riley. He, Schag, and Parker were sitting in the NCIS conference room.

"He identified himself to the petty officer as Special Agent Tom Riley." Schag answered. "But all she saw was a badge. She didn't know the difference. She'd never seen an NCIS badge before."

"Why me?"

"Have you ever met a PI named Gavin?" Schag asked.

Riley shook his head. "Doesn't ring a bell. Who is he?"

Schag sat at one of the computers in the conference room. "There's only one private investigator in this area named Gavin. Full name is Terry Gavin. Has an office east of here in El Cajon." He typed a command into the computer and a service file flicked to life on the wall screen. It showed a heavyset man in his late thirties with closely cropped hair and wearing the khakis of a Navy chief. "He retired from the Navy a few years ago as a chief master-at-arms. In fact, his last duty station was this base. I should say he was allowed to retire."

"Allowed?" Riley repeated. "Caught with his hand in the cookie jar?'

"Something like that," Schag said, nodding. "Originally, Gavin was an IT specialist. But he got bored in that rate and switched to master-at-arms. He used his computer knowledge a lot in his MAA investigative work. Got praise for it, too. Then he hacked into a suspect's personal email to look for evidence. He found it. The defense attorney discovered how it was obtained and got the case kicked out. The suspect walked, and Chief Gavin was forced to retire."

Riley nodded. "I remember that case now," he said. "NCIS got called in to investigate Gavin's action, but when he agreed to retire, we dropped the case."

"That before you became SAC?" Schag asked. Riley nodded. "That's why he called himself 'special agent' instead of your current title. He didn't know about your promotion." Schag typed more instructions into the keyboard. Another photo of Gavin appeared on the wall screen. In this one he was older, the stubble of hair grayer. "After retiring, he got a state PI license and opened an office in El Cajon. He doesn't seem to have learned his lesson, though. His practice is a bit shady and he's got a few complaints filed against him, but nothing that could be substantiated so he's never had his ticket pulled."

"What kind of complaints?"

"Hacking personal computers, email, and social media accounts."

"Same kind of stuff he did with Commander Clarke," Parker said.

Riley grunted. "He should have gone to work for the NSA."

"There have been some physical altercations, too," Schag continued. "He's not afraid to get his hands dirty— or bloody."

"Well, I guess we should have little talk with Mr. Gavin sooner or later. Tell him to stop pretending he's me." Riley rapped the table and stood. "But, unfortunately, it's too late for your good doctor and her girlfriend. That train's already left the station."

"I think sooner rather than later," Schag said. "In fact, I was planning to pay Gavin a visit this afternoon."

Riley tensed. "Why?"

"Someone hired him to rat out Commander Clarke," Schag said. "I want to know who and why."

"To what end?" Riley demanded again.

"Because I think it has something to do with Bill Butcher's case," Schag said. "I can't say why I think that, but I do. She shows up at the sheriff's briefing and the next day this scumbag is spying on her. It's too coincidental. I think it has something to do with why Bill went rogue."

"You mean that medication stuff," Riley said, his voice tightening. Schag nodded. "It's still not our case, Lin."

"Well, technically, this is our case," Parker said. Riley shot him an angry look. "I mean, this guy is impersonating a federal law enforcement agent. That's a federal felony. And if he impersonated an NCIS agent, that makes it our case."

"You heard the lad, Tom," Schag said, smiling.

Riley's face was red with anger, but he took a deep breath and relaxed.

"Fine," he said. "Go talk to this guy. However, if you find anything out that has anything to do with Butcher, you bring it to me, and I'll give it to the sheriff. And that's it. Understood?"

Schag nodded, unable to hide his grin. Riley looked at the agent once, twice, then shook his head and walked out of the conference room, slamming the door behind him.

CHAPTER 15

THURSDAY
Office of Terry Gavin, Private
Investigator
El Cajon, California
1400 Hours

SCHAG, WITH PARKER RIDING SHOTGUN, found Gavin's office in an industrial area a few blocks from Gillespie Field, El Cajon's municipal airport. The office sat between a computer repair shop and a pilot's supply store. Parker read the sign on the glass door aloud. "Special Investigations. Terry Gavin, Chief Investigator."

"There's nothing like truth in advertising," Schag said as he parked the car on the street a few doors down from Gavin's office.

As the two agents walked past the pilot's supply store, a customer stepped out and eyed Schag's flight jacket.

"Nice jacket," said the customer, a man wearing a navy-blue ball cap. Across the front of the cap, embroidered gold letters said: FLIGHT INSTRUCTOR. "You a Navy aviator?"

Schag shook his head and kept walking. "Nah. I won it in a poker game."

"Oh," said the man, disappointed.

The glass door to Gavin's office was unlocked and the two agents walked in. The office wasn't much bigger than the notary public's. A variety of computers and monitors cramped what space there was, the screens flashing with data either being scanned or downloaded. An electronic bell chimed in the back of the office, activated when the door was opened. Gavin appeared through a door that led to a back room, dressed in khaki pants and a loose-fitting beige polo shirt. He was chewing something. When he saw Schag and Parker, he stopped chewing and swallowed hard, trying to force the food down his throat so he could speak.

"May I help you gentlemen?" Gavin's eyes shifted warily from one man to the other.

"Terry Gavin?" Schag asked. Gavin nodded. Schag pulled his credentials wallet from his jacket pocket and flashed his badge. "NCIS. You were identified as a man who misrepresented himself as an NCIS agent to a Navy petty officer in order to trick her into signing an affidavit confessing to an improper relationship with a superior officer."

Gavin looked at Schag's badge, then at Schag and Parker. His mouth turned down into a half moon, and he shook his head. "Nope, not me," he said. "Don't know what you're talking about." He sat in a chair and looked at one of the computer screens. "Now if you'll excuse me."

"You were seen with the petty officer at a notary public," Parker said. "The notary saw your PI license when you paid her in cash. She saw your name."

Gavin shook his head, not looking at the two men. "Some other guy named Gavin," he said. "Lots of

Gavin's around."

"Only one PI in this area is named Gavin," Schag said. He leaned across Gavin's desk and pressed the power button on the monitor he was watching. Leaning close to the detective, he said, "We showed the petty officer your photo, chief. She identified you."

Gavin blanched. Whether it was news that Clarke's lover identified him or the use of Gavin's former Navy rank, Schag couldn't tell. He knew, however, Gavin's facade was starting to break.

"We know about your Navy record, Gavin," Schag said. "About your use of computers to get evidence illegally." Gavin's eyes flicked up to Schag's face, then away again. "We figure you used similar skills to find out about the petty officer's relationship with Commander Clarke. Are we right?"

Gavin sighed and leaned back in his chair. "Okay, I did a job for a client," he said. "That's no federal case. You've got no jurisdiction."

"We do since you identified yourself as an NCIS agent," Parker said.

"I did not!" Gavin protested. "I never told her I was NCIS. I said I was with criminal investigations. I showed her my PI badge. If she misunderstood me, that's not my fault."

"Criminal investigations?" Schag repeated.

"Well, I do criminal stuff," Gavin insisted. "Employee thefts and stuff like that. So I stretched it a little. It's still no crime—and it isn't no federal or Navy crime. So you still have no jurisdiction."

"You used Tom Riley's name with the petty officer," Schag said.

Gavin shrugged. "Who's Tom Riley?"

"He's the NCIS agent who investigated you for

computer hacking before you retired," Schag said. "He's now Special Agent in Charge of the entire NCIS Southwest Region—and you've really pissed him off."

Schag may have exaggerated Riley's reaction, but the impact on Gavin was plain to see. The idea he used the name of a powerful Navy law enforcement agent made the detective visibly shrink in front of the two agents.

Schag smiled. "Look, chief," he said politely. "We're only here to ask you a few questions. That's all. Like who was your client and why?"

"You know I don't need to tell you squat, agent," Gavin mumbled. "That's privileged information."

"Which are you impersonating now?" Schag asked. "A lawyer or a priest?"

"I've got privilege, too," Gavin insisted.

"Only if you're working for an attorney," Schag said. "So, is your client an attorney, chief?"

Gavin's eyes brightened. He started to answer, but Schag held up a cautionary finger. "Remember, it is a federal crime to lie to a federal agent when he is conducting a line of inquiry into an official matter."

Gavin's face darkened. "What are you talking about. What official matter?"

"The matter of William Butcher." Schag replied.

Gavin jumped to his feet. "That guy they're looking for? The guy with The Butcher's Bill?" Schag nodded. "I got nothing to do with that!"

"Commander Clarke was assisting NCIS and the local authorities with the Butcher case, chief," Schag said smoothly. "I think whoever hired you wanted to discredit the commander and shut her up. Now, who hired you, chief?"

"That's bullshit!" Gavin yelled. He was sweating heavily now. "You're bullshitting me. I'm not falling for that. Get out! Get out of here now!"

Schag shrugged. "Well, if you insist," he said calmly. He picked up one of Gavin's business cards from a holder on his desk. "You know what they say, chief. Don't leave town. We'll be back in touch."

Schag waved the card at Gavin and motioned Parker toward the door with nod of his head.

They sat in their sedan and waited. Fifteen minutes later, Gavin stepped out of his office and locked the door. He turned from the door, slipped on wrap-around sunglasses, and glanced up and down the street before rushing off toward the parking lot.

"He looks like he's in a hurry," Parker observed.

"Yeah," Schag said. "Just for kicks, let's follow him."

Aidan Black was driving west on Interstate 8 when his cell phone chirped. He closed his eyes as if in pain, and reached for the phone. The last few days had made him wary of phone calls. They'd all brought bad news.

Without looking at the caller ID, he answered the phone. "Aidan Black." The voice on the other end was nervous, uncertain.

"It's me, Gavin. I just had a visit from two NCIS agents asking me questions about that damn Navy doctor of yours."

Shit! Black thought. After a moment, he asked, "How did they find you? I thought you said nothing could be traced back to you."

"That fucking bitch of a notary public saw my name when I paid her. They talked to her and traced me."

Black pounded the steering wheel, trying to vent his anger. *Another foul up.*

"What did you get me involved in, Aidan?" Gavin demanded.

"I don't know what you mean. What did they tell you?"

"That this Navy doc was involved in helping the cops trying to catch that Butcher guy," Gavin said. "The guy that attacked your compound the other night."

Jesus Christ! It just gets worst, Black told himself.

"Where are they, the agents?" he asked.

"I kicked them the hell out of here," Gavin said. "But they said they'd be back. What did you get me into, Aidan?"

"Nothing, nothing. Just relax. We'll meet and talk this over." Black paused for a moment, deciding on a good meeting place. Somewhere quiet. Somewhere not crowded. "You know the national cemetery?" he asked. "Meet me there . . ." Black checked his watch. "In an hour and a half. The bay side, at the Bennington Memorial, okay?"

Gavin agreed. Black hung up and dialed a number. "It's Black," he said. "You still following that NCIS agent?"

The man at the other end of the call sat in the front passenger seat of black Ford SUV parked in the trolley station outside the main gate of the 32nd Street Naval Base. His name was Gott and he shook his sleeping comrade as he spoke. The other man, a tall, thin operator named Kasitz with mousey brown hair and a thin moustache started cussing, but Gott put a finger to his own lips to shush him.

"No, sir," Gott said. "We trailed him from the coroner's office back to the Navy hospital, then to a notary public. We reported that already. Then we tailed him to the 32nd Street Navy base. We've been waiting at the main gate since then. But he could've have left by another gate."

"He did," Black told him. "He and another agent. I've got another job for you. I have a meeting with a guy, and I need to be alone with him. Schag and that other agent might be following the guy I'm meeting with. I need you to cover me and run interference for me. Are you two up to it? It might need to be dirty."

Gott turned to Kasitz, who was listening in on the call. Kasitz shrugged and nodded. "We're up to it, sir," Gott said calmly.

"Good," replied Black. He gave them the details of what he needed done. When he finished, he ended the call and put the phone back in his pocket. He reached under his seat, removed a 9mm Berretta concealed there, and slid it into the back of his waistband.

"Damn," he muttered.

CHAPTER 16

THURSDAY
Fort Rosecrans National Cemetery
San Diego, California
1545 Hours

KNOWN TODAY FOR ITS NAVAL installations, San Diego's Point Loma peninsula used to be an army fortress. The Spanish built the peninsula's first fort, Fort Guijarros, in the 1790s to guard the entrance to San Diego Bay. The Spaniards only fought one battle in the fort, firing its cannon against an American brig called the *Lelia Byrd*, which was trying to escape after being caught smuggling furs. The second and last time the Fort Guijarros fired its cannon was also against a fleeing American smuggler, but this time the cannoneers were Mexican soldiers. The fort remained under Mexican control until the *USS Cyane* sailed into the harbor in 1846 and claimed control of San Diego for the United States.

In 1873, the U.S. Army started construction on Fort Rosecrans in the same area of Fort Guijarros, and for the same reason—to defend San Diego Bay. Named after a

Civil War general, Fort Rosecrans grew to include massive artillery emplacements burrowed into the peninsula's rock face. The emplacements housed large, long-range cannon designed to fight off an invading naval force. Such guns protected the bay through two world wars. Those impregnable warrens are still there today. So, too, are many of the fort's old administration buildings built on Point Loma's bayside. Instead of overlooking artillery, however, those buildings today overlook submarine pens—docks for the Navy's Los Angeles-class fast-attack submarines. The only memory that Point Loma was once an Army fortress is the name of the cemetery that sits atop part of the peninsula looking seaward to the west and bayward to the east: Fort Rosecrans National Cemetery.

One of the most prominent monuments at the cemetery is the memorial dedicated to the memory of sixty-six sailors who died aboard the *USS Bennington* on the morning of July 21, 1905. While lying at anchor in San Diego Bay that morning, one of the gunboat's boilers exploded, spewing scalding steam throughout the wrecked ship. Efforts to save the ship and rescue the injured earned eleven members of her crew the Medal of Honor. One crewman aboard the Bennington that morning was John Henry Turpin, a black sailor with the distinction of having survived both the explosion onboard the *USS Maine*, which led to the Spanish-American War, and the explosion onboard the Bennington.

The memorial is a sixty-foot obelisk built of unfinished granite blocks. It stands like a rough-hewed Washington Monument overlooking the graves of the Bennington's dead.

Aidan Black didn't live in San Diego, but he had

gotten to know many of its landmarks during the months of regulatory red tape Gideon had gone through to get permission to build its training center in the backcountry. Though a prominent feature of the cemetery, Black knew the Bennington monument stood in one of the graveyard's oldest sections and that the mourners of those buried there had long ago passed away themselves. It was doubtful any mourners would disturb his meeting with Gavin.

He stood in front of the towering memorial, the winter winds whipping through his dark hair. He buttoned his suit coat more to keep the wind from revealing the pistol in his waistband than from cold. Occasionally, he glanced around, ensuring himself there were no history-minded tourists approaching. A hundred yards downhill, a black SUV parked. Two men got out and walked through the headstones, heads bowed as if looking for a familiar name. They stopped at one marker and stood in silence, heads still bowed. To anyone but Aidan Black, the two men looked like mourners paying their respects to a friend or family member. Black knew, however, they were his men, Gideon operators.

Black turned at the sound of another vehicle approaching. It steered toward the monument. Black flexed his gun hand nervously, as if warming it up. The sedan stopped, and Gavin climbed out, looking around as he did, and eyeing the two ersatz mourners suspiciously. He shrugged and walked toward Black.

"Terry!" Black said, sticking out his hand as if greeting an old friend.

"Aidan," Gavin said dully, and shook the offered hand. "I don't know what you got me into, but those Navy feds have got me nervous. They're saying I'm linked into this Butcher's Bill thing."

"Not here," Black whispered. He glanced at the two men downhill, as if suspicious of them, causing Gavin to do likewise. Black nodded toward a copse of trees a little farther uphill. They walked in silence, Gavin in the lead. Gavin stopped once and started to turn, but Black urged him on further. When they were deep into the shadows of the trees, Black said, "Okay, Terry, this good."

Gavin stopped, but before he could turn, Black jammed the barrel of his 9mm hard into the base of the detective's neck, using his other hand to pull the detective into the gun, and squeezed the trigger. It was a technique he perfected in Iraq to dispose of troublesome business associates—corrupt Iraqi government officials, greedy insurgent leaders, even a British army officer on the take. Gavin's own head muffled the gunshot. The bullet tore through the cervical spine, destroying the spinal cord, and dropping the victim like a marionette with its strings cut. Fragments of the bullet and shattered bone shredded the cerebellum, the part of the brain that controls the autonomous nervous system, stopping the victim's breathing and heartbeat.

Black let Gavin's body drop. He took a handkerchief from his pocket and wrapped the pistol in it before placing it back in his waistband. He looked quickly around, saw no one nearby, and walked from under the trees to his car.

Schag parked the car a hundred yards from where Gavin parked, and watched him walk uphill to the monument, where he met a man in a black suit. At that distance, neither he nor Parker could see the other man clearly. Schag had a pair of binoculars in his go bag in the trunk, but he didn't want to draw attention by retrieving them. Instead, the two agents milled about the headstones, blending in with the two mourners they saw. They walked through the graves, meandering but always working themselves closer toward the monument and the trees beyond, where Gavin and the other man had disappeared. Then they heard the pop of a muffled gunshot. The other two in the cemetery either did not hear it or took no notice. To trained agents, however, the noise was unmistakable.

Schag and Parker exchanged glances and sidestepped away from each other, expanding the tactical distance between them so a shooter couldn't hit both with a quick double shot. As they walked, their hands went to the automatics at their waists. Their pace quickened. Weapons still in their holsters, they stepped past the two mourners. Up ahead, they saw a man in a black suit step away from the trees. It was the same man who greeted Gavin, but he was still too far away to identify. Schag reached for his Glock. At the same time, he yanked the badge off his belt to show the man as they approached him.

Schag was never sure which his brain processed first, the gunshots or the bullet slamming into his back. He was aware he was thrown forward and of intense pain in the right shoulder. He lay on the ground, his face buried in grass, unable to move. To his right, where Parker had been, he heard a scream followed by car doors slamming, an engine roaring to life, and tires screeching on pavement.

It seemed like minutes before he could move his body again, but it was only seconds. He rolled onto his left side and looked about. The two mourners were gone and so was their car. He heard a groan and a whimper, turned and saw Parker ten feet away, writhing on the ground. His right pant leg was dark with blood. Schag crawled to the agent, the ten feet feeling like a trek through the desert, and saw bright-red blood jetting from Parker's thigh. Schag pulled his necktie loose and wrapped it twice around Parker's thigh, tied a half hitch in it, then fumbled in his leather jacket for his pen. This he placed in the center of the half hitch, and tied a knot over it. He twisted the pen until the blood stopped pumping out of Parker's leg. Parker screamed in agony. Schag wrapped the remaining loose ends of the tie around the pen and secured it in place.

Somewhere in the distance, people were yelling. Schag tried to sit up and look around, but the pain in his back shot through him like an electrical shock. He fell backward, the sky swirling around him. Hitting the ground again repeated the shocking pain. Schag closed his eyes, and all around him went dark and quiet.

CHAPTER 17

THURSDAY
Aboard the Coronado Ferry
San Diego Bay
1715 Hours

AIDAN BLACK PARKED HIS SEDAN on the street near the *Star of India*, an iron-hulled ship that sailed the seas in the 1800s, before becoming a maritime museum piece. Tourists milled about the harbor front, exploring the *Star* and her historic sister ships, or waited in line for a table at one of the waterfront restaurants. Black quickly buried himself in the crowd and made his way to the docks, where tour boats tied up. He bought a ticket for the ferry to Coronado Island and boarded, finding a place to stand near the stern. Then he waited.

Black stared at the oily water beneath the ferry's stern, his hands gripping the handrail, his teeth clenched as tightly as his hands. Killing Gavin didn't unnerve him. He'd killed before. It was his philosophy that a man had a right to do whatever needed to be done to further his own interests. He had no qualms about lying, cheating, stealing, or even killing. This philosophy served him well as a psychological operations officer in the Army. Many psy-ops officers he served with were uneasy with the deceits their job forced them to embrace. Aidan Black, however, had no such reservations.

What upset Black at that moment was the *need* to kill Gavin. The private detective had been a loose end he hadn't counted on, and there had been too many loose ends of late, starting with Bill Butcher. Black blamed himself for that. He had tried to be clever in disposing of the threat Butcher posed to Gideon and the others. Far too clever. He should have taken him out as he had Gavin. Quick and clean. Instead, he worried about the information Butcher had. He felt he needed to discredit Butcher the way he had that Navy doctor. But the whole operation was screwed up from the beginning—from the loss of the two assassins sent after Butcher, to Cavendish's murder, to the loss of the assault team in the cabin explosion. SNAFU, Black thought. Situation Normal—All Fucked Up.

A flurry of activity on the dock caught Black's attention. Crewmembers cast off mooring lines, and the ferry's engines growled as it pulled away from the dock. As the vessel picked up speed, the cold sea air drove most of the tourists inside the ferry's deck housing. Black turned up his collar, but stayed where he was. The ferry motored across the bay and swung alongside an aircraft carrier tied up at Coronado's North Island Naval Air Station. With the passengers' attention centered on the massive warship, Black slipped the handkerchief-clad pistol from his waistband, gave it one more covert wipe-down, and let it drop into the bay.

Minutes later, the ferry docked at the Coronado landing. Black walked ashore and found the first restaurant with a bar. He downed two double vodkas on ice, and then took the next ferry back to San Diego.

Bill Butcher sat in his darkened motel room, staring at the luminous glow of his laptop screen. The motel was in a cheap section of town. It had nothing to offer a visitor except the management took payment in cash for a day or a week at a time, and paid little attention to its guests after that. The room was small and crowded by a single twin bed, a small, marred desk, and one chair. Besides the computer, jars of makeup and two wigs—one black, one red—cluttered the desk. An ancient clock radio played an all-news station while Butcher worked at the computer, organizing files, annotating them, and transferring them to a micro-memory card. The news station kept him up-to-date on the renewed manhunt. He finished transferring the last file when the news station broke into its normal broadcasting with a report of the shooting.

"We now have reports of a shooting at the national cemetery on Point Loma," a female announcer said. "This just coming in, and we don't have any details yet. But it seems three men were gunned down at the Fort Rosecrans National Cemetery out there on Point Loma. And ..." the announcer paused as if listening to someone. "And we now have reports that at least two of the victims were federal agents. What's that?" Another pause. Butcher, staring at the clock radio, willed her to continue. "Yes, federal agents, members of NCIS. That, you probably know from the popular TV show, stands for Naval Criminal Investigative Service."

Butcher rolled his eyes and shook his head in disgust.

"We don't have any information yet on the names of

the victims, or who the shooter or shooters may have been," the woman continued. "Police officials are not saying yet if this shooting was the work of the notorious Butcher's Bill killer—that is, William Butcher, the former NCIS agent who has been the subject of a massive local manhunt."

Butcher slammed his fist on the desk and switched off the radio. He stood in the cramped room, his smooth head drooping, his eyes closed, and sighed. Somehow, he knew one of the shooting victims was Linus Schag. And he knew it was his fault.

Sitting back at the desk, Butcher removed the small memory card and stared at it before removing the hiking boot from his right foot. He pulled back the padded insert, and placed the card beneath it. He replaced the boot on his foot, tied its laces, and sat back, a hand squeezing his eyes until they hurt.

In the background, he heard music he knew didn't exist.

CHAPTER 18

SCHAG SAT ON THE EDGE of his hospital bed and rolled his shoulder, testing its range of motion. He had spent the rest of the day and the night at the hospital, under observation for any potential problems arising from the beating his shoulder had taken at the cemetery. The Kevlar vest he wore beneath his shirt and jacket stopped the round that slammed into his back, but the impact had left his shoulder and back sorely bruised. X-rays revealed no bone fractures, but the doctors warned Schag not to overuse his right shoulder and arm. The bullet also had left a thumb-sized hole in the back of his precious leather flight jacket. Schag figured another cruise patch could cover it.

Tim Parker had not fared so well. The first shot slammed into his lower back. Parker's body armor stopped that one, but a second shot struck him as he fell, punching through his inner thigh back to front, and nicking the femoral artery. The doctors in the emergency room said Parker would have bled to death before reaching the hospital had Schag not jerry-rigged a tourniquet. Parker underwent surgery to repair the blood vessel, and was recuperating in a hospital room.

Schag may have saved Parker's life, but that didn't make him a hero in Tom Riley's eyes. Just the opposite. The senior agent had barely determined Schag's own condition before unloading a variety of expletives on him.

"Damn it, Lin, just what the hell were you thinking?" Riley demanded. "I thought you were just going to question this guy Gavin, not get involved in the goddamn gunfight at the O.K. Corral."

"It was a pretty one-sided gunfight, Tom," Schag protested, as he dressed. He winced as he slipped his injured arm into a shirtsleeve. "We never got a chance to draw our weapons. More of a bush-whacking than a gunfight."

"I don't give a rat's ass about that," Riley said. "I'm talking about how you got the hell to that cemetery. Why did you decide to tail Gavin? Who gave you permission to do that? What did you think you were doing?"

"My job," Schag said, buttoning the shirt one-handed. "Gavin impersonated a federal officer and blackmailed an active-duty Navy officer. That gives us jurisdiction."

"Well, not anymore," Riley said, turning toward the door. "Gavin's murder is now a local crime. It's up to the local cops. Keep your nose out of it."

"Come off it, Tom." Schag's voice was tight and loud. "Gavin was killed on a federal reservation—a naval reservation. That gives us enough of a nexus to take jurisdiction."

"No!" Riley spun on his heels, his faced contorted

with rage. "Enough of this, Schag. We have enough to keep us busy, especially now you got one of my agents shot. You *will* stay out of anything that even smells of Bill Butcher or this guy Gavin. No ifs, ands, or buts. You're officially off duty for the next two days. Doctor's orders. Rest that arm. That's official, goddamn it."

Riley turned back to the door, and slammed it on his way out.

Flashing amber traffic lights warned the yellow cab to slow as it neared the main gate of the submarine base. Signs advised the driver to dim his headlights. Two guards in blue-and-black Navy camouflage were huddled in the guard shack. At this time of night, few cars entered the base. On approach of the taxi, however, the guards stepped from the shelter of the shack and stood on either side of the entry lane, ready to challenge the newcomer.

The cab driver was black, with a headful of dreadlocks that fell to his shoulders. The guards saw him swaying as he approached, as if keeping time to music. He wore dark glasses despite the time. As he got closer, they could hear the driver singing to a reggae rhythm. The guard standing on the left held out his arm. When the car rolled to a stop, the guard leaned down to the driver's window.

"Hey, mon," the driver said in a Jamaican accent. Besides the dreadlocks, the driver also had a beard. "Me looking for a fare called Mista Schag," the driver said, handing the guard a copy of his cabbie's license. "He be staying at the Gateway." He continued swaying in a rhythmic motion.

The guard stepped into his hut and consulted a clipboard. "Oh, right. Mr. Schag called and said you were coming," the guard said, handing the license back. "Just stay on this road and take the last left. The Gateway will be on the right."

"Thank'e, mon," the driver said, bobbing his head. "I am totally overstanding," he added, using the Rastafari *Iyaric*, or dialect, word for understanding. "You've been most upfulness, mon. You enjoy this music?"

The guard looked puzzled but nodded, and the cabbie drove away. His partner gave him a questioning look.

"What was that guy saying?" the second guard asked. "Sounded like gibberish."

The black guard, who enjoyed listening to reggae himself, shook his head. "He said he understood my directions and that I'd been very helpful. That's not what's weird, though."

"What then?"

"He asked me if I enjoyed his music."

"So?"

"There wasn't any music playing," the guard said.

Schag stared out at the night beyond the window of his room at the Gateway Inn, massaging his shoulder and testing its range of motion again. The pain from the movement encouraged him to take another sip of Scotch, and he was once again thankful he wasn't on a dry Navy ship. Offshore, the oil tanker still swung at anchor, her deck lights dancing on the waves lapping at her sides.

After Riley left the hospital, Schag had visited Parker in his room. Painkillers left the young agent drifting in and out of consciousness, and Schag didn't stay long. He took a taxi to the police impound yard and recovered his rental car, where it was towed after homicide detectives finished their investigation at the cemetery. Then he returned to his hotel room.

He still could not understand Tom Riley's reluctance to get involved in any of the investigations that seemed to be growing around Bill Butcher. Sure, he could understand the manhunt for Bill was a job for the local agencies, but there were other federal agencies lending them assistance. While Riley could argue the murder of Gavin was a local matter, the subsequent ambush of two of his own agents gave NCIS the nexus, or the connection to the crime, that it needed to claim jurisdiction. It was arguable Gavin's impersonation of an NCIS special agent with the apparent intent to blackmail Lieutenant Commander Clarke—or at least neutralize her role in the search for Butcher —also gave the agency the nexus it needed. Schag had known senior agents before who shied away from controversial cases, but Riley seemed determined, even eager, to keep his hands clean of anything dealing with Bill Butcher, and that raised the hackles on Schag's neck.

A knock on the door stirred Schag from his thoughts. He glanced at his watch. It was a little after ten-thirty. Late for a social call. Moreover, he didn't know anyone in town who would want to be social with him. Stepping to the door, he removed the small, rolled-up piece of tissue he always placed in the peephole of hotel doors—most people didn't realize those peep holes were two-way—and looked out. All he could see was a shoulder and long, black dreadlocks.

"Who is it?" he called.

"Taxi for Mista Schag, mon."

"I didn't call a taxi," Schag said.

"No, mon, Mista Riley—he called. Said he want to see you but you all busted up. Couldn't drive, mon."

Schag shook his head, barely able to understand the

man's accent. Normally, Schag would never open the door to a stranger unless he had his pistol in his hand. On the other hand, he was on a protected Navy base—a base with nuclear submarines and the security force to protect them. He opened the door.

"I'm sorry but I don't und—"

A black man with shoulder length dreadlocks and dark glasses stood in the doorway. He held a savage-looking .45 caliber automatic pointed at Schag's stomach. His mouth parted in a big toothy smile.

"Don't you want to let an old friend in, Lin?" the man asked.

Schag recognized the voice and the smile.

Bill Butcher.

CHAPTER 19

THURSDAY
Naval Base Point Loma
San Diego, California
2245 Hours

SCHAG BACK PEDDLED INTO THE room. Butcher, his gun still aimed at Schag, followed him inside and closed the door. Butcher removed the dark glasses, revealing blue eyes that quickly scanned the room. Satisfied they were alone, Butcher turned to Schag.

"Well, how do I look," he said. "Not bad for a dead man, eh?"

Schag gestured to the black makeup on Butcher's face and hands. "A little charred, perhaps."

Butcher puzzled at the remark, looked as his hands, chuckling once he understood the reference to the cabin fire.

"Yeah, well, the cops are looking for a big, bald white guy," he said. "It was this or a Hispanic, and Yolanda always said my Spanish accent was crap."

"You got on base disguised as Rastafarian cab driver?"

Butcher shrugged. "The cab I stole added some validity."

"How'd you know I was here?"

"I figured you be staying at a Gateway, so I called each one asking to talk to you until I found the one where you were checked in. Then I called the main gate, told them I was you, and that you were expecting a taxi to take you to the airport."

"Are you going to keep that cannon pointing at me all night?" Schag asked.

"Do I need to?" Schag shook his head. "Good. Then I'll put it away as soon as you assure me you don't have a cannon available to point at me. Do you?"

"My service pistol is in the desk drawer," Schag said, turning and pointing to the desk where his laptop sat.

"And that pea-shooter you keep as a backup?" Butcher asked.

"Same place." Schag said, pulling up his pants legs to reveal his ankles.

Keeping Schag covered, Butcher eased over to the desk, slid the drawer open, and peered inside. Both of Schag's weapons lay inside. Satisfied, Butcher closed the drawer, stuck the .45 in his waistband, and tugged off the wig.

"If that's a bottle of whiskey on the dresser over there, I could sure use some."

Schag moved to the dresser and poured two stiff drinks. When he turned around, Butcher was pulling the remnants of his fake beard from his face. With the wig and the beard gone, only the middle portion of his face was dark with makeup. He looked like an over-grown raccoon. Schag couldn't stop from laughing, which made Butcher grin. The wide grin only added to his raccoon appearance, making Schag laugh harder, and causing him to slosh the drinks.

"Give me my damn drink before you spill it, Lin," Butcher said. He took the drink and walked into the bathroom. After washing his face and hands, he went back into the room and found Schag looking at him, the laughter replaced with a look of sorrow. "What?"

"Yolanda is worrying herself to death over you, Bill," Schag said. "You know that?"

"Of course, I do," Butcher said. He dropped into a chair and took a long swig of Scotch, closed his eyes, and sighed. "I didn't start this, Lin," he said, looking up. "I didn't bring this on."

Schag studied his friend for a while, noticing the lines on his face were deeper, and his crisp blue eyes a little duller, wearier. It looked as if Bill had aged ten years since the last time Schag saw him.

"Then who did, Bill?" Schag said. "Start at the beginning."

Butcher pursed his lips, then nodded.

"It started back in Iraq," he said. He sipped his Scotch and looked at Schag. "Remember when we had dinner in Bahrain?" Schag nodded. "I told you about the money, right?"

Schag nodded again. "The eight or nine billion in cash that disappeared. You were on a joint task force investigating its disappearance and you all were told to drop the case."

"And that didn't make sense, Lin," he continued. "We were losing thousands of dollars in equipment and supplies each month. We knew much of it went to the insurgents. We'd find their dead and wounded wearing our bandages and our plastic explosives in their IEDs. How could we be certain that missing money didn't go to the insurgents, too? Eight point nine billion would buy an awful lot of AK-47s and ammo, not to mention an Abrams tank or two."

"Did it?" Schag asked.

"No fucking idea," Butcher said, shaking his head. "I heard about some guy from D.C. who supposedly was sent out to find out what happened to the money. Met him a couple times. He said he found some of it stashed in a bunker in Lebanon. Lebanon!"

"Did he retrieve it?"

"Never had a chance. A short while later he was in a helo that went down. Killed everyone aboard. The official verdict was a mechanical malfunction. But I saw the accident investigators' notes, and according to the eyewitnesses, the helo blew up in mid-air."

"Shoulder-fired missile or rocket-propelled grenade?" Schag asked.

"If it were, why not just say so in the report?" Butcher said. "I mean, we were in a combat zone."

Schag sat back, looking at Butcher. "You're saying it was a bomb?"

Butcher paused a moment before answering, collecting his thoughts.

"I can't say for sure, Lin," he said. "But it was sure damned convenient for whoever took that money."

"And no one ever followed up?"

Butcher shook his head.

"But you did."

"Yep."

"And what happened?"

"Got my leash yanked—hard," Butcher said. "I tried to keep it on the down low, unofficial. But word got back to our offices in Bahrain, and they read me the proverbial riot act."

"How did they find out?" Schag asked. "You were in

Baghdad. They couldn't have had that much oversight."

Butcher shrugged and sipped his drink.

"A spy," he said.

"What?"

"Some of us had suspicions there was a mole in our system, either there in Baghdad or somewhere higher up. We'd be conducting an investigation and suddenly the suspects would disappear. We'd plan a raid on some place where we suspected black marketeering was going on, and when we launched the raid, the place would be empty. It happened repeatedly, like someone was tipping them off."

"And you think the mole tipped off regional headquarters in Bahrain?"

"No, no, not like that," Butcher said. "I think the people who stole the cash tipped off the mole."

Schag sat back and digested what Butcher had said. If whoever stole the cash had tipped off the mole inside NCIS, then the mole had to be working for them. Not only was the mole informing on investigations, but blocking them, too. It was something that sounded too familiar to Schag.

"Tom Riley was your supervisory agent, wasn't he?" Schag asked.

Butcher nodded. "Why?"

"What do you think of him?"

Butcher shrugged. His mouth turned down in thought, and he shook his head.

"I have no grief with him," he said. "He's political, a ladder climber, but that's not unheard of in the agency."

"But he'd be the one who pulled your leash, right?"

"Yeah, but . . ." Butcher paused, understanding where Schag was going. He shook his head. "No, I don't think it was like that, Lin. He's not a bad guy. He's fair. And he didn't have the power to kill the original task force investigation. That had to come from much higher up. In fact, he was as pissed off about it as I was. When he came down on me later, he was just following orders. They told us to stop, and he was just making sure we did. That's the kind of agent he is—by the book, make no waves. But like I said, that's not unusual in the agency."

Butcher's opinion of Riley was the same as Schag's. Career climbers like Riley never took chances, never risked a rebuke. They attended the right parties, shook the right hands. There were people like that in every large agency or corporation. Hell, they were in the military, too. In truth, Schag felt relieved to hear Butcher dismiss his suspicions.

"Okay, let's get back to what's been happening to you," Schag said.

"I followed Riley's orders until I got back from Iraq," Butcher continued. "I was working out of the Northwest Regional office then. I just couldn't stop thinking about that money, about who took it, where it went. It was like a little voice whispering in my ear. You ever hear things like that, Lin?"

Schag tensed, remembering Lieutenant Commander Clarke's description of agueloquine psychosis. "You mean like a hunch?" he said. "Like a voice in your head alerting you to something before it happens?"

"No," Butcher said. "More like someone actually speaking to me, but there's no one there. I'd hear this voice saying, 'Look here' or 'Look over there,' and then I'd have to go look. I couldn't stop myself. I kept looking, digging into the financial record of contractors working in Iraq, checking their tax returns, their financial statements. Every spare minute I had, I kept looking."

Schag remembered what Yolanda told him about Bill's

obsession, but he didn't think this was the time to mention it. "Then what happened?"

A triumphant grin spread across Butcher's face.

"I found the son-of-a-bitch who stole the money."

CHAPTER 20

THURSDAY
Naval Base Point Loma
San Diego, California
2330 Hours

BILL BUTCHER REMOVED HIS RIGHT boot. Reaching inside, he pulled back the inner sole and removed the micro-disk he had placed there earlier. He flipped it to Schag as if it were a coin.

"Your laptop read those?" he asked. Schag nodded. "Then let's put it in."

They both crowded around the desk as the laptop read the tiny disk and opened its directory. Dozens of folders crowded the screen. Schag clicked on the first folder. It opened to reveal more folders inside. He looked at Butcher.

"I've been a busy boy," Butcher said, smiling proudly. "Go back to the beginning." When Schag complied, he pointed to a single file standing alone. "Click on that."

The file blossomed into a spider diagram. At the center was a circle inside of which was the name

"Gordias LLC." Dozens of lines reached out like tentacles from the center circle to touch other circles. Inside each of those circles appeared another business name. From those circles, more lines stretched out to touch additional circles with names, and lines from those circles touched others. It looked like so many victims stuck in the grip of an intricate spider web.

"Ever hear of Gordias, LLC?" Butcher asked. Schag shook his head. "Know the myth of Gordias?"

"As in the Gordian Knot?" Schag said.

Butcher nodded. "Gordias was a poor Macedonian farmer who rode his ox cart into the kingdom of Phrygia. The Phrygians had lost their king, and an oracle told them the first man to enter the kingdom would be their new leader. Gordias was that man. Gordias's old ox cart stood in the palace for years, tied down in place by his son with a knot impossible to untie—the Gordian Knot."

"Like this diagram," Schag said, nodding at the picture on the laptop screen. "This represents business relationships among . . . must be a hundred different companies."

"One hundred and twenty-three," Butcher said. "And that's just upper levels."

Schag knew that drug cartels used multiple layers of businesses—some real, some only on paper—to launder their profits. Even legitimate corporations used layers of businesses to hide profits from the IRS. However, he had never seen anything this elaborate. Like the Gordian Knot, an investigator could go around and around all these holdings and never find the end.

"Cartel?" Schag guessed.

"Define *cartel*," Butcher said. Schag looked at him, and Butcher shook his head. "No drugs that I could find. But let's say the business practices of Gordias, LLC, aren't much different than a cartel's."

"Are these real companies?"

"For the most part, yes," Butcher said. "Some might bend the definition of 'real,' but they're not false fronts the way you're thinking."

"And Gordias owns them all?"

"Owns them, runs them, or controls them," Butcher said. "Let me start at the beginning. Gordias is both an investment group and a business management group. It offers companies long-term management services for a fee. That's called a fee stream. They take that fee stream to a bank—always one of a half a dozen banks Gordias always does business with because it has management services contracts with them, too—and they leverage the fee stream against a Standing Letter of Credit. That's as good as cash. They use that letter of credit to buy or invest in another company. They sign management services contracts with those companies, which produces another fee stream, and that is used to get still another letter of credit, and so on. All along the way, they seed these companies with their own handpicked personnel so even those companies they don't own in full or in part answer to their demands. Take those six banks Gordias always uses. Gordias doesn't own them, but it does pick who runs them."

"So, they are basically buying companies without risking any of their own money, right?" Schag asked.

Butcher slapped Schag on the back.

"You go to the head of the class, Lin," he said. "They take out a letter of credit for, say, ten million bucks. They invest half of that in buying some company and the rest goes to various fees that filter back to Gordias as profit. Slick."

"How'd you figure all this out?"

Butcher slapped Schag lightly on the back of his head. "I didn't get my master's degree on a football scholarship, Lin," he chided.

"This is all real clever, Bill, but I don't see anything illegal about it," Schag said. "Corrupt and greedy, yes, but not necessarily illegal. What's it got to do with you and Gideon?"

Butcher reached across the table and pointed to a small circle with even smaller type at the bottom left corner of the screen.

"Can you read that?"

Schag adjusted his glasses and squinted at the screen. "Gideon?" he said. "They own Gideon?"

"At least in part," Butcher said, nodding. "It's hard to tell sometimes how much of a company they own. But Gordias had its tentacles wrapped around damn near half the contractors we used in Iraq and Afghanistan."

Schag studied the screen, thinking. He still didn't see what Gordias had to do with all that had happened over the past few days. Butcher seemed to sense Schag's thoughts.

"Gideon is Gordias's own private army," he explained. "Gordias uses its influence to get Gideon contracts with our government and others. But Gideon also does all of Gordias's so-called security work."

Schag's years as a Wall Street lawyer gave him an insight to how large corporations worked. "You mean strong-arm work," he said. "They're Gordias's henchmen."

"I told you their business practices weren't much different than a cartel's," Butcher said. "Anyway, a few days ago, Gordias sent two of Gideon's apes after me."

"After you?" Schag asked. "As in a hit?"

"They were supposed to make it look like suicide,"

Butcher said, nodding again. "I took care of them before they could execute their plan, the fucking amateurs."

"But why would Gordias put a hit on you?"

Butcher's tooth-filled grin stretched across his face.

"Because I discovered it was Gordias that stole all that money from Iraq," he said.

They moved from the small desk and were sitting in chairs with renewed drinks in their hands.

"How?" Schag asked. "Why?"

"Gordias was making a fortune off the war in Iraq," Butcher continued. "But the people running Gordias got arrogant and started making errors. They spent megabucks buying a company without doing proper due diligence. It wasn't until after they completed the buyout that they realized the company was being threatened with a class-action lawsuit over an industrial accident that killed a few dozen workers. The value of that company nosed dived to less than half of what Gordias paid for it."

Butcher sipped his Scotch before continuing.

"About that time, the economy faltered and some of those companies Gordias had management contracts with went under. Gordias not only had a worthless new company, but the fee streams for the letters of credit used to buy it had dried up. They were facing bankruptcy, dissolution, criminal charges, who knows what else? That's when they decided to steal the Iraqi money."

"Wait a minute, Bill," Schag interrupted. "Who is *they*?"

"The SOBs who run Gordias."

"And they would be?" Schag asked.

"At the executive level, the CEO is a former U.S.

Senator," Butcher answered. "The board of directors has a couple former prime ministers, a former U.S. president, and a variety of other well-heeled, influential political hacks."

"What?" Schag exclaimed, stunned. "A president, a senator, and a prime minister?"

"Two prime ministers," Butcher corrected. "A couple sheiks and what-not, too. It's part of their operation. They sell political influence more than anything else. Who says 'no' to a former president or prime minister?"

"Okay, I'll bite," Schag said. "Which U.S. senator? Which president?"

Butcher shook his head. With his drink in hand, he pointed toward the laptop.

"It's all in there," he said. "But they don't matter because they don't actually run Gordias. There's a silent partner who prefers to stay in the shadows. He's the guy in charge."

Butcher sipped of his drink, and smiled as Schag leaned forward expecting him to continue. Butcher loved being on stage, loved an audience, and he was soaking this up.

"Well? Go on, damn it," urged Schag. "Who?"

"Charles Bennett the Third."

"Bomber Bennett?" Schag said, finding his voice. "The next secretary of defense?"

Butcher nodded. Schag remembered the offer of an NCIS bodyguard Tom Riley made during their videoconference with Bennett, and told Butcher.

"We wondered why he would prefer Gideon in light of . . ." Schag paused, choosing his words. "In light of current events. He said he wasn't assistant SecNav anymore and wouldn't take it."

Butcher understood the euphemism and let it pass.

"Bennett always uses Gideon, going back to when he was assistant navy secretary," he said. "Government bodyguards are required to log every place they go and every person their charge meets. Gideon doesn't do that. Bennett can go wherever he wants and meet whomever he wants in secret."

"But how does he figure into the missing money?" Schag asked.

"Remember, before he was assistant SecNav, Bennett was in the State Department," Butcher said. "It was his idea to send the Iraqi money overseas in cash. They could've done wire transfers, but he argued that would have left it in the hands of corrupt Iraqi officials." Butcher made air quotes around the word 'corrupt.' "Better to send it in cash that could be handed directly to the contractors doing the reconstruction."

"And the State Department bought that?" Schag asked.

Butcher shrugged. "Who could refuse?" he said. "Bennett likes to hide in the shadows, but he's got a lot of power. He pulls a lot of strings."

After taking another sip of Scotch, Butcher continued. "Anyway, Bennett was in charge of organizing the money transfer. Surprise, surprise. He hired a Saudi financier named Awadi to be his front man in Baghdad. Awadi organized everything from the time the cash arrived in Iraq to its final dispersal, including all security for the cash. And guess who he hired to provide that security."

"Gideon," Schag said flatly.

"Bingo," Butcher said, raising his glass in salute.

"Bennett's people determined a single Air Force C-130 could carry $2.4 billion in shrink-wrapped bricks of $100 bills. So once or twice a week, a C-130 loaded with dozens of pallets of cash landed at Balad and handed it all over to Awadi—that is, to Gordias. When the airlift operation was finished, so was Awadi. A vehicle he was riding in conveniently got hit with an IED."

"You're saying Gordias simply walked off with nine billion in cash and no one noticed?" Schag said. "I can't believe that."

Butcher leaned forward. "You don't understand, Lin," he said. "It wasn't just nine billion. It was more than forty billion." Butcher watched Schag's face go slack with disbelief, and nodded. *"And most of it is unaccounted for."*

Butcher let that sink in before continuing.

"Most of it probably did go to contractors, but there are no receipts showing who got how much and what for," he said. "Whether those contractors ever built anything to earn the money is another question. The corruption in Iraq was unmanageable. Hell, Congress approved $61 billion in taxpayer-funded reconstruction in addition to the $40 billion of Iraqi money, and most of it went into shit work. All that's known is that *at least* eight point nine billion magically disappeared. It arrived at Balad, then no one saw it again." Butcher shrugged and shook his head. "There might have been more, but no one knows how much. My hunch is some of it went to the insurgents to get a free pass out of the country without being blown up by IEDs. Hell, that's how we got them to stop blowing up our troops."

Butcher referred to an Army program that paid insurgent leaders and their followers one hundred dollars per month per man. The program was more effective at reducing the violence in Iraq than the so-called Surge pushed by the White House.

Schag nodded and sat quietly, thinking about what Butcher told him. "I admit, Bill, that's pretty convincing conjecture, but that's all it is. How do you know the missing money went to Gordias?"

Butcher smiled again. "Because as soon as the cash transfers were complete, Gordias was flush. All those companies that had no money were feeding Momma Bear again. Even the companies whose failures caused Gordias's money problems in the first place started paying their fee streams, even though they were no longer in operation."

"They were laundering the money through dead companies?"

"Spotting that was what unraveled the knot for me," Butcher said. "It was just like Alexander the Great using his sword to cut the Gordian Knot. It all just fell apart."

"And they found out what you knew and put a hit on you?"

Butcher shook his head.

"Not right away," he said. "Somehow they knew I was still looking into that missing nine billion. That's when things started going badly for me at NCIS. I kept getting called on the carpet for all kinds of minor things. Got bad evaluations. Given all the crap assignments. You know office politics. You become the goat and soon everyone is against you."

"Mobbing," said Schag, remembering what the psychologists at the task force meeting had said about the phenomenon. Butcher looked at him questioningly. "It's what the head shrinkers call it when the people in an organization start harassing an individual."

"Huh," Butcher said. "Mobbing. Yeah, well they did a mobbing on me, that's for sure. I finally resigned, *under pressure.*"

"Did you ever find out how Gordias knew what you were doing?" Schag asked.

"Nah," Butcher said, shrugging. "Maybe it was a mole

like we had in Iraq. Maybe even the same person. Alternatively, maybe they caught wind of all the Internet research I was doing. No way of knowing."

"They figured you'd stop looking into them if you lost your badge," Schag said.

"Well, the fuckers thought wrong," Butcher replied. "It wasn't until I stumbled on those dead companies that Gordias sent Gideon after me."

"Tell me how that all happened," said Schag.

"I was up north visiting Yolanda and the kids," Butcher said. "You know we separated?" Schag nodded. "That's a whole different story. Anyway, I noticed these two goons following me as I started back south. I recognized one of them as a Gideon merc I knew from Iraq. They followed me as I headed up to the cabin. I didn't know if they were tailing me to see where I was going or whom I was meeting. So, I figured I needed to have a talk with them. That's when one of them told me about the hit. After that, well, you know the old saw—the best defense is a good offense."

"Jesus, Bill," Schag said, "you killed and beheaded them."

"Only one," Butcher insisted. He added more quietly, "I know. I know. But it seemed like a good idea at the time." He sighed, shaking his head. "I don't know where I get these ideas anymore, Lin. It just happened."

"And the man at the Gideon compound?"

"Fucking Cavendish," Butcher spit. "I needed him to confirm what the other guy told me. Cavendish was the one who told me about that fake suicide letter on Facebook. Hell, I don't even have a Facebook account. Cavendish gave me the password and later I added to the letter."

"What the media is calling your Bill of Demands."

Butcher nodded. "Yeah, I hear they're also calling it The Butcher's Bill. Very clever."

"Why?" asked Schag. "Why not just delete the damn thing?"

"Nothing is ever really deleted from the Internet, you know that, Lin. At some point, someone would find it and it would just play into Gideon's and Gordias's hands. That's why I left it and added my demands. If something happened to me, it'd still be out there for people to find. You know, make them think a bit."

Butcher paced the room. "Who am I kidding? I don't know what I was thinking." He patted his head. "Things aren't always right up here, Lin. They haven't been since I got back from Iraq. Yolanda mention that?"

Schag nodded. "Why did you write my name on the wall?"

"Because I need your help, Lin," Butcher said. His face looked strained. "I don't think I'll get through this." He turned and dipped his head toward the laptop. "I want you to keep that disk. Get it to the right people if I can't. Someone who can do something with it."

"Like the media?" Schag asked.

Butcher sneered. "Did you know almost all major news outlets in this country are owned by five corporations?" Schag shrugged, shaking his head. "Well, they are. And guess who has some tie to each of those corporations."

"Gordias," Schag said. "So the news media wouldn't do anything with it.

"You figure out who can do something with it," Butcher said. "But not now. And don't let anyone know you have it. If Gordias finds out you know anything about what I found, they'll be after you next."

Butcher stood, pulled a cell phone from his pocket,

and tossed it to Schag.

"It's a burner," he said. "Registered to no one and prepaid in cash. I have its mate. You need to get hold of me, use it, and I'll do the same. But don't leave it on. Power up every hour and check for messages, then turn the damn thing off again."

Schag slipped the phone into his pocket. Butcher moved toward the door.

"Bill, wait."

Butcher turned back, and looked at Schag, waiting.

"About the problems you've been having," Schag said, tapping a finger on his head. "There's a Navy doc I know who thinks it's because of some medicine you took to ward off malaria. It causes problems in some people."

Butcher took a step forward. His eyes widened, hopeful. "Is there a cure?"

"Honestly, she doesn't know. But she said she might be able to help you, but only if you're still alive."

The hope in Butcher's eyes faded. "Oh," he said. After a moment, he asked, "You said she's a Navy doc?"

"For now," Schag said. He explained how the private detective Gavin had uncovered Commander Clarke's love affair with a female sailor under her command.

"Gavin? That's the guy you were following when you got shot?"

"Yeah."

Butcher fell silent a moment, then asked, "And you think what Gavin did was to discredit the doc's research into this ... what'd you call it?"

"Agueloquine."

"Check those files I gave you," Butcher said. "Gordias has an interest in one or two pharmaceutical companies. Maybe there's a connection there."

"I'll do that," Schag said.

Butcher turned back to the door, stopped, and turned around.

"If you're planning to call anyone to tell them about this meeting, Lin, just do me a favor," he said. "Give me ten minutes to get off base. Will you do that for me?"

Schag nodded, and Butcher left. As soon as the door closed, Schag reached into the night stand drawer for his Blackberry. He opened the directory, but paused before dialing. After sitting still for a minute, he replaced the phone and slid the drawer closed.

CHAPTER 21

SCHAG SPENT THE REST OF that night and most of the next morning going through Butcher' disk, opening one file and reading through it, then the next. Some of the best law enforcement investigative work was based on the painstaking tracking of minute details in documents. Elliot Ness and his Untouchables didn't bring down the Prohibition gangster Scarface Al Capone. An accountant going through Capone's business ledgers discovered Scarface was not paying his taxes, and that put the gangster in federal prison.

Schag had the television on low, half listening to the reports about the manhunt for Bill. Now and then he stopped his work to watch a report if it seemed to have new information. So far, though, Bill Butcher seemed to have disappeared. Throughout the day, Schag powered up the burner phone Butcher gave him and checked for messages. There were none, so he continued reviewing the files.

The amount of information Butcher had on Gordias, LLC, was massive. The firm had its tentacles in everything—banks, manufacturing, trans-oceanic shipping, air cargo. It even owned an interest in a Middle Eastern port operations firm that had contracts to run a few of the United States' largest commercial ports. Schag wondered for a moment how, in the post-9/11 era, the country tolerated such a major security compromise. But he soon remembered what Butcher had told him about Gordias's board of directors—a former U.S. president, a couple of prime ministers, and an Arab sheik or two. Schag shook his head and moved on through the files.

Gordias's financial records were just as interesting. After being drummed out of the Naval Academy for a deadly accident that wasn't his fault, Schag went to law school. He married a woman whose father was a controlling partner in a large Wall Street law firm, and Schag married into his father-in-law's business as well as his family. When Schag's wife ran off with a hirsute college professor a few years later, the Wall Street job went with her. While he regretted losing his wife, he didn't regret losing the job. Schag's sense of right and wrong was too well honed and his dedication to country too strong to work in a field where sociopathy and limitless greed were required job skills. Yet the time he'd spent on The Street gave him perspective on how the wealthiest corporations and persons conducted—and sometimes hid—their business activities. As uncomfortable as he had been with those machinations, the experience proved useful when he became an NCIS agent.

As Bill had told him, Gordias was using a variety of

purported revenue streams to back up letters of credit. It wasn't illegal, but it was dangerous—essentially a legal Ponzi scheme. That type of risky business activity was, in part, responsible for the worldwide economic collapse of 2007. As in a Ponzi scheme, when things went sour, the people at the bottom of the pyramid paid the price, not the schemers at the top. Even considering the corruption that led to that economic collapse, Schag had never seen an operation on such a wide scale as Gordias. The only reason no one ever questioned Gordias's operation was the names of the men at the very top of the organization.

Schag wondered if Bill had been correct about Bomber Bennett. Nothing in the documents on the disk showed Bennett had any role in running Gordias's day-to-day business. There was a news profile on Bennett that mentioned he helped found the firm, but beyond that, he seemed to have little or no connection with it. The same profile, however, described Bennett as a kingmaker and power broker, an Ozian man-behind-the-curtain who placed men in the spotlight of leadership but shunned it himself. Bennett had served as an assistant secretary of state and assistant Navy secretary. Both were powerful though anonymous positions. It struck Schag as odd that Bennett would now allow himself to be considered for the high-profile post of defense secretary.

If Bill was right about Bennett's power over Gordias, and Gordias was linked to the missing Iraqi money, Bennett's future in politics and business—both in the spotlight and in the shadows—would be destroyed. That kind of motive could easily drive a man to order another's murder. Schag remembered what Bill said about the fates of Awadi, the man Bennett hired to handle the Iraqi money, and the official who discovered some of the missing money in a Lebanese bunker. Both died under suspicious circumstances. In Schag's mind, the first two deaths made Bill's story—including the attempt to make his murder look like suicide—more credible.

Clicking through more folders, Schag found one of particular interest: Medico Pharmaceuticals. Butcher said Gordias owned a pharmaceutical company, and urged him to check them for any connection to agueloquine. Switching to Google, Schag entered the firm's name. Hundreds of hits came back. Scrolling through the pages, he spotted one that mentioned "anti-malarial" in the headline. Schag click on it. The article described the problems a few takers of the drug were having, and pointed out that most pharmaceutical companies had stopped its production—but not Medico Pharmaceuticals. It continued to make agueloquine for distribution throughout Africa, where it was much cheaper than other prophylactics. Despite being cheap, it was still profitable to Medico—and hence to Gordias— which appeared to have a monopoly on its sales in the African continent.

There were links to more stories about the problems with agueloquine. Schag clicked on several and read the articles. As Commander Clarke had said, only a small minority of people given the drug ever had adverse effects, while millions died of malaria each year. Still, those who did have problems with the drug found themselves in horrifying real-life nightmares, the worst of which led to violence and murder. Too many of those were veterans of the Iraq and Afghanistan wars. Despite these stories, Schag found none indicating the nation had paid any real attention. It was as if someone had taken great pains to damp down the bad publicity.

Just as someone had sent a group of psychologists to aid in the manhunt for Bill Butcher, and to deflect any questions about whether agueloquine was responsible for his behavior. Just like someone hired Gavin to discover information to discredit Commander Clarke.

Schag now understood who that was—Gordias and Charles Bennett III.

Something on the television caught Schag's ear. An overly excited reporter said there was breaking news in The Butcher's Bill manhunt. The reporter had no details, but the video feed showed police cars from multiple agencies speeding away, sirens blaring, and red and blue lights flashing.

Schag's Blackberry buzzed. Tom Riley's name flashed on the screen.

"Hey, Tom, what's up?"

"Where the hell are you?" Riley demanded.

"In my room at the Gateway resting my injured shoulder for two days as you ordered," Schag retorted, not liking Riley's tone.

"I don't give a fuck what I said," Riley said. "Get your god damn ass back in the office here. Bill Butcher just kidnapped his wife from the safe house, and killed our agents in the process."

CHAPTER 22

Yolanda Butcher closed her cell phone and wiped a tear from her eye, careful not to smudge her makeup. She had been speaking with her family—her parents and her kids—and the sound of the children's voices made her terribly homesick. The children knew their father was in trouble, but they had no idea how bad. Yolanda's parents had avoided watching news programs or leaving newspapers lying around that would have alerted them. Likewise, Yolanda avoided discussing Bill with the kids, deflecting any questions they asked by changing the subject. Still, she could hear the worry in their young voices, and that broke her heart.

The doorbell rang and, thinking—hoping—it was Schag, she rushed from the bedroom and down the hallway. She heard one of the bodyguards call out, "Who is it?"

"Pizza delivery," a man replied. "A Tom Riley ordered a pepperoni and sausage pizza for you. He said he called you about it?"

The agent, who had been in the field less than a year, glanced at his partner. The older man shrugged. "Tom's done that kind of thing before when we were on stake outs and such. Can you see the guy?"

The younger agent peered through the peephole and saw a tall man with a red ball cap with the logo of a well-known pizza chain sewn on.

"Looks legit," the agent said.

His hand on his pistol, he cracked the door for a better view. The deliveryman grinned at him and gestured with a large cardboard pizza box he held in both hands, one hand on top, the other on the bottom. The agent could see a pizza delivery van parked at the curb, He relaxed, opened the door wide, and reached for the box. As he did, the deliveryman pulled the trigger on the automatic pistol concealed beneath the box. The impact of the bullet slammed the young agent against the opposite wall, where he collapsed in a heap, blood spilling from a hole in his throat. The blood spread out to mix with pizza slices thrown from the box.

The older agent jumped from the chair he was sitting in, his hand moving swiftly to his weapon. It wasn't fast enough. The gunman stepped through the door and fired twice, hitting the agent in the head. As soon as the gunman was inside the house, a second man rushed inside. Like Bill Butcher, he was tall and husky, with a cleanly shaved head. As the first gunman checked the bodies of the dead agents, the second scanned the living room looking for Yolanda. Not finding her, he started down the hallway where Yolanda stood frozen, her eyes transfixed, lips trembling. At first, she thought the tall, bald gunman silhouetted by the light streaming from the open door was her husband, but that thought was fleeting. As the gunman came toward her, she turned and fled back toward the bedroom.

It was too late. He was on her in a few steps. She felt his beefy hand grab her shoulder and jerk her backward. She let herself fall onto her back, slapping the floor with her arms to absorb the impact as Bill had taught her. Using the momentum of the fall, she continued to roll as if doing a backward somersault, and slammed her feet into the face of her assailant as he bent over to grab her again. He fell with much less grace. Yolanda jumped to her feet, kicked the man in the face again, and turned to flee.

The sound of the gunshot froze her.

"You fucking bitch," screamed the man on the floor. "You fucking bitch!"

"Shut up, you idiot," growled the man in the pizza hat. "You let her smack you around like that? You're fucking disgusting. Now get up and tie her hands."

The bald man did as told, pulling a set of zip cuffs from his pocket and securing Yolanda's hands behind her back. Faced with a gunman she knew had already killed twice, she didn't struggle. They led her out the front door, without regard to the neighbors peering cautiously out windows in response to the sound of gunfire. Shoving Yolanda into the parked van, the first gunman climbed into the driver's seat and said to his partner, "Now do your act."

The bald gunman turned toward the gawking neighbors and fired his pistol twice into the air.

"Tell them Bill Butcher was here," he yelled. "That's

me! The Butcher!"

"That's enough, goddamn it," the driver said. "Get in."

The gunman complied, and the van drove off with a screech of tires.

"It was Butcher," Captain McManus said. The San Diego Police captain was again in charge of the SWAT action, in and around the NCIS safe house. "Two men, one in a red ball cap, the other big and bald. Driving a stolen pizza delivery van. One of our units found the van abandoned about a mile away. Empty."

"How can they be sure it was Bill?" Schag said.

"Big bald guy like they've seen on the news for the past several days," McManus answered. "And he screamed his name out to them." McManus looked at a notebook in his hand. "According to witnesses, he yelled, 'Tell them Bill Butcher was here. That's me. The Butcher.'"

Schag shook his head. "Bill never refers to himself as The Butcher. That's only something our academy classmates called him. Why would he shoot up the neighborhood?

McManus shrugged. "He wanted their attention?"

"What about the second guy?" Schag asked. "Who the hell was the second guy? Bill's on the run alone."

The police captain sighed. "Look, agent, I know is this guy's your friend, but people *saw* him, the whole fucking block saw him."

"They saw a big bald guy with a gun," Schag retorted. He waved his hand at the police officers and detectives milling around the safe house. Many of them were beefy and sported closely cropped hair or shaved heads. "We already mistakenly identified a big bald guy as Bill. How can we be sure this time?"

"No, *you* mistakenly identified some big bald guy as Bill," Riley corrected. He held a hand between Schag and McManus to quiet the agent. "Frankly, I really don't care if Santa Claus shot up the neighborhood. Two of my agents are dead and Bill Butcher is the prime suspect. That gives us the nexus to cut in on this thing. I want my own crime scene techs to go over this house, too."

McManus nodded. "Seems we all have jurisdiction now," he said, turning to walk away. "Your dead agents, in my jurisdiction, and Gideon's people in the sheriff's jurisdiction. It's getting pretty damn crowded on that dais during press conferences."

Schag waited until McManus was several yards away before turning to Riley and saying, "None of this makes sense, Tom."

"Why? Riley said. "Because Bill's your friend?"

Schag bit the inside of his mouth. He was churning inside. He didn't believe for a second Bill Butcher kidnapped Yolanda and killed the agents. Someone else did, someone who had Yolanda. Fear for her safety left a sick ache in his stomach. He wanted to grab Riley by the collar of his expensive suit and shout, *No. because I spoke with Bill last night and he was just fine!* He knew he couldn't. Instead, he said, "Because Bill would never do anything that would endanger Yolanda."

"You don't know that," Riley said. "You said yourself that medicine maybe made him crazy. No telling what he might do. Besides, who else would do it?"

"What about Gideon?"

Riley looked at Schag curiously. "Why would Gideon want to snatch Butcher's wife?"

Schag couldn't explain the connection between Gideon and Gordias, and the plot to kill Butcher and make it look like suicide. "They attacked him at the cabin," was his weak answer.

"That was a rogue group of Gideon men out for revenge," Riley said tightly. "Look, Lin, I understand where you're coming from. Bill's your friend. But like you said yourself when I first called you in on this, you're too personally involved. You can't be part of this investigation, especially now that we're part of it. However, you know Bill better than anyone else except his wife, and now she's gone. I still need you close by to bounce stuff off, but you've got to maintain some semblance of objectivity to be of any good to us. You understand?"

Schag's jaw clenched. He was being pushed out of the way, but he knew Riley was right. Even if NCIS had nexus, there was no way he could be an active participant in the investigation. He had to sit it out. His jaw loosened. He nodded.

"Understood," he said.

"Good," said Riley. "Now get back to the office. Take care of some paperwork, whatever. Just keep busy."

Riley turned to leave, but Schag stopped him.

"Tom, assuming it was Bill who did this, how did he know about the safe house? The only people who knew Yolanda was here were you, me, and those two dead agents."

Riley glared at Schag. "How the fuck should I know?" he said. "Maybe someone told him." Riley eyed Schag. "Did you?"

"No, I didn't," Schag said. That much was true. "When could I?"

"Well, neither did I," Riley said. "Maybe his wife called

him. Now get back to the office."

Riley walked off. Schag turned and walked to his car. Inside, he started the engine, strapped himself in, and put it in gear. After a moment, he put the car back into park. It wasn't the top of the hour yet, but he pulled out the burner phone and turned it on. There was a message waiting.

"Not me," was all it said.

CHAPTER 23

"I CAN'T BE HERE WITH that woman," Charles Bennett complained. He paced the captain's cabin of the *Mars Venture*, which had been his safe house while he hid from Bill Butcher. A sheen of nervous perspiration glinted off his baldpate. He finished the drink in his hand and poured another from the captain's supply. "Why the hell did you bring her here, Aidan? What were you thinking of?"

"We needed a safe house," Black replied. He had his own drink, which he sipped. "Every cop on the Butcher case will be looking for her. We needed to take her some place where she wouldn't be seen."

After abandoning the pizza delivery van, the two Gideon men had put Yolanda into a Ford SUV with darkened windows, and drove her to a rendezvous with two more Gideon operators. Those Gideons had a truck from a local port services company. The company provided food and other supplies to the merchant ships visiting the Port of San Diego, so no one paid any attention when the men unloaded a large container from the truck and placed it aboard a tender boat heading out to the oil tanker anchored offshore. Inside the container, bound, gagged, and sedated, lay Yolanda Butcher. Within an hour, the container was aboard the tanker and Yolanda placed in captivity in the chief engineer's cabin.

"But here?" Bennett paced again, shaking his head. "I don't like this, not at all. I don't like being this close to her. Hell, Aidan, I don't like being this close to *you*. It's not safe. We've always maintained distance for security. You know that."

"You mean we keep a distance so you can maintain— what do you call it in politics? *Plausible deniability*."

Bennett stopped his pacing again, turned to face Black, and shook his finger like an angry schoolmaster.

"Don't you get fresh with me, Aidan," he said. "My ability to work inside government is what keeps you and the rest of us in business. It's too damn important for us to get sloppy. We need to keep our distance."

Keep you safe, you mean, Black thought, sipping his drink.

"And what if Butcher comes here looking for his wife? My God, man, I'm trying to keep my distance from him, too. No telling what that crazy man would do to me."

Yep, keep you safe. He took another sip.

"Why would Butcher come here?" Black said. "How the hell would he know about this ship?"

"Who knows how crazy men think?" Bennett said.

"You want to see her?" Black asked, changing the subject.

"See who?"

"The woman. Butcher's wife," Black said, smiling inwardly. "She's quite attractive."

Bennett looked horror-stricken. "Good Christ, no!" he said "Of course not. What have we just been talking about?"

"Then what are you going to do, Mr. Bennett?"

Bennett thought for a moment, looking around the cabin.

"I'm getting the hell off this ship," he said.

✿

Black watched the running lights of the tender boat disappear amid the myriad of lights speckling the shore. Bennett didn't lose a second escaping from the tanker. He tossed what few personal items he had aboard into a suitcase. Black laughed inwardly at the sight of the powerful businessman and politician scuttling about the cabin, checking drawers and under the furniture for anything linked to him. My God, the man even used a handkerchief to wipe off fingerprints from items he may have touched!

Like rats leaving a sinking ship.

Yes, a sinking ship. That's what everything was becoming. A fucking ship of fools foundering in a sea of lies and treachery. He poured himself another drink and sat down. Why the hell couldn't Bennett stay in the shadows? All these years, he had been successful at manipulating the twin worlds of politics and business, pushing malleable politicians into the right positions of power, using them to put into place the right laws and regulations, the right foreign diplomacy, even the right wars to bolster his business profits. Hell, he even pulled off the biggest bank heist in history. And he did it all behind the scenes, hidden in the shadows, the man without a face.

But now? Now the son of a bitch wants to come in from the dark, to show his face in the limelight. Now he wants to be secretary of defense. Why?

On the surface, Bennett said it would allow him to have more direct power over the billions of dollars of contracts the DoD handed out each year, to steer them to Gideon and other Gordias holdings. Black didn't believe that. Bennett could do that without becoming SecDef. No, this was pure ego. Since pulling off the Iraqi heist, Bennett had become too full of himself. He wanted real recognition. Hell, the asshole might even be thinking of running for president.

If it weren't for the nomination, Bennett might have left Butcher alone. Working from the shadows, Bennett could have diffused any scandal that arose from Butcher's allegations. The media wasn't interested in scandals involving second-level bureaucrats. But with him expecting to become defense secretary, Bennett feared any whiff of scandal, and he was enough of a sociopath— or perhaps a psychopath—to demand more extreme measures be taken to protect himself.

Black drained his glass and turned his thoughts to what to do next. Butcher would already know they had his wife. It was all over the networks and newspapers, and even though they made the media and the cops think Butcher was the kidnapper—Black congratulated himself on that neat touch—Butcher would know damn well it was Gideon.

Black needed a way to contact Butcher, to dangle the bait and lure him into a trap. But how? And where to lure him to, where to set up the ambush? Black hadn't had time to figure that out. Bennett wanted the woman as bait, and Black's men went and got her. Perhaps, he could use that agent named Schag? They were close friends. Butcher demanded he be brought into this mix, demanded it in Cavendish's blood. Perhaps the two were in secret contact. If they were, Black thought, maybe he could make Schag lure Butcher into the ambush.

Black stood, yawning, and decided to check on the woman. Maybe he could learn something from her. Maybe *she* knew how to contact her husband? He'd have to be careful with her, try to manipulate her. It wouldn't do any good getting rough with her. She was no shrinking violet, that was for sure. From what he heard, she'd put up quite a fight. He'd have to make certain his men were guarding her properly.

As Black neared the chief engineer's cabin, he could see something was wrong. The two men posted there— Gott and Kasitz, the same two he'd called in for backup at the cemetery—were arguing. Gott held a hand to one eye. Kasitz was nursing a bloody nose, the blood matting his thin moustache.

"What the hell happened to you two?" Black demanded.

The two guards straightened themselves as Black approached. Despite the gesture, neither could retain much dignity. Gott lowered his hand and revealed a massive shiner beneath his left eye. Kasitz kept snorting blood onto the deck.

"The bitch tried to escape," Gott said.

"He let her punch him out," Kasitz complained, his voice muffled by his battered nose.

"She asked for water," Gott explained. "When I brought it to her, she blindsided me."

"She decked him like a schoolyard bully," Kasitz wheezed. "Then when I tried to grab her as she ran out of the cabin, the bitch slammed her elbow into my face. I think she broke my nose, Mr. Black."

Black rolled his eyes, stepped nearer, and growled, "Where the fuck is she?"

"Back in the cabin," Kasitz said. "We got her back in there . . . the two of us."

Black stepped to the door and put his hand on the knob. "Is it safe to go in there?"

Gott nodded. "Yes, sir. We put the zip cuffs on her again."

"Good," Black said. He opened the door.

Yolanda Butcher stood in the middle of the living room of the spacious cabin, almost as large as the captain's own accommodations. Despite her hands being zip-tied together, she clutched a desk lamp like a club. Her dark eyes blazed with anger and her lips curled in a grimace. Blood from the guard's broken nose spotted her shirt.

Black held up his hands and said, "Please, Mrs. Butcher. I only want to talk."

CHAPTER 24

LINUS SCHAG LEANED BACK IN his chair and glanced at his watch for the . . . well, he couldn't remember how many times he'd checked his watch. Time seemed to be stuck, moving neither forward nor backward. He looked at the papers on his desk, then at the documents on his computer screen, and sighed. He looked at his watch again.

Schag sat in Riley's office working on administrative matters, sorting through documents related to other cases, reading, and commenting on subpoena requests— the work Riley would be doing if he weren't occupied with the other agents trying to find Bill and Yolanda.

Yolanda. Schag felt a sickening jab of pain in his stomach thinking of her. It was bad enough having the feelings he had for her and the guilt they produced, as if he were actually cheating on Bill. But with Yolanda . . . who knew where? Worry and fear gnawed at his gut and compounded all the other emotions.

Riley left it to Schag to call Yolanda's mother and father to tell them what happened. He told them the official story—that Bill Butcher found the safe house, killed two agents, and kidnapped Yolanda. Yolanda's parents seem to doubt that as much as Schag did. Despite everything Bill had done, they still believed he loved Yolanda and would never harm her in any way. Still, Schag could hear the worry and fear in their voices. He wanted to tell them he had talked to Bill, and he was not the madman the media and law enforcement officials were making him out to be. What difference would it make? He'd have to tell them hired killers had kidnapped their daughter. How would that make the ordeal better for them?

Sitting in this damned office was killing him. He wanted—he needed—to be out looking for Yolanda. Riley and the others were wasting time trying to find Bill, thinking that would lead them to Yolanda. Schag knew it wouldn't. He was certain Gideon was behind the kidnapping.

Schag had copied Butcher's files to a CD, and hid the micro disk in his shoe as Butcher had done. The CD was in Riley's computer and when no one was near the office, Schag studied the files. Between brief looks at the Gordias data, he worked on the files Riley needed completed.

Schag looked at his watch again. At last, the minute hand had moved. It was almost an hour since he last checked the burner phone. He stood, stepped to the opened door, and looked out. The hallway was empty. He stepped back to the desk where his battered flight jacket was hanging from the back of the chair, jammed his hand into the right side pocket, and pulled out the phone. Powering it up, he checked the text messages. There was one new message.

"Need your help.

Tonite 2200. B @ phone booth 2303 Shelt Is Dr"

Schag hadn't spent much time in San Diego, so he wasn't sure what "Shelt Is" meant. Pulling up his Web browser, he typed "2303 Shel." The search page's auto find function showed him it was an address on Shelter Island Drive. Schag knew Shelter Island, a popular tourist attraction filled with hotels, restaurants, and nightclubs jammed between boatyards and yacht brokers. The island was very near the sub base where Schag was staying, and he had eaten dinner there only the night before. The map that popped up on his search screen revealed the address was a hotel on the southern tip of the island.

Schag looked at his watch again. It was 6 p.m., 1800 hours in military time. Four more hours. He wanted to get there at least half an hour early to surveil the area. Even though he trusted Bill, he didn't want to blunder into an ambush. It could take an hour or more to get from 32nd Street to Shelter Island, depending on traffic. To get there before the meet, he'd have to leave NCIS headquarters no later than 2030 hours—8:30 p.m. About two and a half hours away.

Schag turned back to the documents on his desk, tackling them with new energy. The sooner he got through them, the sooner he could concoct an excuse to leave.

"Where the hell are you going, Schag?" Riley demanded.

Schag finished slipping on his leather jacket. It was 8:30 p.m., and he was eager to get going. He didn't stop to answer Riley, but walked past him and the other agents in the Hole.

"Back to the Gateway," he answered.

"Really?" Riley said in mock disbelief. "How lucky for you."

"You don't need me here, Tom," Schag said, still moving.

"What about the paperwork?"

"Done and on your desk or in your email queue."

"That's doesn't mean you can just take off."

Schag stopped and turned to face Riley.

"Tom, I can't be involved in this investigation. You said so yourself. The paperwork is done, and you're just wasting my time now. So, I'm getting some dinner, a drink, and some sleep. I'll see you in the morning—*if* you need me."

Schag turned and walked through the door.

"Schag!" Riley shouted, but the door closed before the word was out of his mouth.

Riley turned, saw the other agents staring at him, and felt his face flush with anger and frustration. "What the hell are you people looking at?" Riley swore under his breath as the other agents turned back to their work. "I'll be in my office," he said, and stomped out of the bull pen muttering, "God damn insubordinate asshole."

Schag pulled into the parking lot at the address Butcher texted him. It belonged to a hotel-marina at the southern end of Shelter Island. The parking lot was packed. Well-heeled couples left their vehicles and walked toward an open-air restaurant. Unable to find a parking space, Schag parked in a public lot across the street from the hotel, and trotted across the road to the lobby entrance. He glanced at his watch as he walked through the doors. It was a little after 9:30 p.m. Glancing around the swank lobby, he spotted a lone pay-phone booth half way down a secluded hallway near the public rest rooms. Schag picked up a complimentary copy of *USA Today* and sat in an over-stuffed chair on the far side of the lobby where he could watch both the entrance and the phone booth.

Minutes ticked by with glacial speed. Schag reread the same three articles in the newspaper, stopping occasionally to glance over the paper at the lobby and the pay phone. He saw nothing out of the ordinary. When the minute hand on his watch clicked into the full upright position, he stood, walked to the phone booth, and stepped inside.

It rang straightaway.

Schag picked up the handset and said, "Yes?"

"Still wearing that old leather jacket, eh, Lin?" Bill Butcher said.

Still holding the handset, Schag leaned out of the booth and looked around. He saw no one.

"Where the hell are you, Bill?" He demanded.

"Somewhere where I can see you but you can't see me."

"How can that be?" Schag said. "I've been watching the lobby and the phone for the past half hour."

"I know," Butcher answered. "I've been watching it for the past hour. Had to make sure you didn't bring any of Riley's boys with you."

"I wouldn't do that."

Butcher grunted. "You might have been followed."

"That I can buy," Schag conceded. "So, are we going to talk?"

"Not here," Butcher said. "I've got my own safe house. A rundown motel, but the owner keeps his nose out of his renters' business. I'm texting you the address. Meet me there in one hour."

Schag took out his burner phone and turned it on. A moment later, it beeped with the incoming message. "Got it," he said, and hung up.

Schag returned to the lobby and looked around, seeing no one who looked even vaguely like Butcher. He looked back down the hallway and still saw no one. With a shrug, he walked out of the lobby, and trotted back to his parked car.

In an office behind the lobby desk, Bill Butcher watched Schag leave the lobby on the hotel's closed-circuit security system. Butcher wore a jump suit emblazoned with the name of the CCTV firm that maintained the hotel's security cameras. A bright-red wig covered his baldpate, and he wore a thick beard of the same color. Earlier in the day, he had disabled a few of the closed-circuit video cameras. Later, changing disguises, he showed up as a repairman saying the company's automated error detection system had alerted them to a problem. He quickly "fixed" the problem, but told the hotel security staff he needed to calibrate the system. Butcher convinced the guard who watched the monitors to walk the premises while he worked.

A wry grin spread across Butcher's face as he watched

Schag leave, looking one way then the other, trying to figure out where Butcher was. With almost perfect timing, the hotel guard returned to the security office just as Schag left the lobby.

"Get it fixed yet?" the guard asked.

"That I did," Butcher answered with a soft Irish lilt that went with his bright red wig. He gathered up his tool bag and smiled at the guard.

"That was fast," the guard said.

Butcher shrugged, still grinning. "Luck of the Irish," he said. He winked once, and left.

CHAPTER 25

SATURDAY
Bill Butcher's Safe House
San Diego, California
0020 Hours

SCHAG'S GPS GUIDED HIM TO the address Bill
Butcher had given him, a boxy, two-story building located
on a two-lane frontage road paralleling the Interstate 5
freeway. A neon sign announced it as the Bay View
Motel. It was the only thing colorful about the place. The
weatherworn paint had grown dull, and the plants that
grew wild along the outer walls of the lobby were a thirsty
brown turning to black. The name itself was misleading.
A freeway stood between the motel and San Diego's
Mission Bay, a massive, man-made aquatic sports
attraction. Schag was certain the only thing seen from any
of the motel's grimed windows was traffic.

Schag parked around the corner on a road leading
uphill. From there he could see that the motel, though
narrow in front, ran deep, with two separate buildings
that stepped up the sea bluff. There was laundry drying in

front of a few rooms, and it was obvious to Schag the motel did not cater to the tourist trade but rather rented out to residents who, for various reasons, couldn't lease an apartment or a house. That included fugitives like Bill Butcher.

The agent walked another block uphill and turned a corner, found a narrow alley, and worked his way back downhill toward the back of the Bay View Motel. There he hopped a wall and found a spot where he could watch most of the rooms and parking spots. Then he waited.

After twenty minutes, he still hadn't seen anyone with the height or bulk of Butcher. He watched a young hooker drag a john into her room and, a few minutes later, push him out. Occasionally, Schag caught a whiff of marijuana. Once he witnessed a minor drug purchase go down outside of a room, the light thrown through the opened door silhouetting the transaction for any narc with a camera. Then he heard the crunch of a shoe on sandy cement, turned, and found a giant shadow hovering about him.

"Lin, you going to sit here all night?"

Schag dropped his head in shame. "How long?" he asked.

"Since you got here," Butcher replied. He nodded over his shoulder. "I was over there in the shadows when you jumped the wall."

Schag stood, shaking his head. "Making sure I didn't bring the cavalry with me?" Schag said, annoyed.

Butcher shrugged. "It was a nice evening," he said. "I was just enjoying it and the music."

Schag cocked an ear. "What music?" he asked, not hearing any.

"It's in my head," Butcher explained. "It's there all the time now. Better than the voices, I used to hear. You think it's because of that . . . what'd you call it? Agueloquine?"

"Yes," Schag answered softly. "Yes, I do, Bill."

"Me, too," Butcher said, his voice gloomy. He stepped closer, and as the light from the motel fell on him, Schag could see he wore a red wig with matching beard.

"Nice look."

"Aye, to everyone here I'm a just a jackeen Irish immigrant," Butcher said in his lilt. He switched to his normal voice and added, "Something I perfected for a role in one of Shaw's plays. Everyone's looking for a big bald guy, not a hairy, red-headed Irishman." He cocked his head toward the motel, and adopted the lilt again. "No more foosterin' now. Let's go, copper."

Schag followed Butcher through a parking lot that bordered the two-story structure.

"I checked out that same route you came through before I rented this place," Butcher said. "Figured it'd make a good escape route. I have a car parked up there, just in case."

As they passed the door where the hooker lived, it opened and a woman with bleached hair and a dress two sizes too small stepped out.

"Well, there you go, you naughty Irishman," she said, eyeing Butcher, then Schag. "Now I know why you don't take me up on my offers."

"Ah, be away with ya, you wicked hoor," Butcher said, smiling. "It's all I can do to keep me hands off ya." He slapped her on the behind, and she giggled like a little girl. "And you w' no drawers, I can tell. Diabolical, you are, temptin' me mate the way you are."

Butcher reached his room and unlocked the door. He held a cupped hand under the latch as he opened the door. A small wad of tissue dropped in his hand. He held it up so Schag could see.

"No visitors," he said, leading Schag inside. "You know, she really is a good kid."

"The 'hoor'?" Schag asked.

"Studies medicine. Knows a lot about anatomy."

"I bet," Schag said. He glanced about the cramped room with its ancient bed, a marred wooden table serving as a desk, and from what Schag could see through the opened bathroom door, plumbing from another century. "All the comforts of home," he added, his voice grim.

Butcher saw the pain in his friend's eyes and tried to lighten the mood. "It has its good points," he said. "The walls are so thin not even a SEAL could get near without me hearing him coming. And if I open the bathroom window, I can get a cheap contact high."

Butcher smiled a grin so infectious it made Schag chuckle before asking, "So, why did you bring me here, Bill?"

The grin vanished and Butcher's face turned serious. "I need your help, Lin," he said. "I've been racking my brain trying to figure out where Gideon took Yolanda."

"You're sure it was Gideon?"

"I'm sure," Butcher said, waving Schag to sit on the bed while he took the chair at the desk and removed the wig and fake beard. "Yolanda and I had a secret method of sending messages to each other. All those times I was away on missions." He shook his head. "It was a breach of security, I know. But—" He shrugged. "Anyway, whenever there was Internet access, guys would spend their down time playing online video games. Yolanda and I would log on to this one online game with fake names, and in our online personas leave messages for each other. To anyone else it would look like we were dissing each other as part of our avatars. But we knew what we meant."

"And you got a message from her?"

Butcher nodded.

"Ever since she was grabbed, I've gone to a nearby library twice each day and logged onto the game using one of their computers. I figured whoever took her would need to communicate with me. And I was right. Today, there was a message."

Butcher's lips tightened into a thin, bloodless line. Schag leaned forward and looked into Butcher's angry blue eyes.

"What did it say, Bill?"

"They want to arrange a meet," he said, his teeth still clinched. "They'll let her go if I give myself up to them. Otherwise they'll kill her."

Schag felt his own chest tighten, as if a giant hand was squeezing him.

"You don't believe them, do you, Bill?" he asked, his own voice tight. "That they'll let her go, I mean."

"What do you think?" Butcher said, shaking his head. "They'll kill us both. They can't leave witnesses." He stood and paced the small amount of empty floor the bed and the desk didn't cover. "We've got to figure out where the hell they've got her and go get her before they can hurt her.

"Did they set the meet yet?" Schag asked.

"No, they wanted my answer first," Butcher said. His hands rubbed the sides of his face. "I haven't acknowledged the message yet. I'm trying to buy time."

"Good," Schag said. "They'll have her in a safe house somewhere around here. Too dangerous hauling a kidnapped woman too far. What about the Gideon compound?"

Butcher shook his head. "First place I went," he said.

"There are still a bunch of cops around there." Butcher chuckled darkly. "I think they're guarding the place against me."

"They have any other property around here?"

Butcher nodded toward the laptop. "That's what I've been doing, going through all my files looking for something local. The only company I found was a port services firm with an office in National City. I checked it out, too. Small office, something of a warehouse down on the docks, but I didn't spot any unusual activity."

A thought formed at the edge of Schag's memory. *Port services. An oil tanker anchored offshore. A Gordias-owned shipping firm.*

"Fire up that thing," he said, pointing to the laptop on the desk. "I've got an idea."

It took a good ten minutes for Schag to wend his way through the labyrinth of files Butcher had collected on Gordias. As he searched, he explained his hunch.

"When I was looking through the micro-disk you gave me, I saw Gordias had some holdings in the maritime industry. If I remember right, one of them was a shipping firm."

"Shipping?" Butcher asked. "Like cargo ships?"

Schag nodded. "And here it is," he said.

The company's name was Trans-Oceanic Transport. There was little information on the activities of the company, only that Gordias owned the firm's controlling stock. Schag copied the Trans-Oceanic's name and opened the web browser.

"No good," Butcher said, leaning over his shoulder. "This place doesn't provide clean towels let alone

Internet access."

Schag cursed, thought a moment, and pulled out his Blackberry. Using its small browser, Schag found a website for Trans-Oceanic that promoted its reputation for safe and reliable bulk transportation.

"Bulk," Schag explained to Butcher, "means uncontained liquid and dry goods."

"Liquids? Like oil?" Butcher asked.

Schag nodded but said nothing. He was too busy typing in a web address he knew from memory.

"This website provides the position of nearly every ship in the world," he told Butcher. "Well, every ship that's not hiding something."

Dozens of small, colorful dots cluttered a map of the world's oceans. Maneuvering around the map, he located the U.S. West Coast, the California coastline, then San Diego. He zoomed in on the coast off San Diego Harbor. The colorful dots emerged as ship-like icons heading in all directions. As he touched each icon, a small window opened and provided the vessel's name, latitude and longitude, and speed. When he found one that showed zero knots, he clicked on it. A new window opened with a photograph of an extremely large oil tanker. Above the photo was the name *Mars Venture* followed by a Liberian flag indicating the ship's registry. Below the flag, it showed the vessel's status: Anchored.

"That's got to be the tanker I can see from my hotel window," Schag said. "It should have the name of her owner, too." He scrolled down further until he found it. He grinned at Butcher. "Trans-Oceanic," he said.

"That's got to be where they have Yolanda," Butcher added.

Schag nodded, but raised a finger in warning.

"Hold on," he said. "We need more intel."

Using his phone's browser, Schag looked up the phone number for the U.S. Coast Guard base he knew sat on the harbor's edge across from Lindbergh Field.

"The Coast Guard's got to have information on the ship," he told Butcher. "People don't just anchor a jumbo tanker off your coast without drawing attention."

Schag dialed the number for the Coast Guard's Marine Safety Office. The office was closed, but a recording provided another number to call in case of an emergency, such as an oil spill or maritime accident. Schag called that number.

"Coast Guard Sector San Diego," a man answered. "Operations center. Senior Chief Dalton speaking. May I help you?"

"Senior chief," Schag said. "This is Special Agent Schag of the Naval Criminal Investigative Service. I have a question for you."

"Of course, sir," the senior chief said. "Fire away."

"There's an oil tanker anchored offshore. What can you tell me about it?"

"She's the petroleum tanker *Mars Venture*," Dalton said without missing a beat. "She's classified as a VLCC—a very large crude carrier. Liberian registry, but out of Bahrain. She had an engine casualty and had to drop her hook in the stream. Too big to get into this harbor. She's bigger than an aircraft carrier. Most of her crew was off loaded and sent home until parts can be flown in and repairs completed. She has a skeleton crew aboard as a live watch."

"How big a skeleton crew?" Schag asked. "Do you know?"

"Despite her size, sir, she has a pretty small crew. Only about 25 when they're underway. Ships like that are highly computerized. I guess only two or three, maybe fewer, left onboard to watch the computer screens, make sure she doesn't drag anchor. May I ask, sir, is this part of an official investigation? I mean something our own law enforcement people should know about?"

"No, no, senior chief," Schag answered. "I can see her out of my window at the Gateway on the sub base, and I was curious. You don't see many VLCCs sitting around on a hook. I'm sorry to have bothered you, senior chief."

"Not at all, sir," the petty officer replied. "But I do have a question for you."

"What's that?" asked Schag, eager to hang up.

"Do you know David McCallum?" Dalton asked. "You know, the guy who plays Ducky on that show?"

The senior chief was laughing as Schag hung up.

"How do we get out to the ship, Lin?" Butcher asked. He reached into the only closet in the room and pulled out a rucksack. "We're going to need a boat."

Schag nodded as he watched Butcher pull the Colt 1911 .45 auto he took off the Gideon assassin and stick it in his waistband. Butcher also jammed two loaded magazines in his pocket.

"I thought you always carried that little Glock in an ankle holster," Schag said.

"I do," Butcher said. "But I left it in the cabin, remember?"

Schag nodded. The Glock was the weapon Butcher used to kill his Gideon doppelganger, and stage the phony suicide.

"That port services company you checked out," Schag said. "Did they have boats?"

Butcher pulled soft body armor from the bag and

looked it over. "Yeah," he said. "Three that I saw. Could be more underway that I didn't see. All of them painted some god-awful shade of orange." He glanced at Schag. "What do you have in mind, Lin?"

"With all that high-speed stuff you learned in the SEALs," Schag said, "did they ever teach you to how to steal a boat?"

Butcher grinned.

CHAPTER 26

SATURDAY
San Diego Port Services Company
National City, California
0315 Hours

THE MATCH FLARED, ITS FLAME cutting through
the dark shadow of the warehouse. Bill Butcher, wearing
the red wig and beard again, studied the flame a moment,
mesmerized by its dancing colors. He touched the match
to the cigarette in his mouth and inhaled. Butcher didn't
smoke, never had. In fact, the cigarette wasn't even his.
On their way south to National City, he and Schag
stopped at a liquor store, where Schag bought the pack of
filtered Marlboros and picked up two books of matches.
Sitting among the garbage dumpsters outside the
warehouse, Butcher puffed clumsily on the cigarette until
its tip was a fierce red. He placed the cigarette inside a
matchbook, with the last of the tobacco touching the
match heads, and wrapped the cover around it.

It was an old trick for improvising a time-delayed fuse.
The cigarette would take about five minutes to burn

down to the matchbook. Once the smoldering embers of tobacco touched the matches, they would flare into life, igniting anything flammable around them. Butcher made sure there was plenty of flammable of material to burn, scraping together a pile of waste paper, cardboard, oil-soaked rags, and pieces of creosote-treated wood from the boat docks.

Butcher laid the makeshift detonator on the pile of debris, and made his way back to where Schag parked the sedan. Schag was at the opened trunk, checking the gear in his go-bag. Both men wore dark clothing—Butcher the same dark pants and sweater he did for his raid on the Gideon compound, and Schag a pair of black BDU trousers and his leather jacket. Over his jacket, he wore a black Kevlar raid vest, the reflective four-inch tall NCIS letters taped over with black duct tape Schag kept in his bag for that purpose. Sometimes it was safer not to announce your presence to the enemy with glowing letters.

Schag closed the trunk and slung the go-bag ruck over his shoulder as Butcher trotted up. "Get it set up?"

Butcher nodded. "Should make a nice bonfire," he said, looking at his watch, "in about two more minutes."

Leaning against the sedan, they waited. Two minutes passed, then three. Butcher looked at his watch, and Schag looked at him questioningly. Butcher nodded and gestured for Schag to be patient. Another minute passed, and they detected a whiff of smoke. A thin tendril of it twisted into the sky behind the warehouse, illuminated by the building's high-power work lights. Excited voices rose above the din of engine sounds and backup warning beeps from forklifts working inside the warehouse. A fire alarm screeched. Workers from around the compound stopped what they were doing and trotted toward the parking lot near the street, obviously a predetermined rally point in case of a fire.

Butcher straightened and whispered to Schag. "Time to go."

They wended their way along the fence line until they reached the docks. Six port services boats painted a dark orange lined the docks.

"You're right," Schag said. "That is a ghastly shade of orange."

"Any one in particular you want me to steal?" Butcher asked.

"The one at the outboard end of the dock," Schag said. "We can make a faster get-away from there."

Butcher nodded. "Let's go."

Boots thudded dully as they trotted down the dock to the last berth. It was a typical work boat, the type Schag had seen in a dozen ports around the world, somewhere between thirty and forty feet long, beamy, all engine and cargo space, with a small opened wheelhouse and smaller compartment below decks, and nothing left over for the comfort of the crew. The single throttle to the right of the wheel showed it was a single-screw monster, difficult to back down, steer on a straight course, or dock. Butcher removed an access panel below the wheel while Schag began to take in the mooring lines. By the time Schag returned to the wheelhouse, Butcher was standing next to a tangle of wires smiling broadly.

"It's all yours, Lin," he said.

Schag opened the engine cover, located the seacock that let in water to cool the diesel engine, and opened it. Back in the wheelhouse, he punched the starter button and the diesel engine roared to life. Schag glanced nervously over his shoulder towards the warehouse. No one seemed to notice the noise. At the stern, Butcher glanced over the transom, saw the overboard discharge of the cooling seawater, and turned to Schag with a raised thumb. Schag cranked the wheel inboard and engaged the engine just enough to kick the stern away from the dock, then backed down. Once clear of the dock, he swung the rudder over, gunned the engine, and circled around toward the harbor channel.

It was a good forty-five-minute run from National City to the harbor's mouth. A full moon peeking through scattered clouds bathed the dark water ahead. Schag kept a wary eye on the boat's radar screen, looking for any sign of the Coast Guard or harbor police. It was one thing for agent to explain why he commandeered a private vessel, a very different thing to explain why he was in the company of a wanted murder suspect.

"Any idea how we're going to board the ship?" Schag asked, leaning toward Butcher's ear, and shouting over the throb of the diesel.

Butcher mulled the questioned. "Climb the anchor chain?" he answered, making a hand-over-hand gesture.

"You've got to be kidding," Schag said. "You have any idea how tall a supertanker is? It's like a high-rise building sitting if it isn't fully laden with cargo." Schag made an exaggerated roll of this shoulder. "Besides, with this shoulder, I could barely get dressed this morning."

"You got any better idea then?"

Schag thought about it a moment, but nothing came to mind. He glanced at Butcher, about to concede that fact when he noticed Bill was still wearing the red wig and beard.

"Yeah," he said. "Yeah, I think I do."

Once past the Zuniga Light, they entered open water. The sea was what sailors called DFC—dead flat calm. Schag was glad for that. Docking a single screw boat in mild to moderate weather was no mean feat; in rough water, it could be impossible for someone out of practice as he was. He set a course for the *Mars Venture*. The ship had dropped its hook at one of the southern-most anchorages, meaning another good twenty minutes before they reached her. Schag had already explained his plan for getting aboard the tanker, so Butcher laid out their gear as Schag steered. Neither said anything for several minutes.

At first, all Schag could make out of the *Mars Venture* were the deck lights that glowed brighter than the shore lights behind her. After a few minutes, moonlight revealed her shape and size. Even from a distance, she looked bigger than anything Schag knew from his personal experience, even larger than the *Halsey*, the aircraft carrier he once called home. So taken up by the massive ship's size, Schag didn't notice Butcher step up beside him until he spoke.

"Lin?"

Schag turned. The lights from the instruments shone on Butcher's face. Despite the phony beard, Schag could see something was plaguing him.

"What is it, Bill?"

"Um, look," Butcher stammered. "You've been a good friend all these years, you know? And, I . . . I know it hasn't been easy on you."

Schag understood what Butcher was talking about, and his breath caught in mid-intake. He looked away, making a show of watching the rising hull of the tanker.

"I don't know what you're talking about, Bill."

"I know you're in love with Yolanda, Lin," Bill said as gently as he could over the growl of the diesel. "I've seen it in your eyes when you look at her . . . at us together. And I know you've never done anything about it, never tried. And I know you're doing this more for her than for me."

Schag pretended not to hear. He stared ahead, not acknowledging his friend. His chest felt tight, as if it might burst. He wondered if Bill was right. Was he about to storm a ship—a ship guarded by armed men—because of his love for Yolanda and not out of friendship for Bill?

"If I don't make it out of this mess," Butcher continued, "I want you to promise to look after her." Butcher's voice thickened, and he struggled with his words. "I mean, you know, it would be okay with me if you two, um, got together."

Schag turned and faced Butcher. The man's mouth was twisting nervously.

"You're a god damn idiot, Bill, you know that?" Schag said. "You think I could ever compete with you in Yolanda's eyes? She loves you, no one else. Your kids love you. That's what you saw in my eyes. Wishing I had something like what you two have instead of the marriage I had. That's all."

Schag thought the lie sounded reasonable. Maybe even a little truthful.

Butcher smiled sadly, unconvinced. "Promise me, bro. Take care of her."

Schag looked back at the tanker, made a course correction to come along her leeward side, where a companionway clung to the side of the ship.

"You'll take care of her yourself, Bill," he said. "We'll rescue Yolanda, and then we'll get you the medical care you need to be well again and get that music out of your head. Look, we're almost there. Get ready to do your act."

Butcher hesitated, then nodded. Forcing a grin, he turned and headed toward the stern.

The hull of the massive tanker loomed over the approaching small boat. Schag tapped Butcher on the arm and pointed up to a symbol painted in white high on the black hull. It was a circle with a horizontal line through the middle.

"That's the load line," Schag said. "If fully loaded, that would sit at the water line."

"So she's empty?"

"Dry as a bone," Schag said, nodding.

"At least we don't have to worry about her blowing up," Butcher said.

"Wrong," Schag said flatly. "An oil tanker is most dangerous when its cargo tanks are empty. Oil itself isn't that dangerous, but its fumes are explosive. They usually fill the empty tanks with an inert gas that replaces the oxygen. Without O2, the fumes can't explode."

"Then she should be safe, right?"

"Theoretically," Schag said. "But let's try not to shoot up the place, okay?"

Butcher frowned and nodded.

In the glare of the deck lights, they both saw the silhouette of a guard watching them approach. From the way the guard held his arms across his chest, he appeared to be carrying an automatic weapon on a three-point sling.

"There's your audience," Schag said, throttling back the diesel. "Go break a leg."

Stepping out of the wheelhouse, Butcher stood at the stern and waved his arm in a slow, elongated sweep of greeting. The man on the tanker raised his arm in acknowledgement, turned and walked aft toward the entry port at the top of the companionway.

Schag sighed with relief. He had guessed Gideon used Gordias's port services firm to run people and supplies out to the tanker—may have even used one of the boats to transport Yolanda to the ship. From the guard's casual response to Butcher's wave, Schag had guessed right. He aimed the bow of the boat at an acute angle to the mooring dock tied to the bottom of the ladder. Waiting until the boat was only a few feet from the dock, Schag put the rudder hard to port and gave the engine a kick. The boat's stern swung parallel to the dock, and Schag backed down on the engine to stop his forward motion. Butcher jumped onto the platform with two mooring lines in hand, and made them fast to the cleats. He turned and looked up to the top of the gangway, and saw the guard standing in the entry port.

"Back again?" yelled the guard.

"Aye," Butcher answered in his lilt. "We've got you a bloody heavy package this time. Lend us a hand, will ye?"

The guard looked around and shrugged.

"Sure," he said, as he started down the rungs.

Butcher met the man at the bottom of the companionway and held out this hand in greeting. "Surely, I'm indebted to ye, mate" he said.

The guard reached out his hand. Instead of shaking it, though, Butcher grabbed the man's thumb and, twisting outward and downward, drove the guard to the ground. Butcher followed the guard, landing on his chest, his knee trapping the guard's weapon while he wrapped one of his muscular arms around the man's neck and squeezed. The flow of blood to his brain cut off, the guard went limp.

Schag was already on the dock, standing over Butcher

and the guard with two sets of handcuffs and the roll of black duct tape in his hands. Butcher used the cuffs to hog-tie the guard's arms and legs behind his back, and sealed his mouth with the tape. Together, Schag and Butcher lugged the guard onto the boat and laid him in the small forward compartment, closed the compartment hatch, and returned to the dock. Butcher picked up the rifle he had removed from the guard and checked it. It was an AK-47, cheap, ancient, and effective. He offered it to Schag. The agent shook his head.

"I've never fired an AK," Schag said, holding up his Glock. "I'll stick with something I know."

Butcher shrugged, slung the rifle, and shoved the .45 into his waistband. He went forward to the small cabin again, and returned with extra AK magazines he took from the guard. He nodded at the ladder. Schag motioned him to go ahead.

Butcher brought the AK to his shoulder and quietly climbed the stairs, his eyes scanning the top of the gangway and the entry port for signs of a second guard. Schag followed behind, his attention and his pistol searching the gunwale behind them. They reached the entry port without seeing another soul and stopped, crouching behind the gunwale. Butcher scanned as far aft as he could and saw no one, then moved to the other side of the entryway and scanned forward, still seeing no one. He signaled Schag to enter the ship first, and move to the left while he would follow and move to the right. *On three*, he mouthed. He held up one, then two, then three fingers.

Schag dashed through the entry port in a crouch and swerved aft, taking up position behind a crane. Butcher came behind him, moving toward the bow, and taking cover behind a giant valve. They scanned the deck, looking for any movement.

Schag was no stranger to cargo ships. On occasion, he had to investigate crimes aboard Navy freighters and tankers, those civilian-manned ships of the Military Sealift Command that fed the fleet food and fuel. Those ships were miniscule compared to the *Mars Venture*. The tanker's main deck was immense, rivaling the *Halsey*'s flight deck. But where the Halsey's deck was flat and wide open when no aircraft were aboard, the *Mars Venture*'s deck was a confusing tangle of pipes and valves.

Amidships two, maybe three pipes as thick as phone poles ran fore and aft atop an elevated platform. Smaller diameter pipes branched off from those, running athwartships. Spaced along both sides of the ship were cranes, like the one Schag was using for cover, which handled the hoses that fed and emptied the huge cargo tanks below decks. At the stern, rising like the White Cliffs of Dover, stood the superstructure, its white facade gleaming in the glare of the deck lights. Painted in four-foot black block letters on its front were the words: NO SMOKING. As if someone needed reminding of that on this ship, Schag thought.

Schag scanned the long, elegant bridge wings stretching out from the wheelhouse the entire width of the ship, but saw no one. He studied the bridge itself, its wide expanse of glass slit dimly from within, and still saw no one. He looked back and found Butcher staring at him with a blank look.

"What's wrong?" Schag asked.

"It's so damn huge. Where do we start?"

"That's the bridge and crew quarters," Schag said, pointing to the superstructure. "Everything below us here is cargo space. Oil tanks and bilge tanks." He rapped his knuckles on the deck plate. "And aft will be the machinery spaces."

Butcher nodded toward the superstructure. "So that's where they'll be holding Yolanda."

Schag nodded. Butcher crouched a little higher and raised the AK to his shoulder.

"Okay. Let's go."

CHAPTER 27

AIDAN BLACK STARED INTO THE darkness, rubbing the new bruise on his left cheek. That bitch had blindsided him with a right hook that damn near knocked him down. All he wanted was to talk to her, get her to tell him the best way to contact her husband and arrange an exchange, and she fooled him. She seemed willing to work with him, but as soon as he let his guard down, she walloped him. Next thing he knew, she was running out of chief engineer's cabin. The guards outside, however, learned their lessons from her earlier escape attempt and were ready for her. The instant she barreled through the door, they grabbed her and pushed her back into the cabin.

"All right," Black growled as he flung her to the floor. "No more fucking around. You tell me how to contact your goddamn husband, now."

"Why? So you can kill him and me both? You won't exchange me for Bill. You'll kill me, too. You have to. I'm a witness." She shook her head, her long black hair twisting angrily with the motion. "I'm not luring Bill into a trap for you. So, you may as well kill me now."

He looked at her, took a deep breath, and let it hiss through his teeth. She was smarter than he thought. Looks and brains. And tough. Black, however, knew she had a weakness. Every mother does.

"Your children are staying with your sister in Texas." Black spoke with acid in his voice. "Your mother and father, too. Your brother-in-law's a cop, and he's protecting them." He watched Yolanda's dark eyes grow wide with understanding.

"How do I know that?" he said. "That's what you're thinking, isn't it, Mrs. Butcher?" He circled Yolanda, keeping a safe distance from her. "The world is full of Judases, all lining up for their thirty pieces of silver. And I have a lot of silver to pass around."

He stopped, hitched up his pants legs, and crouched in front of her.

"Now, if you play nice and tell me what I want to know, and if—" He wagged his index finger at her. "—if you don't throw anymore tantrums, then your children will be fine. But if you don't . . ."

He didn't need to say any more. Sometimes a threat was more powerful if left unsaid. Let the victim's mind conjure its own horrors. *Basic psychological operations,*

That had been ten hours earlier, and at that moment he was resting in the captain's cabin. Yolanda had given up the secret way she and her husband communicated through the online game. Pretty damned clever, he had to admit. He'd have to use it himself someday.

There was a knock at the door.

Black rose from the couch he was lying on and snapped on a table lamp.

"Enter!"

Hans Jürgen, the Gideon operator in charge of the guard detail on the tanker, entered the cabin. He was a tall, thin German. A cigarette hung from his mouth, its ash growing by the second. His right hand rested on a handgun slung in thigh rig. He'd been in the German army's special forces—the Kommando Spezialkräft—until they learned he was an ardent neo-Nazi and kicked him out.

"We've got visitors, sir," he said in a thick accent. "Meier's standing lookout on the bridge, monitoring the CCTV monitors. He reports seeing a port service boat come alongside."

Oh, crap, Black thought. *Did Bennett decide to come back aboard?*

"And?" he demanded.

"Meier reports two men came up the gangway," Jürgen said. "And they are armed."

Black blanched at the news.

"Who are they? Cops?"

Jürgen shook his head and shrugged. "One man is bearded," he said. "The other wears a tactical vest but no markings are seen."

"Bearded?"

"Yes, sir," Jürgen said. "Meier's said he has red hair and a beard."

"Don't you have a man patrolling on deck?"

Jürgen frowned and cleared his throat. "Yes, sir. Melito. But we . . . don't know where he is. And . . ." Jürgen paused with discomfort. "The bearded man is carrying an AK like the one Melito was carrying."

Black took a deep breath, sighed, and shook his head.

"Get everyone up and armed," he ordered in a low, angry voice. "Post them in every ladder way. We'll let them come up to us."

"Yes, sir," Jürgen said, turning.

"And . . ."

Jürgen stopped and turned back to Black.

"Sir?"

"Bring that damn bitch up to the bridge."

As he crossed the massive main deck, Schag felt like he was moving through No Man's Land after the sheltering darkness is shattered by a star shell. Only the exposing light on the main deck didn't fade away after a few seconds. The glare of the powerful deck lights never ended. Though he scanned the deck in front and behind them, Schag couldn't shake the feeling they were being watched.

Reaching the superstructure, they crouched against the bulkhead and rested, taking deep gulps of air to slow their heavy breathing. Schag was glad to hear Butcher's breathing was as heavy as his own. Over their breaths, he could hear the familiar hum of machinery below decks, though it was not as loud as he knew it would be if the ship was underway and its single, gigantic diesel engine was making turns. Schag figured only the main generators were running to supply power to the lighting, pumps, and ventilation systems.

He turned to say something to Butcher but laughed instead. Butcher looked at him oddly.

"You know you're still wearing that beard and wig?"

Butcher felt his chin. "I'd forgotten," he said, grinning.

He pulled the fake hair from his face and head, tossed it on the deck, and rubbed his skin with the palms of his hands to remove any lingering adhesive.

Schag glanced around their immediate surroundings. They were crouching in an air castle, an opened area covered by the first of five upper decks towering above them. Stairs, called ladders aboard ships, rose at an acute angle from the main deck to the first upper deck. Additional ladders zigzagged their way up to the four remaining decks. A hatch stood open next to Butcher. Schag stood and saw the bulkhead he was leaning against was a cutwater, a short, pointed wall designed to keep any waves coming over the bow from striking the superstructure with their full force.

He looked over the cutwater and muttered a curse.

"What is it?" Butcher whispered.

Schag lowered himself, a look of disbelief on his face.

"It's a swimming pool," he said. "They have a damn swimming pool on board."

"Nice work if you can get it," Butcher muttered. He was looking through the opened hatchway to his right. "Should we go in here?"

"Wait." Schag moved past Butcher and stood listening at the hatch. It opened into a passageway. Midway down the passageway stood another set of stairs. He raised an index finger to his lips.

A ship is never quiet. Besides the always-constant cacophony of machinery, there's the dull ring of boots on the rungs of metal ladders, and the murmur of voices reverberating off steel walls. Living conditions on merchant ships are much better than those aboard warships. Wood paneling lined the passageways, and the furniture was as plush as any found in a hotel. Nevertheless, for those not accustomed to moving about a ship, remaining quiet is near to impossible. Schag could hear the dull echoes of hurried boots, muffled voices, and the clang of weapons carelessly banged against equipment. The latter made Schag frown. Metal on metal contacts can cause sparks, something to avoid aboard ship, particularly when the ship was a floating pipe bomb. He crouched next to Butcher.

"Too many people in there, going up and down an internal ladder." He pointed to the first flight of stairs leading to the deck above. "We'll clear top to bottom."

Butcher nodded, stood, and stepped to the ladder. Shouldering the AK, he moved up the stairs. At each landing, they paused, Butcher sweeping the deck with his rifle. Once confident the deck was clear, they climbed the next ladder, moving swiftly but quietly, taking each rung flat-footed to reduce noise.

At the third deck, they passed a lifeboat perched on a ramp canted at a 45-degree angle to the sea. Schag had seen them before. In an emergency, the crew would enter the enclosed boat from a stern hatch and strap themselves into chairs. When ready, the coxswain would pull a lever, releasing the boat, and letting it slide down the ramp and free-fall to the ocean below. Though it sounded like an amusement park ride, it provided a much faster escape than conventional lifeboats held by davits and cradles along the sides of the ship. Merchant sailors appreciate speedy escapes, especially when the vessels they're sailing have a tendency to explode.

They reached the fifth deck, which housed the bridge from which the crew piloted the tanker. Butcher scanned the landing, saw no one, and stepped up onto it, followed by Schag. The open deck encircled the wheelhouse, and Butcher signaled Schag to go along the back of the bridge and enter it from the port side. Schag nodded his understanding, moved behind the bridge with his weapon raised while Butcher advanced on the starboard bridge door.

A loud electronic screech made both men freeze.

A voice boomed from an unseen speaker.

"Welcome, gentlemen," it said. "Mr. Butcher, I see, and I assume Special Agent Schag of NCIS. Won't you join us on the bridge? We've been waiting for you."

CHAPTER 28

SATURDAY
Aboard the Mars Venture
Anchored off the San Diego coast.
0420 Hours

BLACK NOTICED A FRESH BRUISE marred Yolanda's face when Jürgen brought her onto the bridge. He also noticed two parallel scratches on Jürgen's face, still oozing blood. He smiled inwardly. There was no sense of chivalry in the German mercenary. He would repay kind with kind, plus change. Jürgen held Yolanda's arm twisted behind her back with his left hand while his right hand tightly clamped the back of her neck, his fingers digging painfully into the nerves there. A slight smile of approval twitched on Black's lips.

"She's a bit of a fighter, this one," Jürgen said, almost with admiration.

"That she is," Black said, nodding, and fighting the urge to rub his own bruised face.

The bridge spanned the entire width of the ship, and was a quarter deep as it was wide. Large windows ran the entire width of the compartment, providing the kind of view one expected from the heights of a high-rise building. The windows let in enough light from the deck lights to let Black see the darkened bridge. He knew nothing about ships and expected to see a large steering wheel, maybe with wooden spokes, and a large brass binnacle holding a compass. This bridge, however, reminded him more of an air traffic control tower than his fantasized idea. A control station set back from the windows wrapped itself in a semicircle in the middle of the bridge. Video displays lined the panels of the station, overlooked by two space-age chairs. The steering station stood back from the control station, a simple metal podium with its own electronic displays and a stainless-steel wheel smaller than found in the family car.

How the hell do they steer a ship this size with that little wheel?

In fact, an automatic pilot steered the ship, leaving the helmsman available to stand lookout.

Meier, the man who had reported the intruders, sat in one of the control station chairs. He stood, caught Black's eye, and waved him over. He pointed to a split-screen video display in front of him. CCTV cameras linked to the video screen looked out over the ship, giving the bridge crew a quick 360-degree view of the weather decks. In one section of the display, Black saw two men climbing a ladder from the main deck's starboard air castle to the second deck. Black recognized the large bald man as Bill Butcher. The second Black guessed was the NCIS agent. *What was his name? Something strange. Linus, like the character in the Peanuts comics he grew up reading. Linus Schag.*

"Where's the bearded man?" Black demanded.

Meier shrugged. "I don't know, sir," he said. "I saw the guy in the black vest come up the companionway with the bearded guy, then I lost sight of them when they entered the air castle. Maybe the bald guy boarded from the stern?"

So, there are more than two, Black thought. At least three, perhaps more. No, probably more. But who? Not NCIS. They wouldn't work with Butcher. Black's mouth twitched. And how the hell did they know we had Butcher's wife out here? It had to be the woman.

Black turned to Jürgen and Yolanda.

"How did you tell your husband where we were?" Yolanda said nothing. He stepped closer, his jaw muscle twitching and his lips pressed thin. "You had to tell him where we were. How?"

Jürgen pressed his fingers deeper into Yolanda's neck until she yelped angrily. "I couldn't I tell him anything," she said. "*I* don't know where the hell we are."

Black thought about that, but decided it didn't matter. He looked at the German.

"Alert the men we've got at least three intruders, and there may be more," he said. "Tell them to watch for a guy with red hair and a beard as well as these two."

"Yes, sir," Jürgen said. "Meier!" The lookout turned and Jürgen nodded toward the stairway. "Go tell them."

Meier nodded and rushed from the bridge.

Black stared at the video display, watching the approaching men. Their element of surprise was ruined. It was his chance to unnerve them, and give himself an unexpected advantage. That was when the idea of using the public address came to him. As he lowered the microphone, he smiled. *Psy-ops.*

Linus Schag popped open a pouch on his armored

vest, tugged something out, and held it up for Butcher to see. It was an olive-drab cylinder about as long as the width of his palm, with what appeared to be holes along its side, and a handle held in place with a pin attached to a ring. Butcher nodded, recognizing the flash-bang grenade, and motioned with his left hand for Schag to continue around the back of the bridge to the port wing. Butcher approached the opened starboard door and peered inside.

There were three men on the bridge, and Yolanda. One he recognized as the Gideon CEO Aidan Black. One man stood behind Yolanda, one arm restraining her. In his free hand, he held a large automatic. The third man stood near Black, shouldering an AK aimed at Butcher.

"Well, Mr. Butcher, I applaud your audacity for storming our little ship nearly single-handedly," Black said. "Please come in, and bring your friends, too. All of them."

Black must have seen a look of surprise on Butcher's face and added, "Yes, we know there are at least three of you on board. You, Agent Schag, and a red-haired man we don't recognize." Black pointed to the CCTV screen on the control center panel. "We've been watching you since you came aboard."

Butcher realized he held the attention of all three men, a bad tactical error on their part. On the far side of the bridge, he saw a shadow dip below a window and understood Schag had reached his position. He looked at Yolanda. Her eyes were large, fearful, but also angry. Better yet, expectant. He nodded to her.

Yolanda shouted, "Bill!" as loud as she could and jerked forward, trying to break from Jürgen's grip but he was expecting the move and followed her motion. That's what she expected him to do. She reversed her forward motion and pushed back against Jürgen, stepping backward, and placing her right leg inside his legs. Then she bent forward, twisting to her left. The move caught Jürgen unprepared. He rolled across her back and landed on the deck. Yolanda leaped over him, running toward her husband. She crashed into her husband, and the two turned and ran toward the ladders.

Before Black's men could respond, a thunderclap exploded within the bridge, and lightning stabbed through the dark. The flash-bang grenade left the three men on the bridge stunned, deaf, and blind.

Schag squatted against the outside bulkhead of the bridge, eyes squeezed tight and hands still clamped over his ears. His right hand ached from holding the safety handle of the flash-bang for so long, waiting for the right moment to toss the device. The instant he saw Yolanda break free from the man holding her, he had tossed the grenade.

Even with his ears covered and his eyes closed, he could hear the thunder and sense the stab of lightning. When it finished, he rose and ran the way he had come. He turned the corner and saw Bill and Yolanda disappear down the stairs. Heading toward the same stairs, he noticed the rectangular box of a closed-circuit camera aimed at the starboard ladder and realized that was how Gideon knew they were aboard.

Butcher and Yolanda reached the first deck below the bridge just as one of Gideon's mercs stepped out of the deckhouse. Butcher pulled his wife behind him, covering her with his body, and raising the AK to fire. He wasn't fast enough. The mercenary's rifle was already pointing at them. Before the Gideon man could pull the trigger, three blasts roared from above and behind the Butchers. The rounds slammed the gunman into the bulkhead. Butcher glanced behind him. Schag stood above him, still in a firing stance, the Glock trained on the crumpled body of the mercenary.

"They'll be waiting for us on the next deck," Schag said, leaping over Bill and Yolanda, and checking the merc for signs of life. There were none. "This way. Hurry!"

He led them inside, toward an inner stairwell that ran the entire height and depth of the ship. Unlike the metal ladders on the exterior of the ship, these looked more like the fire escape stairwell found in a hotel—wider, more solidly built, and bordered by shining chrome handrails. As Schag started down the stairs, he heard the clatter of men climbing from below. The agent backtracked, directing Yolanda and Butcher to follow the interior passage to the portside door. Butcher made a quick glance out the door to ensure no one was on that side of the ship, then slipped out, Yolanda and Schag following.

"How many of them are there?" Schag asked Yolanda.

"I don't know for sure," she said. "Six, seven. Maybe eight, including that bastard Black."

"Did you see how she handled that guy on the bridge?" Butcher asked, looking at his wife fondly. "That's my girl." He kissed her on the cheek. She turned and kissed him full on the mouth.

Schag watched two men run out of the stairwell and out the starboard door. Despite their battered faces, Schag recognized them as the two men who ambushed Parker and him at the cemetery. They glanced at their dead comrade and hurried down the outside ladder.

"Come on," he whispered. "Fight now, fornicate later."

He led them back into the deckhouse and down the interior stairs. At the next landing, he saw a merc waiting on the starboard weather deck. He motioned the Butchers down one more deck. Butcher, in the lead, peeked around the corner and saw two more two mercs on that landing, too. They looked worse for the wear, one with a bloody nose, the other with a swollen black eye.

"More out there," he whispered.

"This is the main deck," Schag said. "We need to get to the starboard gangway to the boat. Below us are the machinery spaces. We need to go out here or go back up and try from there. Maybe go down the port side and cross over to starboard to the gangway."

The decision was made for them. Voices of the mercenaries in the starboard air castle became louder, moving inside the superstructure toward them.

"Up!" urged Butcher, pushing Yolanda and Schag up the stairs they had just come down.

They hadn't taken three steps when they heard boots pounding down the stairs from above.

"Down!" urged Schag, nearly knocking over Yolanda and Butcher. "Go down!"

As if to emphasize the point, one of the gunmen above fired a round down the stairs. It ricocheted down the stairwell in front of them, like a ball in a pinball machine. Schag, trailing the Butchers, fired blindly at their pursuers. It, too, ricocheted off the metal walls. This time, however, Schag heard a satisfying yelp of pain from someone above.

More boots joined the pursuit above them, and someone let go with a short burst of automatic fire. A few rounds punched holes in the thin steel walls but most, striking at acute angles, skipped away, showering Schag and the others with stinging chips of paint.

Like the other landings, the next one opened into a long passageway extending the width of the superstructure. Butcher tried to open a door opposite the landing, but Schag yanked him back and pointed to a sign representing fire, explosion, and asphyxiation hazards beyond the door. The door led to the pump room, which housed all the pumps used for loading and unloading the cargo tanks. Schag had investigated the accidental death of a merchant sailor who had died aboard a fleet oiler when he entered the pump room without taking the proper precautions. The volatile fumes accumulated in the pump room had instantly asphyxiated the seaman. "We was lucky," a gruff chief engineer told Schag at the time. "A spark from opening that door could've set off those fumes and blown us sky high."

Schag led them down the next stairway into another long passageway. There were unmarked doors along each side of the passage. One was grimier than the other doors.

"This way," he said, opening the door.

It opened into a changing room. Jump suits of varying colors hung in open cabinets. On top of the cabinets sat safety helmets. Schag opened a heavy watertight door, and the room flooded with the roar, warmth, and stench of machinery. Stairs angled steeply into the bowels of the ship. Bill and Yolanda clambered down the rungs. At the bottom was a cavernous compartment filled with machinery of such monolithic proportions it made Bill and Yolanda feel like Lilliputians.

There were no decks among these mechanical behemoths. Catwalks meandered among them, like fragile trails winding around precipitous metallic peaks. In some places, half decks hung from the bulkhead like cliffs, reached by more catwalks and ladders. On one of those landings was the control room. A large window spanning the width of the ship revealed a bank of green, high-voltage control panels stretching as wide as the window. In front of the electrical switchboard sat a control station as wide as the power panels. Colorful lights from a multitude of digital read-out displays reflected off the green paint of the control room.

Schag closed and dogged the door behind them, then bounded down the stairs, using his hands to slide past several steps at a time as he would on the Halsey. When they reached the bottom of the stairs, Butcher turned and said something. Schag cuffed his ear, showing he couldn't hear.

"Where are we?" Butcher asked, stepping closer to Schag and leaning in toward his ear.

"Main engineering," Schag said.

Yolanda had her hands clamped over her ears, trying to muffle the noise. Butcher was rubbing his own ears.

"This noise is deafening," he said.

"It'd be a lot worse if we were underway and that main engine was running." Schag pointed to the main engine, which towered three decks above them.

"They only have a generator or two running at this point to keep the power on."

"Where do we go now?" Butcher asked.

Schag shook his head.

"Nowhere," he answered. "This is as far as we can go."

CHAPTER 29

SATURDAY
Aboard the Mars Venture
Anchored off the San Diego coast.
0510 Hours

AIDAN BLACK PALMED HIS EYES, trying to rub away the searing light trapped beneath his lids. The ringing in his ears stabbed deep into his brain, leaving his wits dulled. He forced his eyes open and waited for the sun-like orb to eclipse and fade, leaving him in the darkness of the bridge. He spotted Jürgen on the deck, sitting up, shaking his head, and blinking his eyes with exaggerated motions, as if that would make the vestige of the flash-bang go away. Meier was on all fours, groaning and cursing.

Black pulled himself onto one of the bridge chairs, still trying to think through the constant ringing in his ears. He looked at the video screen Meier had shown him earlier, with the displays from multiple closed-circuit deck cameras. One view showed the backs of three figures descending the stairs from the bridge to the deck below.

He turned, looking for Jürgen, who was standing next to him, leaning against the console, still dazed but watching the video screen, too.

"Give me your handheld," Black ordered. Jürgen handed it to him, and Black thumbed push-to-talk button. "The prisoners are heading for the deck below the bridge! Everyone there, now!" He turned to Jürgen and Meier. Both had gotten to their feet, but still needed to steady themselves against the console. "You two. Go!"

Jürgen pulled his pistol and Meier recovered his AK, and both rushed from the bridge. Black pulled a Sig Sauer P238 from the back of his belt—a replacement for the Beretta he tossed into the bay—but stayed at the console watching the video display. He saw Butcher and the woman running down the stairs until stopped by one of his men. Before Black could direct more men to assist the gunman, he saw the mercenary thrown back by multiple gunshots. Then he saw Schag come into view and lead the Butchers back inside the deckhouse.

"The inside stairs," he yelled into the radio. "They're going down the inside stairs!"

Black continued watching the video screen, but there were no cameras on the inside of the superstructure and the displays remained empty. With a final curse, he slammed his hand onto the console, turned, and followed his men down the stairs.

Jürgen and Meier pounded down the stairwell, almost colliding with Gott and Kasitz rushing into the well from the outside. Meier leaned his AK over the stair railing and fired a burst. A moment later, a single pistol round answered the burst. It bounced off the metal bulkhead two or three times until it slammed into Meier's shoulder. The mercenary stumbled backwards with a shout of pain, dropped his rifle, and collapsed on the stairs. Jürgen leaped over Meier, picked up the dropped AK, and threw himself onto the next set of stairs, firing a sustained burst to clear the stairwell ahead. Gott and Kasitz followed close behind.

Black paused and crouched as he heard the firing below. The angry whine of ricochets echoed through the stair well. When it became quiet again, he went on, taking two steps at a time. He found Meier on the stairs below, bleeding heavily from a shoulder wound. Black didn't stop to help him either. He stepped over the man and moved on. At the next landing, he found Jürgen, Gott, and Kasitz. A fourth and final member of their team, a former bounty hunter named Paudert, had joined them. They were standing in front of the pump room door, weapons at the ready, preparing to enter the room.

"Stand down!" Black ordered. The men looked at him. Black pointed to the warning signs. "Can't any of you read? You need protective equipment to go in there." He jabbed his Sig Sauer at the next flight of stairs. "They had to keep going down! Hurry!"

Jürgen motioned the three mercenaries down the stairs and followed with his rifle shouldered. Black went last. They moved more cautiously, wary of an ambush at the next and final landing. There was none. They spread out along the passageway, trying doorknobs until Gott opened the door leading to the changing room. They entered one at a time, weapons raised, and scanned each corner until Jürgen hollered, "Clear!"

Black entered, his eyes quickly sweeping the room. They landed at the watertight door, and he nodded at it. Jürgen tugged on the handle and realized door was dogged shut. He motioned to Paudert, who took position to the side of the door and waited, weapon ready, as the German turned each dogging lever one by one.

"What do you mean this is as far as we can go?" Butcher demanded.

"This is pretty much the bottom of the ship," Schag said. He pointed to what appeared to be a catwalk leading from the giant main engine to toward the stern. Beneath the steel grating, the Butchers could see a metal shaft at least two-feet in diameter. "That's the propeller shaft. Past this, it's only the bilges and the ocean."

"You!" a voice hollered with a distinctive Asian accent.

The trio turned, Schag and Butcher raising their weapons. They found a middle-aged Filipino in a blue jump suit and white safety helmet. The two guns aimed at him did little to tame the anger on his face or in his voice.

"You not supposed to be down here," he said. "You people supposed to stay up there." He pointed upwards with a large wrench his right hand. "And I stay down here. That's agreed. Remember?"

Schag realized the man must be a member of the merchant crew, not one of Gideon's mercenaries. He pulled his ID wallet and flashed his badge.

"Federal agent," Schag said. "Who are you?"

The Filipino looked at the badge, confused. He lowered the wrench and said, "I am Chief Engineer Ocampo."

"What are you doing here?" Schag demanded.

"The captain got orders to anchor here," Ocampo said. "We had to say my engine needed repairs." He pointed the wrench at the gargantuan diesel in the middle of the compartment. "Engine works good. I keep it that way."

Schag nodded, and prodded the man on.

"I was left on board to be the live watch. But those men up there tell me to stay down here. They even take my cabin and make me sleep in the engineering cadet's quarters."

"Is there another way out of here?" Butcher asked.

Ocampo nodded, pointing with his wrench to a ladder climbing from the engine room's main deck straight up the bulkhead. A few feet above the deck, a semicircular metal tube enveloped the ladder and continued up the bulkhead until ended in a watertight scuttle.

"Escape ladder," Ocampo said. "Leads to main deck."

Butcher took Yolanda's hand and led her toward the ladder, Schag following close behind.

Schag heard a familiar scraping sound from above them and whirled around, pistol raised toward the watertight door at the top of the stairs. One of the dogging levers turned. Butcher swung his rifle in the same direction and, pulling Yolanda with him, moved into better cover. Schag did the same with Ocampo.

"No guns! No guns!" The engineer insisted. "Too many fuel lines in here. Start big fire." He pointed up toward the pump room. "Pump room ventilation fans not working. Fire down here, go up there and boom!" His hands mimicked an explosion.

"It's not up to us, chief," Schag said. He pointed to the stairs. "Bad men up there. Better stay down."

Schag adjusted his position and leveled his pistol at the door. One by one, he watched the dogging levers turn.

Then the heavy metal door groaned open.

CHAPTER 30

"MR. BUTCHER! AGENT SCHAG!" AIDAN Black's voice rose over the ambient noise of machinery. "We don't have to do this. There's no reason for more violence. I'm a businessman. I just want to make a deal."

Black waited for a response. He knew there was nowhere else for the three to run. Even as little as he knew about ships, he understood the engine room was as far down as someone could go. The only way they could go was up, and to do that they would have to get past his men. A little psychology might bring them up without more shooting. Therefore, he waited for their reply.

None came.

Hunkered down behind the machinery, Schag looked

around trying to figure out a plan. He spied the escape ladder again, and called to Bill Butcher.

"Bill, you and Yolanda go for the ladder. I'll cover you." Schag nodded at the ship's chief engineer. "Take the chief here with you."

Every fiber in Butcher's body rebelled against leaving the fight, not to mention leaving behind his friend. He looked at Yolanda. Her dark eyes were wide with fear. Her mascara ran with tears. He took a deep breath, and nodded.

"Okay, take this," he said, sliding the AK over.

Schag picked up the rifle and checked the action. Bill tossed Schag the extra magazines, and the agent stuffed them into the pockets of his vest. Schag patted Ocampo on the shoulder. "Go with them, chief."

The engineer shook his head. "No, I stay. This is my ship. I'm responsible for her."

"Chief, any second now those men will come down here with machine guns," Schag said. "They won't differentiate between us and you. Besides . . ." He nodded toward Bill and Yolanda. "They need you to guide them out."

"Come on now, people." Black's voice rose again over the machinery. "We don't have much time. I know you have nowhere else to run. So, let's be grown up and talk this over."

Ocampo looked at Schag and nodded. Schag patted the engineer on the shoulder again and sent him scurrying over to the Butchers. Bill had him squat on his far side, nearer to the escape ladder. He turned back to Schag.

"I'll get them going up the ladder, but I'm not going up until you join us," he said.

Schag nodded and said, "Get going."

Black looked at his Rolex Submariner for the fifth time in the past minute and a half. He was losing patience. He leaned toward the hatch again.

"Come, come, Mrs. Butcher," he called down. "Surely you want this all to end well. You have your children to go home to. Talk some sense to your husband and Agent Schag, and whomever that bearded man is. All of us want to go home tonight, don't we?"

Black glanced at Jürgen. The German mercenary was growing even more impatient than Black.

"Maybe they aren't even down there," he said.

"They're down there," Black replied. "There's nowhere else they could be. They aren't on this deck or the decks above us, and the only way off this deck that we don't have covered is down those stairs."

Jürgen nodded but stepped to the mercenary posted to watch the passageway outside the changing room, and made his own inspection of the corridor to satisfy himself.

Several more minutes passed along with one last appeal to Yolanda. Black glanced at his watch again, then nodded to Paudert. The mercenary opened the hatch a little wider, shoved the barrel of his AK further out, and pulled the trigger.

Ocampo scuttled toward the escape ladder, followed by Yolanda, then Butcher. The first spray of bullets went high above them, screaming like angry bees. Rounds slammed into a bulkhead across the compartment, some punching through the thin steel into a smaller compartment labeled "FUEL PUMP ROOM." Others found their way through an open door leading into the same compartment. To conserve ammunition, Schag moved the AK's selector switch to semi-auto. He took careful aim at the opened hatch and fired three shots.

The automatic fire from the top of the stairs stopped.

The whine of the power generators dropped to a lower pitch. The engines that turned the dynamos coughed and died. The overhead lights faded and died, replaced by battery-operated emergency lamps that provided dim, spotty illumination, casting much of the engine room into deep shadows. Despite the sudden darkness, Schag saw Bill watching him. Schag nodded and Butcher prodded Yolanda and Ocampo to start moving again. Ocampo didn't move. He stared behind them in horror. He yelled something in Tagalog and pointed.

All three of them followed Ocampo's finger. Through the door to the fuel pump room came another light—the wavering, flickering glow of flames. The rounds entering the compartment severed one or more lines providing fuel oil to the generators—explaining why their engines died—and set the fuel ablaze.

Still screaming something incomprehensible, Ocampo ran toward the pump room, his arms reaching for a fire hose coiled on the bulkhead next to the door. As he reached the hose, a burst of gunfire stitched him across the back, throwing him into the bulkhead. His body crumpled to the deck, and didn't move.

"Go, damn it! Go!" screamed Schag as more as more gunfire came from the top of the stairs. Bullets shrieked through the air, ricocheting off machinery and hurling metal shards and chipped paint through the compartment.

Butcher pushed Yolanda to the deck, sheltering her

body with his. After a moment, he rose into a squat and fired three rounds from his stolen .45. The Gideon mercs responded with a fusillade of bullets. Butcher fired four more quick rounds, then the slide jammed open. The pistol was empty. He reached for another magazine.

There weren't any.

Frantic, Butcher glanced around in the dim light but saw nothing. Somewhere during the flight from the bridge, the two spare magazines must have fallen out of his pocket. He cursed himself for not securing them better. He looked at Schag, who gestured for him and Yolanda to keep moving. Butcher realized there was too much gunfire to make it to the escape ladder, and shook his head. He reached down, pulled up a trouser leg, and drew the KaBar from his boot.

It was his only weapon left.

At the top of the stairs, Aidan Black slapped the mercenary named Paudert on the shoulder and yelled, "Go!"

Paudert swung open the metal door, fired a burst from his rifle, and took the stairs two or three at a time. In the compartment below, Schag fired twice. One round hit Paudert in the side, throwing him against the bulkhead. The mercenary tumbled down the steep ladderway until he sprawled at the bottom.

Gott and Kasitz knelt at the open door and sprayed the engine room with bursts of automatic fire. They paused only long enough to let Black and Jürgen move through the door, then resumed firing as the two men rushed down the stairway. The heavy fire forced Schag to keep his head down. Black leaped over Paudert's body.

Jürgen grabbed the dead man's AK-47 and tossed it to Black. They took cover behind machinery, and motioned to Gott and Kasitz to join them. The two mercs rose from their kneeling positions, but threw themselves backward as three more single-shot rounds from Schag's AK pounded the hatch.

"Shit!" cursed Black. Regaining control, he tried to play the psychology card again. "Gentlemen, we are more plentiful than you, and better armed. I saw my man Paudert took out one of you. I certainly hope it wasn't Mr. Butcher—for Mrs. Butcher's sake."

Bill Butcher looked at Yolanda and raised his hand to his lips in a hushing motion, and moved several feet away.

"No, I'm still here," Butcher hollered.

Several rounds of AK fire slammed into the machinery around him, aimed at his voice. He looked over at Schag, some sixty feet away, and cupped his ear, followed by a gesture toward the Gideon men. Butcher was planning to triangulate their position by sound. Schag nodded, not realizing that Bill had no weapon except the knife.

"Perhaps it was Agent Schag, then?"

Butcher silently moved to another listening position.

"Sorry to disappoint you, Black, I'm still here, too," Schag called out. He moved to another position as gunfire raked the machinery where he had been.

"Then it must be the third man, the one with red hair and beard. We never did learn his name. What was it?"

A smile crept across Schag's lips. Black and his people still thought there was a third member of their raiding team. He could use that.

"You're wrong again, Black," Schag yelled. "That was Ocampo, the chief engineer that your man killed. Red is still alive and well . . . and up topside radioing the Coast Guard."

Schag moved again, but there was no gunfire from the mercenaries.

"Nicely played," Black said. "But I don't believe you. I think this Red is right down here with us."

"Then that's too bad for Red," Schag shouted. He was watching the flames in the fuel pump room grow in intensity. "Because in just a few minutes this ship will go up like a Fourth of July celebration."

He moved his position again, but he didn't wait for a reply.

"You see those flames, Black? That's only the fuel pump room for the engine and generators. Right above us is a much bigger pump room, as wide as the ship, used for loading and unloading the cargo oil. And Chief Ocampo told us the evacuation fans in that compartment haven't been working all week. The buildup of explosive fumes in that room makes this ship the biggest pipe bomb you've ever seen. And it's just a matter of minutes before the flames down here set it off."

As if to emphasize the point, a roar emanated from the fuel pump room. The growing heat in there created a flashover, super-heated gases that ignite with a violent explosion. Yellow sheets of flame, called Angel Fingers by firefighters, shot out of the door and burning fuel spewed into the engine room and splashed along the deck, creating pools of pure flame.

"Time's up, Black," Schag shouted.

CHAPTER 31

SATURDAY
Aboard the Mars Venture
Anchored off the San Diego coast.
0545 Hours

AT THE TOP OF THE stairs, Kasitz and Gott exchanged wary glances as they listened to the exchange between their boss and Schag. Kasitz used the back of his hand to wipe sweat from his moustache. When the fire in the fuel pump room flashed over, they both recoiled in horror.

"Holy goddamn shit!" Gott cried, dropping his rifle. "I didn't sign on for this crap." He scrambled to his feet and headed toward the door to the passageway.

"Me, neither," Kasitz agreed, following Gott. "Black don't pay us enough to sit here and get blown to shit. Never liked this whole plan anyway."

Down in the engine room, Black turned and signaled Gott and Kasitz to come down, only to see the two men drop their weapons and run from the hatchway. He cursed and looked at Jürgen.

"Forget those swine," the German said. "Keep the agent occupied. I will move around their right flank."

Black nodded, and as Jürgen moved off into the shadows, he shouted, "Very convenient, Mr. Schag. But I don't believe you. It's a big ship and that's such a small fire."

In fact, the fire scared the hell out of Black. Every fiber in his body screamed to get the hell out of there, but he knew he and Jürgen stood no chance of climbing those stairs as long as Schag and Butcher were still alive and armed. So, he kept playing the psy-ops card.

"We can still reach an agreement, agent," he said. "Let's put down the weapons and talk this over. For the sake of Mrs. Butcher and her children."

Schag moved his position again so he could see Yolanda. She looked at him, eyes wide with fear. Despite her terror, she shook her head. She didn't believe Black either. Schag was about to bellow his answer to Black when he saw movement behind Yolanda. Before he could react, Jürgen pulled her to her feet by her hair and placed the muzzle of his AK against her head.

"Do not try anything, agent," the German growled. "Drop your weapon or I put a round right through this pretty fräulein's head."

Schag froze. Yolanda looked at him, eyes fearful, but defiant. "Don't listen to him, Lin—"

Jürgen jerked her hair to the side and jammed the barrel of the rifle harder against her head. "Shut up! Do as I say, agent."

Schag raised his empty hand in a sign of surrender, and laid the AK on the deck. Jürgen smiled like a hungry wolf and shoved Yolanda to the deck. He lowered his AK to cover them both, and shouted, "I have the woman and the agent!"

Jürgen's words barely left his mouth when he stiffened, his head jerking back. The rifle slid from his grip and he dropped to his knees and fell forward.

Bill Butcher stood behind Jürgen, the hand with the KaBar at his side. "No, you don't," he said.

Bill stooped, lifted Yolanda to her feet, and sat her against a piece of machinery. With his empty left hand, he touched her face, and smiled. Yolanda tried to smile back but what she saw in Bill's smile and his eyes terrified her—a solemnity and finality.

"Bill?"

He hushed her by touching his finger to her lips. Then he backed away into the darkness.

The fire in the fuel pump room growled again and belched more flame into the engine room. Schag watched the fire grow and knew their time was running out.

"Bill, we've got to get out of here!" he yelled.

Hearing nothing in return, he lifted his head above his cover looking for his friend. As he did, he heard a yelp and saw an AK-47 hurtle through the air. It landed with a clatter on the deck and careened into a stanchion. Schag turned toward where the rifle had come and saw two heads rise above the machinery, one with black hair, the other bald. Bill Butcher held Aidan Black from behind, the KaBar pressed to the mercenary leader's throat.

"Coming out!" Butcher shouted. He pushed Black out into the open.

Schag stood, his Glock drawn. What he saw was like a scene from Dante's Inferno. All along the deck, pools of fire burned. Flames licked at the darkness, casting an eerie, undulating glow across Butcher and his prisoner.

Black's face was twisted with fear. What shocked Schag, however, was the expression on his friend's face—the look of the tormented wreaking revenge on the tormentor.

Schag stepped from his cover, his pistol trained on Black.

"I've got him covered now, Bill," he said, reaching into his vest and pulling out plastic zip cuffs. "You can let him go."

Butcher didn't respond. He moved closer, the knife still tight against Black's throat. In the flickering fire light, Butcher's blue eyes looked like dead black holes.

"Bill?" Yolanda gasped. She stood next to Schag, her hand covering her mouth. "Honey?"

Butcher and Black continued forward, and for the first time Butcher spoke.

"Why?" he demanded.

"What?" Black's voice was barely a squeak.

"Why all of this?" Butcher said. "The Facebook post. The hit team that was supposed to make it look like I committed suicide. Everything. Why?"

"Don't know . . . what you . . . mean," Black answered. His eyes rolled over, looking at Schag. "Agent, you've got me now. Arrest me. Get him . . . off . . . me."

Schag kept his weapon pointed at Black, but he began to worry Butcher might be the more serious threat.

"Bill, put the knife down," he said. "We've got to get off this ship, fast."

Butcher shook his head. "Not until this motherfuck admits everything."

"We'll get him into custody and interrogate him," Schag said. "Nothing he says here will be of any use legally. You know that."

"Don't care," Butcher growled. "I want to hear him

confess or I'll cut his god damn throat."

As if to emphasize the point, he drew the blade tighter. Black's face twisted in pain, and a small amount of blood snaked down his neck.

"Don't do this, Bill," Schag pleaded. "I can't let you do this. I'm still a cop. We get off this ship and he'll talk. We'll get you back in NCIS."

Butcher shook his head again.

"Too late," he said. "The music. The voices."

"We can get you help, honey," Yolanda said, her voice pleading. She put her hands on Schag's shoulder. "Lin knows a doctor who can help you, don't you, Lin? Tell him."

"I told him already," Schag told her, quietly. To Butcher he said, "Yolanda's right, Bill. Now let the bastard go."

"Tell them!"

Butcher did something to cause Black more pain, and the mercenary leader grimaced. Slowly, nearly imperceptibly Schag shifted his aim from Black to Butcher's head.

"Fine!" Black blurted. "It *was* the money. You know that."

"What money?" demanded Butcher, though he knew the answer.

"The nine billion in cash we stole in Iraq," Black said. "Yeah, we stole it, you were always right about that. It was that bastard Bennett's plan. He manipulated the whole thing. He virtually owns Gordias, and Gordias owns Gideon. We were just following orders. Stealing the money, going after you—just orders. That's all."

"Isn't that what the Nazis said after the war?" Schag said.

"Nothing like . . . that," Black said, grimacing as

Butcher adjusted his hold. "Just business. Bennett . . . Gordias needed . . . cash. It was just business."

"Okay, Bill, we've heard him," Schag said. "Now let him go and let's get off this damn ship!"

Bill Butcher didn't let go. He looked directly at Schag.

"No," he said.

CHAPTER 32

"BILL!" YOLANDA CRIED. "DO WHAT Lin says!"

Butcher looked at her, his eyes sad. He seemed to think about it, but his head almost imperceptibly shook no, and his face hardened again.

"Bill, I can't let you do this," Schag said, his pistol aimed solidly at Butcher.

The ex-SEAL glanced at Schag. "I know," he said. He turned himself and Black a quarter turn to the left, revealing his body to Schag.

At first, Schag believed Butcher would release Black and push him away. That hope quickly evaporated when Butcher again tightened the knife against Black's throat. Schag's hands shook as he realized he might have to shoot his friend. He thought about Yolanda standing next to him, how she would watch him gun down her husband. He could feel the grip of his pistol grow wet

249

with sweat.

Then it hit him. All the chances Bill had taken since this nightmare began. Hiding in his family's cabin, knowing either the police or Gideon would trace him there. Coming to Schag's hotel room on the submarine base in disguise. Living in a cheap motel in the middle of a police dragnet. Even coming out here to the ship. Butcher could have eluded the police any time he wanted. His training in escape and evasion techniques assured that. But he stayed and repeatedly took chances no sane man would take.

Sane.

The word echoed in Schag's mind. Bill Butcher wasn't crazy, but the agueloquine had done something to his head. Bill acknowledged that in Schag's hotel room, outside Butcher's motel, and again a few minutes ago. *The music. The voices.* And the way Butcher was talking on the port services boat coming out here. If something happened to him, he wanted Schag to take care of Yolanda. It then made sense. Bill not only expected to die, he *wanted* to die. Maybe it was the medication making him think that way. Maybe he didn't want to live with its side effects. Or maybe, with everything he'd done in the last few days, he knew he was past the point of no return.

Bill wanted to die, but he couldn't do it himself. He was Catholic. Like many Catholics, Bill believed suicide meant eternal damnation. That was why Yolanda refused to believe the corpse in the cabin was Butcher. Maybe Bill expected to be killed in this crazy rescue attempt. The odds certainly leaned in that favor. Despite the odds, they were all still alive. *Bill* was still alive. But he was trying to change that. He was trying to do what so many desperate people have done. He was trying to die through what the media called "suicide by cop."

Schag shook his head.

"I won't play this game, Bill," he said. He lowered his pistol and holstered it. "Go ahead. Cut the bastard's throat."

"You . . . can't!" Black gasped.

"Lin?' Yolanda complained. Schag held up a hand to hush her.

The muscles in Butcher's arm holding the knife tensed. The knife moved as if Bill was preparing to slice. Then the knife stopped. The muscles relaxed, and the arm lowered. A look of defeat replaced the demonic anger. He let Black go. Schag sighed with relief.

A burst of gunfire shattered the lull. Several AK rounds struck Black's chest, killing him. Butcher collapsed to the deck as a 7.65mm bullet slammed into his right flank, cutting a swath through his abdomen and blowing out a large chunk of his left side. Yolanda screamed. Schag turned toward the sound of gunfire and saw Jürgen, shirt bloodied from Bill's knife wound, half-crouching, half kneeling, and firing the AK with one hand. In one motion, Schag swung Yolanda behind him, drew his pistol, and fired four times. The German's body jerked with each impact and tumbled over backward. As he fell, his finger remained tight on the rifle's trigger. An arc of bullets pounded through the overhead into the cargo pump room above.

His pistol still trained on Jürgen, Schag approached the mercenary, kicked the AK away from his body, and made certain he was dead. He holstered his weapon again, and walked back to Butcher. Yolanda was at Bill's side, cradling his head, sobbing. Schag pulled an Israeli dressing from a gunshot kit on his vest, opened Butcher's shirt, and did his best to bandage the entry and exit wounds. All the time, he kept muttering, "It'll be okay.

It'll be okay," as if it were a mantra.

Butcher reached up and touched his friend's shoulder, a slight smile on his lips.

"No," he said, "it won't, and you know it." He glanced at his wife. "Forget about me and get her out of here, Lin."

Schag looked at Yolanda and immediately knew she wasn't leaving her husband's side. He glanced at the overhead where Jürgen's rounds had punched holes. A slight haze drifted down from them. Fumes, he thought. Explosive fumes. He looked back at Butcher, shaking his head.

"Not without you, Bill," he said.

With Yolanda's help, Schag got Butcher to his feet, raised the ex-SEAL's arm over his own shoulder, stooped, and grabbed his leg in a fireman's carry. Butcher was a good thirty pounds heavier than Schag, and at first, the agent thought he would collapse under the weight. One look at the appreciation in Yolanda's eyes, however, steeled Schag. He motioned to Yolanda to head for the stairs, while he followed close behind with Bill.

It was warm in the engine room, and Schag was already sweating from the exertion of the escape and the gun battle. Carrying Butcher's limp body up the flight of metal stairs to the changing room made the perspiration soak his clothing and roll down his face. Sweat stung his eyes and flooded over his glasses. The muscles in his legs screamed with each step. The climb was no more comfortable for Butcher, who groaned in agony with every movement. At each utterance, Yolanda turned to comfort her husband. Schag urged her on.

The climb from the changing room to the main deck was easier, partly because the stairs were wider, and partly because Schag's fear of an eminent explosion pumped his body full of adrenalin. Still, Schag completed the last part of the climb blinded by the sweat stinging his eyes and smearing the lenses of his glasses. When they reached the starboard side of the deck, he lowered Butcher into a sitting position. Yolanda went to Bill's side. Schag took a triangular bandage from his gunshot kit and used it to wipe his own face and glasses, then studied the next leg of the trip. The path from the deckhouse to the companionway leading down to the port services boat was flat but had to be half the length of a football field away. Carrying Butcher down those stairs would be as hard as the climb from the engine room.

Schag reached to pick up Butcher again when something caught his eye and made his blood turn cold. A half mile from the ship was a boat. Schag could tell from the position of the running lights—the portside red light on the left, the green starboard light on the right—that the boat was heading away from the ship, not toward it. Leaning over the side of the ship, he looked for the port services boat tied up to the companionway. It wasn't there.

Yolanda saw the look on Schag's face. "Lin, what is it?" she asked.

Schag leaned heavily against the railing, his head down.

"The boat Bill and I came out here in," he said. "It's gone. Those two Gideon men who fled must have taken it." He pointed to the running lights in the distance. "That's it there."

Schag turned and faced Yolanda.

"That was the only way off this ship," he said.

CHAPTER 33

SATURDAY
Aboard the Mars Venture
Anchored off the San Diego coast.
0627 Hours

SCHAG LOWERED HIMSELF INTO A sitting position on the deck next to Butcher and leaned his head back in exasperation. He stared at the bottom of the deck above. A hundred ideas flooded his head, but each ebbed away. Could they swim to shore? Maybe if they had lifejackets? Bill would never make it, not in his condition. Hell, it was doubtful he or Yolanda would make it to shore, he decided. It was winter, and even in San Diego, the coastal waters were cold enough to cause lethal hypothermia. Maybe he should climb up to the bridge again and use the radio there to call the Coast Guard? Maybe they could get a helicopter out to them before . . .

There was another rumble from deep below decks, another flashover, probably spewing flames into the engine room.

No time to call the Coast Guard, Schag concluded.

Maybe swimming was their only chance. Maybe he could find a Stokes litter with a flotation collar to put Bill in. Schag stared at the bottom of the deck above them and banged the back of his head against a stanchion, trying to shake loose a solution. Nothing came.

Schag felt a tap on his leg. He turned to find Bill looking at him through half closed eyes. His hand was making weak movements up and down. The agent looked away again, and again felt the tapping on his leg. Butcher's hand made the same up and down motion, as if he were trying to gesture. His lips moved, but made no sound.

"What is it, Bill?" Schag asked, leaning closer.

"Life . . ." Butcher whispered. "Life . . ."

"What?"

"Li . . . boat . . ."

Schag finally understood the hand gesture. Butcher was pointing to the boat deck above them where the ship's single lifeboat stood in its free-fall davits.

"Damn it," Schag cursed, jumping to his feet. "Of course."

Yolanda jumped at Schag's voice. "Lin, what is it?"

"There's a lifeboat two decks above us." Schag pointed to the ladderway. "Get up there now and get the entry hatch opened. I'll bring Bill."

Schag again lifted Butcher into a fireman's carry and started up the ladder. He felt neither the pain in his legs nor Butcher's weight. All he felt was an elation that there was, just possibly, a way off this death ship.

When he reached the lifeboat, Yolanda was turning the last of three dogging levers that made the hatch watertight. With a grunt, she heaved the door open and stood back as Schag eased Butcher through.

Two rows of high-backed chairs ran the length of the

boat, separated by a single aisle. Designed to secure survivors as the boat plunged into the ocean, each seat faced the stern and had a four-point harness.

Schag lowered Butcher into the first seat and strapped him in, noticing for the first time the blood soaking through his bandage. Butcher's breathing was labored, and his skin spectral white. His eyes opened and looked at Schag, and he muttered something the agent could not hear. Schag leaned closer.

"What, Bill?"

Butcher's voice was a croak, but strong enough for Schag to make out the curse.

"I'm still goin' . . . to get that bastard . . . Bennett," he said. "You'll see. I will . . ." Butcher's clenched fist tapped Schag's arm. "I *will* get him."

Schag nodded and continued strapping Bill in. Yolanda sat in the chair beside Bill and strapped herself in. When Schag finished, he swung the watertight door shut, and slid the dogging levers in place. Stooping, he rushed forward to the boat's cockpit, a raised platform from which the coxswain launched and steered the vessel. As he strapped himself in the cockpit, Schag glanced out of the aircraft-like windshield at the ocean dozens of feet below, and he felt a moment of vertigo. He scanned the instructions on the instrument panel, choked the engine, and pressed the starter. The motor roared to life.

"Hang on!" he yelled to Yolanda.

He pulled the launching lever, and the boat slipped toward the ocean below.

The lifeboat cleared the ramp at the moment the ship exploded. The shock wave slammed into the stern of the small craft, flipping the boat over as it hit the surface and driving it deep underwater. Schag could hear Yolanda's screams behind him as the inverted boat landed in the water. Only the safety harnesses prevented them from flying about the interior of the boat. Schag watched frothing seawater skid past the windshield as the boat sank deeper. He thought briefly of submarines and crush depths, and wondered how deep this little boat could go before the water pressure crushed its hull.

He felt a heaviness press him hard into the straps of his harness. At first, he thought it was the crushing force of the ocean, but then he realized it was gravity pressing him against his harness. The boat had stopped sinking and was rising toward the surface, increasing the g-forces on its occupants.

The boat broached keel up and after a moment of hesitancy, righted itself. Seawater streamed down the windshield. When it cleared, Schag could see stars outside. After rocking side to side, the boat settled, and bobbed gently in the swells.

Unbuckling his harness, Schag slid out of the cockpit and inspected the boat for leaks. The motor stopped while submerged, and the only light came from two small emergency lanterns. Schag took one from off its mount and studied the deck and the watertight hatch for leakage. The boat was dry.

Schag heard sobbing and made his way aft. He founded Yolanda and Bill still strapped into their seats. Yolanda held Bill's left hand to her cheek. Tears streamed down her face. He didn't need to look at Bill to know why.

Bill Butcher was dead.

Schag choked back his own grief, and made his way forward to the coxswain platform. He climbed into the seat and thumbed the engine start button. After three tries, it kicked in. He engaged the engine and pressed the throttle forward. As the little boat made way, he turned the rudder to port and brought it about until he could see the *Mars Venture*. The massive superstructure of the ship was splayed open. Flames licked at the remains of the deckhouse. The ship was heavy by the stern, already taking on water and sinking.

The agent roused himself from the spectacle and turned the boat out to sea, making a long, slow arc around the ship, looking for survivors. He found only debris and patches of burning fuel. With Yolanda's sobs echoing from the stern, he turned the boat toward the harbor entrance and headed for shore.

CHAPTER 34

MONDAY
Shelter Island
San Diego, California
1000 Hours

MORNING BROKE LIKE THE CALM after a storm. The sun shone in a cloudless sky. Only a pillar of black smoke from the still smoldering hulk of the *Mars Venture* marred the view.

It had been two days since the massive oil tanker exploded. Once they had reached the harbor, Schag steered the lifeboat to the San Diego Harbor Police docks at the tip of Shelter Island. Harbor policemen were running back and forth, preparing the fire-fighting equipment on their boats to battle the blaze aboard the *Mars Venture*. Schag was pleased to find the stolen port services boat tied up to the police docks, and the three Gideon mercs—Gott, Kasitz, and, Melito, ship's guard he and Bill left tied up in the boat's cabin of—handcuffed and sitting in the back of a patrol car. The three had been caught by a harbor police boat alerted to the theft of the workboat.

Schag and Yolanda spent the two days since telling and retelling the whole story of Bill Butcher, from Gideon's botched attempt to kill him, to Yolanda's kidnapping and subsequent rescue, and ending with the explosion aboard the oil tanker. In trying to explain their possession of the stolen boat, Gott, Kasitz, Mielto unwittingly confirmed the story Yolanda and Schag told investigators in separate interrogations. When the local police and the Coast Guard finished with Schag, it was time for the NCIS's own internal watchdogs to talk to him. After explaining his actions to them, he provided a few answers to questions they hadn't asked.

When Schag made it back to his hotel at the sub base, he found his room ransacked, his laptop and all other computer equipment missing. Base security and the local police chalked it up to a routine burglary, but Schag knew otherwise. Schag later learned Butcher's motel room had also been searched, and his laptop computer stolen.

Schag knew there were still loose strings left dangling in this matter, and he was about to pull on them.

No longer fearing the wrath of Bill Butcher, Bomber Bennett took up residence in a hotel on Shelter Island. Schag walked through the hotel's parking lot holding in his hand a compact disc. The search of his hotel room had been thorough but the information the prowlers sought wasn't there. Expecting such a move, Schag had left the CD with Bill's files on Gordias taped to the bottom of a drawer in Tom Riley's own desk, the same desk Schag had been working at before meeting up with Bill to rescue Yolanda, and the last place he knew anyone connected to Gordias or Gideon would look.

A flash of his shield convinced the desk clerk to answer Schag's questions about Bennett's whereabouts. Schag found him ensconced in a meeting room with members of his war council, discussing strategies to ensure approval of his appointment as defense secretary. As Schag opened the door, a tableful of hostile eyes turned to inspect him. Two beefy men in ill-fitting business suits rose to stop his entrance, but Schag stopped them with an outstretched arm, a withering look, and a flash of his badge.

"This is a private meeting," one of them said.

"Not anymore," said Schag. He strode the length of the table until he reached Bennett, and tossed the disc onto the table in front of him. "Is that what you wanted?"

Grumbles rose from the men sitting around the table, but Bennett hushed them with a raised hand.

"Agent Schag, isn't it?" Bennett said, recognizing Schag from the VTC teleconference only days before. He picked up the disc and examined it. "And what is this?"

"That's what your goons were after when they trashed my hotel room and stole my computer," Schag said. "It's what Bill Butcher died for."

More complaints rose from the table, but they abruptly stopped when Bennett stood.

"Gentlemen, let's take a break," he said. "Mr. Schag and I need to speak in private."

With a smattering of murmurs, the men pushed back their chairs and filed from the room until only the two bodyguards remained.

"You two also leave," Schag said. "You're both out of jobs now, anyway. Federal agents from Alcohol, Tobacco, and Firearms raided the Gideon compounds here and back east this morning looking for illegal weapons, like

AK-47s."

The two mercenaries glanced at each other but stood motionless, their faces blank. Bennett motioned for them to leave, then sat back down and looked at Schag. "What is this about, agent?"

"It's about everything on that disc," Schag said. "About how you destroyed Bill Butcher's life over it."

Bennett raised his eyebrows in innocence and shook his head.

"Aidan Black told us everything before he died," Schag said. "Or should I say before he was murdered?"

Bennett simply stared, saying nothing.

"At first," Schag continued, "I thought Jürgen was trying to kill Bill and hit Black by mistake. Later, I realized with the way Black was stitched across the chest, Jürgen had to be aiming at him, not Bill. I wonder if Black ever suspected you might think of him as a loose end that needed taking care of?"

"And why would I wish to kill Aidan?"

"Black and his mercs did all your wet work," Schag said. "They stole the nine billion in American cash from Iraq on your orders. They planted the bomb on the helicopter the state department investigator was using after he found some of the money in Lebanon. They hired that private investigator to find dirt on Commander Clarke because you were afraid her work might interfere with your profits from agueloquine sales. Then they killed him when they thought he could lead me back to Gideon."

"And why would I care about Gideon? I'm only one of many clients they have," Bennett said, glancing at his watch as if bored.

"Gordias owns Gideon," Schag said, "and you own Gordias."

Bennett made a sour face and shook his head. "Agent, I am merely an investor in Gordias, one of many. I'm a capitalist. I have investments in many corporations, many of which have investments in other corporations. That's the American way. Free enterprise."

"If I remember my college economics correctly," Schag said, "There's a difference between free enterprise and capitalism."

"Enlighten me," Bennett said.

"Free enterprise is providing a service for a fee. Karl Marx was the first to coin the word 'capitalism' to describe those who abused the free enterprise system to amass wealth and power, and subjugate the masses. People like you."

Bennett's demeanor changed abruptly. He slammed his fist on the table and stood. "Who the hell do you think you are talking to me like that?" he demanded. "Do you understand who I am?"

"Oh, I know who you are," Schag said, nodding. "And what you are. You're Charles 'Bomber' Bennett, a Vietnam draft dodger, born rich and who grew up to start wars for his own profit. Where I come from, they call that a hypocritical coward."

Bennett's mouth tightened and his face crimsoned. "I don't have to stand here and be insulted."

"Then I suggest you sit down," Schag said, kicking Bennett's chair into his knees. Bennett fell back into the chair. "I came here to give you that disc because I want it to end here. Bill Butcher was an idealist. He believed in things many people don't believe in anymore. Like service, sacrifice, and justice. So, he went tilting at windmills. Unfortunately, it was your windmill, and you destroyed his life for it. I wish I were half the man Bill Butcher was."

The last time Schag saw Yolanda Butcher flashed across his mind. It was only the day before. He had driven her to the airport for a flight that would take her and Bill's ashes to her parents' home in Texas. She gently kissed Schag on the cheek and said good-bye. From her eyes, Schag knew it was the last time he would ever see her. Yolanda would not allow Schag to keep his promise to Bill.

Schag shook the memory from his head.

"Well, I want none of that," he said. "I had my fill of sociopaths like you when I was a lawyer on Wall Street."

Schag recognized the look that flashed across Bennett's face—disbelief that someone would leave a lucrative Wall Street job for the bread-and-butter pay of a government employee. Well, maybe I tilt at windmills, too, he thought.

"That's why I brought you that disc," Schag explained. "That's everything Bill knew about Gordias and the theft of cash from Iraq. It's yours. Keep it. Just leave me alone."

Bennett picked up the CD, studied it, and then snapped it in two. He looked at Schag, a cruel smile on his lips.

"Oops," he said. "So much for your bargaining chip, Agent Schag."

Schag's Glock was in his fist and aimed at Bennett's head so fast it took Bennett several seconds to register it. The sneer left his face, and his eyes widened with fear. Sweat beaded on his forehead and a muscle twitched at his jaw.

"I forgot to mention the other part of my deal," Schag said. "You send someone after me like you did Bill, and I'm not settling for taking out one of your minions. I'm coming straight for you. One of your people so much as sneezes in my direction, you're a dead man."

Schag returned the Glock to its holster, and walked toward the door. Bennett sputtered behind him, struggling to overcome his fear so he could have the last word.

"Agent, I can have you transferred to the filthiest scow in the American fleet!" he said. "You'll never see land again!"

Schag paused at the door and turned.

"As long as I'm not around you and your kind," Schag said without turning, "that's fine with me."

Schag swung the door open. The members of Bennett's war cabinet were waiting outside, but the two Gideon bodyguards were nowhere in sight. As Schag walked down the hallway, he heard Bennett's voice call out.

"Gentlemen, Mr. Schag is leaving—finally," he said, recapturing a small amount of his forced bravado. "Let's return to matters and finish this meeting. Tomorrow or the next day, I leave for a much-anticipated cruise up the coast in my yacht, and I still have many preparations to make."

Tom Riley was in fine voice when Schag returned to regional headquarters. Schag could hear him yelling as soon as he walked through the doors of the NCIS offices. He could also hear the name Riley was yelling was his own.

"Schag!" Riley's face was red and sweat beaded on his forehead. "Get your sorry ass into my office now!"

Schag walked into Riley's office and shut the door without being told to do so. Riley paced the office, muttering to himself, shaking his head. He looked at Schag, as if surprised he was already standing there.

"What did you do?" Riley asked, forcing his voice to a normal level. "I just got a call from Charles Bennett saying you disrupted a meeting he was having with some of the most powerful men in government."

"More like some of the most powerful men *behind* our government," Schag said.

"I don't give a damn what you think, you insolent bastard," Riley said, pointing a finger in Schag's face and waving it. "I am sick and tired of your insubordination and disrespect. I'm writing you up this time, Lin. I'm writing you up good."

Schag shrugged, removed his flight jacket, and placed it over a chair.

"All we did was discuss our mutual futures," he said. "We agreed to ignore each other for the rest of our lives."

"Well, he's not ignoring you. He just called me to complain."

"The last gasps of frustration," Schag said. "He'll get over it."

"Well, I won't," Riley said. "I'm going to make a decision about your future in the very *near* future."

"Sit down, Tom," Schag said. Riley looked at him as if not understanding the command. "I said sit down, damn it!"

"Who the hell do you—?"

Schag moved forward quickly and shoved Riley into his chair. Riley's face flushed with rage, but when he tried to stand up, Schag blocked him. Riley's gun hand went to his waist, but found nothing.

"It's locked in your desk drawer, remember?" Schag said. "Leave it there. We have some talking to do about *your* future, Tom. And your past."

"My what?"

"Your lack of a future here with NCIS," Schag said, "and the very real possibility of you spending the next several years in the federal prison at Leavenworth."

"What the hell are you talking about?"

"When Bill Butcher was deployed to Bahrain, he suspected there was a mole in the NCIS organization there, someone who kept tipping off Gideon and other contractors to investigations and raids being planned. You were the supervisory agent there, Tom, and I think the mole was you."

"That's redicul—"

"Bill said any time they planned a raid, someone got tipped off. Didn't matter who the subject was. Investigations are compartmentalized. You know that, Tom. Only the primary investigators know all the details—except the supervisory agent. In Bahrain, that was you. You were the only one with knowledge of *all* the ongoing investigations."

"You're not making sense," Riley complained. "Why would I—"

"It happened again, right here," said Schag. "Only three people knew about the cabin Bill's family had in the Cuyamacas. Yolanda told you and me. I took Yolanda to the safe house and you were supposed to notify the sheriff's department. But you called Gideon first, and that allowed them to move in on Bill before the sheriff could."

Riley said nothing. He was sweating more, and nervously licking his lips.

"Then there was the safe house," Schag continued. "Only five people knew where it was—you, me, Yolanda, and the two agents assigned to guard her. Yolanda was kidnapped and the guards killed. That leaves you and me,

Tom, and I didn't call Gideon."

"And you think I did?"

Schag nodded. "There were only two people who knew where I was staying. You had the office here reserve me a room at the Navy Inn at 32nd Street, but I made my own reservation at the sub base Navy Inn and told you so. I never told anyone else. Someone had to tell Gideon where I was staying so they could break into my room and steal my laptop. It had to be you."

Riley's mouth twisted into a frown. He snorted and the frown became a sardonic grin. He shook his head and chuckled.

"You are really a piece of work, Schag," he said. "You know that? You go hassle one of the most powerful men in government, then come here and accuse me of being some kind of spy with no proof of anything, only supposition. I don't understand what you're trying to prove."

Schag opened the office door and glanced out into the squad bay before turning back to Riley.

"I don't need to prove anything, Tom," he said. He nodded toward the open door. "They do."

Riley stood and walked to the door. Outside, he saw two men chatting with agents in the squad bay. They were not agents under his supervision, but he recognized them. They were the two internal watchdogs who had been grilling Schag for the last couple of days.

Schag picked up his flight jacket and slipped it on.

"They're here to talk to you, Tom," he said. "I told them everything I told you, and they're very interested in hearing what you have to say. They've already checked calls you made on your office phone and your issued Blackberry. They know you were calling Gideon."

Schag started out the door, but stopped and turned.

"By the way, I'm taking a week of leave starting—" He glanced at his watch, then back at Riley. His eyebrows arched in amusement. "Now."

CHAPTER 35

WEDNESDAY
Naval Station Point Loma
1015 Hours

LINUS SCHAG SAT ON THE outdoor dining patio of the Navy Gateway Inn sipping coffee and staring out at the still-smoldering wreck of the *Mars Venture*. Four days after the explosion—two since Schag's confrontations with Bennett and Riley—the salvage crews had arrived to start the hard, if not impossible, work of refloating the massive ship or, barring that, to break her apart.

The day before, Tim Parker had called Schag to tell him that Tom Riley confessed to being Gideon's mole. There had been a woman in Bahrain and photographs of their trysts, photos that would have ruined both his marriage and his career. To save both, he agreed to pass information to Gideon. When Tom returned to the States, he thought his problems with Gideon were over. Then the whole Butcher's Bill thing started and Aidan

Black contacted Riley again, reminding him that Gideon still had those photos.

"Tom said he had no choice but to provide them information again." Parker said. "Word is Washington wants to keep this all quiet, so they're going let Tom resign. But can you believe he got caught in a honey trap?"

A honey trap was the oldest of espionage snares, using a woman to get to a man who had information the spies wanted.

"You know what they always say," Schag said. "Too many men think with the wrong head."

Since leaving Tom's office, Schag had contemplated his own future. He expected a reprimand or worse, even wrote a letter of resignation to throw on some high official's desk if he considered the rebuke too harsh. He placed the letter along with his NCIS credentials and badge in a locked drawer in his room at the Navy Gateway Inn, and waited.

Then the unexpected happened.

That morning he awoke to find an email on his Blackberry from NCIS headquarters in D.C. relieving him from his duties at China Lake and ordering him to report for duty aboard the *USS Halsey*. Someone in Washington wanted to get Schag as far from Charles Bennett and his associates as possible, and punish him, too. The *Halsey*, homeported in Sasebo, Japan, was about as far away from D.C. as they could get him. The paper pushers in the Beltway no doubt also thought sending Schag back to sea, to what many in the agency considered an NCIS backwater, would be a punishment. But the *Halsey* was the assignment Schag wanted.

Schag's badge sat on the table next to his coffee. Morning sunlight glinted off its gold surface. He picked it up and snapped it into place on his belt, taking comfort in its familiar weight on the left side of his trousers.

His Blackberry beeped. He looked at the screen. Parker again.

"Hey, Tim," Schag answered. "What's up?"

"You been watching the news?" Parker's voice was excited.

"No. I'm on leave," Schag said. "I try to stay away from that stuff when I'm on vacation. Something big happening?"

"Bomber Bennett is dead," Parker said.

Schag straightened in his chair, bumping the table hard and almost knocking it over. He grabbed the table to steady it and asked, "What? How? When?"

"Sometime last night, they think."

"Who thinks?"

"The Coast Guard," Parker said. "Bennett left yesterday for a cruise up the coast on his yacht, the *Free Enterprise*. This morning, another boater found debris in the water off Oceanside and called the Coast Guard. The Coast Guard found the debris and confirmed it was Bennett's boat, but they couldn't find any sign of Bennett."

Schag stared at the wreckage of the *Mars Venture* and remembered Bill Butcher's last words to him. "I *will* get him."

"Lin, do you think Bill was involved somehow?"

Schag recalled the reported sighting of Butcher at the yacht club. Bill certainly had the training and skills to sink a boat. Could he have planted a bomb with a delayed action fuse on Bennett's yacht?

"I will get him," Bill had said.

"Yeah, I do, Tim." Schag finally said. "I think he was."

"Well, the crap's hitting the fan," Parker continued.

"Ever since the news got out that Bennett's dead, people all over the country, in government and out, are calling for an investigation into his business activities. Seems old Bomber made an awful lot of enemies in his time, but he was too powerful to fight. Now they want their revenge. We're getting calls from the FBI, IRS, ATF, and every other alphabet soup agency asking us what we know about the allegations Bill made in his Bill of Demands. It's a shame you gave Bennett that disc with all of Bill's research on it. Probably a lot of people would like to see it now."

A sad smile crossed Schag's lips. He leaned over, removed his right shoe, and set it on his lap. He reached into the shoe and pulled back the inner sole, removed the micro-disc hidden there, and held it in front of his face.

"Funny you should mention that, Tim," Schag said.

AUTHOR'S NOTE

THE BUTCHER'S BILL IS A work of fiction with a plot inspired by historic fact. During the Iraq War, the Bush administration decided to empty frozen Iraqi bank accounts in the U.S. and send the money to Iraq. In a decision that continues to confound observers, the White House chose to send the money in cash. Forty billion dollars in greenbacks was flown to Iraq and handed over to contractors—some say in duffle bags—with no receipts or other forms of accounting. Nearly $9 billion—$8.9 billion to be precise—simply vanished, presumably stolen as part of it was found stashed in a bunker in Lebanon. (Fortunately, the person who discovered it was not killed afterward, as in this book.) To my knowledge, it was largest bank heist in history, and all attempts to investigate the theft were blocked by the White House and its supporters in Congress.

Operation Iraqi Freedom saw the largest number of private contractors used in a combat zone in history. At one point during the conflict, there were more contractors in Iraq than U.S. troops. The cost of using these contractors was exorbitant, and the financial burden continues to be carried by the taxpayers today. In particular, the use of "security contractors" proved problematic. Many of the security contractors possessed questionable backgrounds; some were even believed to be former members of South American death squads. Not surprisingly, many security contractors were suspected of illegal activities, including the reckless use of force, weapon- and drug-smuggling, black marketeering, and sexual assault. As they were granted immunity from prosecution for most actions, few were ever punished.

Agueloquine is a fictitious drug. There is, however, a real antimalarial that, during the Iraq War, was linked to psychotic reactions in a very small percentage of people who took it. The tragic incidents Lieutenant Commander Clarke described as linked to Agueloquine psychosis actually occurred. However, as the good doctor told Schag, the number of such incidents is very small. When compared to the millions of lives saved from malarial deaths each year, the math adds up in favor of using the drug. In this book, I use the fictitious Agueloquine simply as a device to explain Bill Butcher's aberrant behavior.

Gordias is a fictional corporation, but its size, complexity, and shady activities were inspired by several real-life firms. Like Gordias, these multinationals are so powerful they often are involved in deciding when and with whom we go to war. Perhaps, someday, a true-life Bill Butcher will come forth and expose these businesses for what they are—a threat to democracy and world peace.

And, finally, yes, it is true—there is no NCIS office in Los Angeles.

ABOUT THE AUTHOR

MARTIN ROY HILL is the author of *Duty: Suspense and Mystery Stories from the Cold War and Beyond*, the military mystery thriller *The Killing Depths*, *Eden: A Sci-Fi Novella,* and the Peter Brandt thrillers, *Empty Places,* and *The Last Refuge*. A former journalist and national-award winning investigative reporter for newspapers and magazines, Martin currently works as a military operations analyst. His nonfiction work has appeared in Reader's Digest, LIFE, Newsweek, Omni, and many others. He has written articles on military history for several publications and web sites. His short fiction has appeared in Alfred Hitchcock Mystery Magazine, ALT HIST: The Journal of Historical Fiction and Alternate History, Nebula Rift, Mystery Weekly, Crimson Streets, and others.

Martin lives in San Diego, California.

Follow Martin Roy Hill on Facebook at https://www.facebook.com/Martin.Roy.Hill, on Twitter at https://twitter.com/MartinRoyHill, or visit his web site at https://www.martinroyhill.com.

If you enjoyed reading this book, please leave a review on Amazon.com, Barnes & Noble, Goodreads, or your favorite review site.